C000182688

A most original and promising new writing talent.

*Russell Stannard, author of 'The Time*
*and Space of Uncle Albert'*

# KALOPSIA

## KEIRA FORDE

Edited by WINSTON FORDE

**author**HOUSE®

AuthorHouse™ UK
1663 Liberty Drive
Bloomington, IN 47403  USA
www.authorhouse.co.uk
Phone: UK TFN: 0800 0148641 (Toll Free inside the UK)
       UK Local: (02) 0369 56322 (+44 20 3695 6322 from outside the UK)

Published by AuthorHouse  06/16/2022

ISBN: 978-1-6655-9925-2 (sc)
ISBN: 978-1-6655-9924-5 (e)

# CONTENTS

# DEDICATION

To those who a genuine smile is foreign to their lips. I love you and I see you.

# kal·op·si·a

[kal-*op*–**see**–*uh*]

a condition, state or delusion in which things
appear more beautiful than they really are

In every story there's a turning point. A point where everything changes, for better or usually for worse. Believe it or not, these changes are normally sparked by the most random of events: a car crash, a murder or even a sudden and totally cliché romance. Now this wouldn't be an issue if these changes were reversible. But they never are. You cannot rewrite the stars nor should you ever attempt to do so. Once you push that button, or text and drive that's it. Over. The problem is, I think we humans forget this sometimes. We act with the spontaneity of those who solely believe there's an Earth 2.0 for us to hop on once we've messed it all up. Maybe, just maybe, if we thought about our actions before jumping into the fire, our world would be a better place. I wish humans had thought like this before declaring World War Three. Because now our world is in ruins. Every country, every landscape, every beautiful mountain with its glowing expanse of greenery and life: dead. My home country, Zayathai, is the bright shining penny among the pile of rusted societies. We are the group that continues to thrive, rising from the ashes like a sacred book surviving a devastating tsunami. 'The happiest place on Earth,' they call it. But we are far from it. This apparent happiness, this beauty and culture, is all a facade. Our smiles bear no sincerity. These grins are forced upon us by an injection, given at the tender age of six. It rids us of all noticeable reactions to pain and stretches a smile upon our lips. Though all displays of pain are lost, the physical and emotional anguish is all too real. You'll never understand the torment of this injection. Nor will I. For my blood resisted it and ruined the tragic existence that is my life.

Walking around Zayathai takes quite a lot of getting used to, even if you are born here. First of all, everything is grey. The houses are grey, the fences are grey, hell I wouldn't be surprised if the few flowers in each garden blossomed a dim shade of soot. The only places where true colour thrives are in the areas where tourists are allowed to roam. The areas where most Zayathian people never have the time or money to go. The only other places that shine are the perfection facilities and the ritual buildings. We'll talk more about them later. The second, and arguably the most important, thing that will catch your eye is that not one person is frowning or showing any physical signs of negativity. Someone could literally be stabbed in the street and their faces would remain in a smile. Once, I saw a young child -probably around the age of eight- skipping down the street. She was in a state of total euphoria, singing and twirling like a spinning top. Her mother followed behind her, carrying the child's book bag. A lone rock made her trip and fly to the floor at an impressive speed. I was closer to the girl than her mother, so I could've helped but I try to limit my social interaction. I have become accustomed to smiling all the time but sometimes my face falters and I frown in public. I dread to think what would happen if the mother were to have seen me do such a treasonous thing. The mother hauled her daughter to her feet, smiling tremendously. When the child stood up, her face was dripping with blood. She stood there smiling as gashes full of dirt and grit patterned her youthful face. She took her mother's hand and, with both of them smiling like Cheshire cats, they headed down the street towards the hospital. The smiles are freaky enough without the knowledge that they still feel pain. That little girl would've been in agony but the injection kept her face in a perfect little smile.

Now, let's talk about the injection for a moment. The medical name for it is MixiMafoew 4-97-5-303. We tend to call it Mixi, for short. There's a number of things that Mixi does to the body. The most obvious effect is that it stretches your lips into a smile. A smile that can't falter. You can pull your face downwards with your fingers, but when you let go, Ping! It'll go right back into place. The second thing Mixi does is force your tear ducts shut. This is to stop the biggest display of distress: crying. However, tears aren't only for emotion. They also help to clean your eyes so many Zayathians are forced to pour water into their eyes to keep them moist and somewhat sterile. Disgusting, I know. The third and final thing that Mixi does is lower your pain tolerance. Now this is just a rumour, but I've done my research and it seems Dianne wants people to truly suffer. So, not only can you not display negative emotion, you'll bear the brunt of pain even worse than normal. Seeing people go through this is quite an unnerving sight, especially as I don't bear the effects of the injection. I sometimes wonder what it is like to be able to break a leg and yet continue to grin. There have been times when I longed to have not rejected the injection. It would be nice to be normal just for a little while.

# 2

The three merciless expressions of the Escobar family stare up at me from my modern history textbook. On the far left, Malcolm Escobar, king of Zayathai. The king is more of the lay-low type of guy. In his prime years, he was boisterous and cunning, but has since aged. His limp silver hair and sagging skin no longer give off the monarchal glow that they used to. Standing closely to Malcolm is his wife, Dianne Escobar. Her short hair is a rustic brown but it's obvious that she's used copious amounts of hair dye to cover up the grey in her locks. Everyone knows she's sixty-years-old yet she strives so hard to deceive us. I guess she doesn't want to be seen to have any weaknesses. She has bright, cunning eyes and an equally bright smile. I've never seen the woman without her crown. I sometimes wonder if it's stuck to her head. It's clear that the queen wears the trousers not only in their relationship, but also in the country. She rules with a cruel hand and a tough regime. Under the control of this ghastly woman, you can't really do anything in Zayathai of your own free will. She controls us like puppets, mocking us at every opportunity.

And finally, standing a tad too far to the right of the picture is Gabriel Escobar, prince of Zayathai. This guy is the heartthrob of our country. He was that baby that mothers always sat around saying dumb stuff about like, 'he's going to break a lot of hearts when he grows up.' His kind words and fountains of compliments has everyone, men and women, obsessed. Only certain types of media are allowed in Zayathai. Books are very limited but any type of positive media about the royal family is allowed. Hell, it's celebrated. On the rare occasion that I'm allowed to go to the library, it hasn't been uncommon for me to see literal fan-fictions about the prince. If you ask me, that is insane. I've read a few of the blurbs and each book has the same plot. A young girl falls in love with the prince and they live a lavish life together in the Escobar's stately home. Borrrringgggggg. I could write something much better than that if I really wanted to, which I don't. I'm sure you won't be surprised to know that Gabriel makes more of a presence than Malcolm. Whilst his dad smiles from the sidelines, Gabriel gives passionate speeches about his belief in the Mixi programme and regularly spews drivel about his adoration for his mother. Of course, people love him and if they don't, they pretend to. If I had to pick one word to describe such a person, I'd go for 'barnacle.' The prince, who's only twenty and a mere two years older than me, clings onto his mother like a barnacle on a blue whale. He is scared, nay petrified, that one day his dear mummy will get rid of him, and he'll be left to perish in the perilous waves of the open societal sea. It's no wonder people love Gabriel so much, he's a 'breath of fresh air' as my mother would say. People crave a young voice to spur them on and reassure them that the world is in safe hands. Besides, people practically swoon at his 'good looks'. The boy's all typical dark floppy hair and magical grey eyes. Although he's not exactly drop-dead-gorgeous, I'm not going to call him ugly. That would be a lie.

"Dakota, get your head out of that book. You know what time it is," my mother tells me.

"Just one more page." I don't even bother looking up as I mutter my response.

The fascination of the World war has sucked me in and I'm finding it hard to escape. I find a certain thrill in the hardship of the war. People sacrificing all they have for the good of their nation, mothers and children waving to their fathers as they're whisked off into battle. Call me weird, but the whole ordeal intrigues me. Don't get me wrong, I think chivalry and patriotism is outdated and weak but that doesn't stop me from finding it interesting. I try to continue reading but the crackling of the open fire beside me is rather distracting. My older brother, Cassius, is poking it with a short metal poker. He comes towards me, brandishing the hot rod. Before I can make sense of the situation, he presses it onto my forearm. I fight every nerve in my body that tells me to scream, because I know he's testing me.

"She said get up." He pushes the burning iron deeper into my skin.

His face is close to mine so I can hear his sharp breaths. I nod, eyes pressed tightly shut. He rips the poker off my arm and I run straight to the basement staircase, not daring to look back. The momentum of my fear-induced sprint sends me flying through the open titanium doorway and into the chair. I look down at the flesh wound on my arm. The skin is bright red and inflamed and it hurts, oh so bad. It's at times like these that I often wish I wasn't a Malsum. That's what they like to call us people who feel pain. It's short for Malum-sensum, which is the blood condition we suffer from. Of course, nobody, bar my family, knows that I'm a Malsum, or I'd be burnt at the stake. The sound of Cassius' heavy-duty boots approaches the chamber. He clambers through the doorway, having to duck because of his immense height. He walks over to me and restrains me to the chair with handcuffs and at least five zip ties. He grabs three fresh needles, attaches them to the tubes coming from the machine behind me and shoves them into my veins. I stare at the bare metal walls whilst he presses all the necessary buttons to get the machine going. After a minute or so, the machine makes its familiar whirring noise and spurs into action. Even after twelve years of blood-shedding I'm still not used to the first shockwave of pain that surges through my body. Cassius doesn't utter a single word to me throughout the whole process. Mind you, he never does. In case you hadn't already noticed, my brother and I aren't exactly best buddies. He flicks the radio on and is even kind enough to start the electric fan. As he trudges to the door, I find myself clearing my throat.

"Cassius." My voice is meek and powerless and I hate it. His head jolts towards me, a picture-perfect grin dancing on his lips. "How long will I be here?" I ask, causing his mouth to curl upwards, while his eyes remain dead.

"As long as we want you to," he grunts as he leaves the room. He swings the door shut behind him with a clunk and locks it using the external keypad.

Although the radio technically counts as entertainment, there's only one channel we can listen to, the Escobar daily. However, I can't bring myself to listen to them drone on and on about their political views, so I've now resorted to watching my blood. It's rather fascinating to watch the crimson stream go up the tubes and into the pouches at the top of the machinery. As much as I hate blood-shedding I do in a way feel better for it. This blood, my blood, will go on the black market so someone can drink it and just for a few seconds they will have the pleasure of displaying emotion and crying like a Malsum. You can only imagine the emotional toll that the injection has on Zayathian citizens. What do you do when you sprain a wrist or go through a messy breakup? You cry. A box of tissues in hand, you watch a soppy romance film and cry. You cannot do that in Zayathai. If you are sad, you smile. If you are happy, you smile. If you are grieving, you smile. If your leg has been severed off by a chainsaw, you smile. Zayathians are stripped of that emotional release. Our suicide rate is horrific. People can't take this internal pain. They have no outlet, and that comes at a devastating price. So, giving my blood does make me feel proud sometimes. Don't get me wrong though, if I wasn't forced to do this, I really wouldn't. The machine is rickety and homemade, so the pain that I face when it vacuums blood from my veins is immense. It makes me faint, nauseous and, for some unknown reason, very hungry. Malsum blood also comes with the defect that our blood replenishes itself every twenty-four hours or thereabouts. It's amazing really. Our defective blood is exclusive to Zayathai. One hundred years ago, when Mixi was first introduced, Malsums did not exist. It evolved only in recent decades, when some people started to resist the injection. I think it's a mutation, though I'm not too sure how the science works.

Mother and Cassius see me as nothing but a source of income. As you can imagine, selling blood or even being a Malsum is strictly illegal, so it must be done very carefully. People go to all sorts of lengths and pay ludicrous amounts of money to get a handful of some blood. Mother relishes in this, so my blood earns us quite a lot of dosh. If I'm being honest, I think my Malsum blood earns more than my mother's standard job at the local arms factory. Not that she turns up to work anyway. The lazy slob is too busy lounging on the sofa or arguing with me. The only reason they haven't killed me on the spot is because my blood pays the rent. Happy families, I know.

The ancient battery-powered fan whirls beside my head as the radio plays the latest oration of Gabriel Escobar. "Good evening, Zayathai. The date is 24th October 2194 and the time is 5:30 pm. As I'm sure you are all aware, on Thursday we celebrate annual injection day. This is such a special day for six-year-olds across Zayathai and I'm sure parents will be delighted to hear the final cries of their children. The youngest of our people are becoming mature, emotionless members of society so I'd like to formally congratulate them on this special occasion."

God, what a load of rubbish. People should be allowed to feel things. Obviously the Escobars are aware of this. They know all too well that their deeds are disgusting. But this injection keeps them afloat. It keeps Zayathai's reputation as the happiest place on earth and it keeps thousands of tourists paying large expenses to come and see us. Tourists can't bring cameras into our country and we aren't allowed out, so people come from all over the globe to witness the sensation that is our country. They marvel at our joy and ask, "How do they do it?" Their words are laced with bewilderment. "Drugs," I sometimes feel tempted to say. "None of this is real, you idiots!" I want to scream from the hilltops. I want to stand at the top of the tallest mountain and shriek, "The Escobars are a bunch of blood-thirsty psychopaths!"

Prince Gabriel's low voice bounces between the titanium walls of the cellar. As much as I hate his propagandistic drivel, it's the only source of entertainment that's available to me. Considering that I spend so much time in the dark depths of this basement, you'd think Mother would allow me some form of decent leisure. It's evident that she hates me. With no good reason, I might add. It's almost as if Mother was sure that she'd give birth to a Malsum. After she shot me in the arm to ensure I had emotions, she brought me straight down to the chamber. It had been fully prepared and waiting for me. The room is all titanium so there's no chance I could break out. It's even passcode-locked and only Mother and Cassius know the combination. Heavens, I've never seen anything as intimidating as the chair I'm sitting in right now. The chair is one of the only things of a nice colour in this room. It's made of a rich wood, most likely from a dark oak tree. There's a set of handcuffs cleverly attached to it to stop me from escaping and it's studded with sharp metal spikes not fixed on the actual seat; Mother isn't that mean. The spikes serve no purpose other than to scare the life out of me. Attached to the back of the chair is the bloodsucking machine. Sadly enough, this machine is the only thing that keeps me company, apart from that wretched radio. The machine makes a sudden jolt which jams the needles in even further. A cry leaps from my mouth and echoes around the sound proof chamber. Imagine caring so little for your daughter that you build a chamber in the basement to lock her in so she can give blood every day of her god-awful life. There are only three things that keep me going in here: the radio, watching my blood and dreams. Hopeless, wonderful dreams.

Just as I begin to question if my body can take much more blood-shedding, I hear the familiar beeping of the keypad. The door slides open with a clunk and the rough face of my brother appears. His blonde locks are askew and flakes of dandruff line each hair. His sharp stubble draws attention away from the many scars that he's somehow obtained.

"Learnt your lesson, Dakota?" He advances on me, his cold blue eyes glaring down at me like icy lasers. I find it in my best interest to simply nod as I don't think I'll survive any longer. Cassius chuckles. A groggy, rancid chuckle that reverberates off the shiny walls and hammers through my skull.

"I must say, you do look rather pale," he quips as he tears the needles from my veins. One, two, three times my fingers tense as each one of them is ripped from my body.

"Of course, I'm pale, Cassius. You left me down here for two hours," I whisper, too weak to speak. His lips curl into an even more menacing smile.

"Two hours? More like five."

"You left me to bloodshed for five hours? You could've killed me!" I hiss.

"Well maybe you'll think about this the next time you want to be defiant." He unties me from the chair and straightens up to full length. "Now get up. Mother's made dinner." His heavy-duty boots thunder up the stairs before I can request assistance to stand up. My legs are so weak I'm convinced they'll buckle under my weight. And sure enough, they do.

By the time I make it to the living room I'm an absolute wreck. As always, I manage to push my emotions down when I spot my little sister Marley perched on the sofa. I couldn't bear to be the reason she's upset. Like Cassius, Marley also has blonde hair, but hers is neat and clean. She wears a pair of brow-line glasses that go perfectly well with her encyclopaedia to make her look like the smartest six-year-old in town. If I saw her down the street, I would've guessed she's eight or nine. Her sophistication and elegance go beyond the abilities of any normal six-year-old. But she isn't normal. None of us are. Both of my siblings are blonde-haired and blue-eyed so I can only imagine Mother's horror when she gave birth to me; a child of dark eyes and thick black hair. Whilst spooning unholy amounts of rice into her mouth, Mother watches the rest of Gabriel's speech and shouts 'hear hear!' at everything he says. She must've taped it because he'd been talking five hours ago, when I first went into the chamber. Obviously, I couldn't see him on the radio, but now here he is in full HD. His piercing grey eyes seem as though they are glaring at me through the screen. Somehow, he's managed to survive teenhood without a single spot on his pristine skin. I wouldn't be surprised if he takes some secret medicine to keep himself looking perfect. It's evident that looks are everything to him. A neat set of floppy brown hair is set on his head and his military-style outfit is nothing short of immaculate. I wouldn't expect any less from the son of a bloodthirsty dictator. There is a kind of roughness to him, though. He may look clean-shaven and well-kept but he looks hungry. Hungry for violence and control. It's almost as if his eyes are sending messages, daring you to step out of line. He most certainly could kill, if he wanted to, there's little doubt about that. You disobey him or compromise his values and you can say goodbye to your life.

"...And now onto the next call of duty, and undoubtedly the most important. My mother, Dianne Escobar, is celebrating her birthday over the coming week and we invite the whole of Zayathai to join the party. We will hold four parties, one in each area of Zayathai. We'll attend the North on Monday, the East on Tuesday, the South on Wednesday and the West on Thursday. Do not be late. The dress code is strictly black. That'll be all. From me and everyone at the Escobar Estate, we wish you a wonderful evening and a splendid night's sleep."

Gabriel flashes the camera a glistening smile before the news channel cuts off. Mother almost sends me into cardiac arrest as she bursts into a fit of spontaneous applause. Sat in her princess costume, my sister starts clapping too, though she has no idea what's going on. She then returns to reading the massive encyclopaedia that's placed in her lap.

"Oh, isn't he just wonderful?" Mother says with a dreamy sigh. I nod just to get her off my case, but Cassius agrees with genuine enthusiasm. Mother's eyes dart to my little sister, realising that she hadn't shown enough appreciation for the almighty Gabriel.

"For Gods' sake child, I wish you would get your nose out of that book once in a while." As you've probably noticed, Mother is also a Malsum. Though she doesn't indulge in bloodshed because she's a selfish cow, but hey ho.

Marley doesn't even acknowledge Mother, which prompts the angry woman to snatch the book from her hands and throw it to the floor.

"I'm talking to you!" she screeches. Marley's face crumbles and she runs upstairs.

"Go and tell her to shut up, Dakota. If the neighbours overhear, they might think you're the one crying."

I find it quite insulting that she thinks my crying

would sound the same as that of a six-year-old girl, but I tread after her all the same.

"Mar?" I knock a few times but there's no response. I push the door open and a meek beam of light stretches across the room. Marley is lying face down on her bed. Her body trembles as she tries to stifle her wails in the pillow. I rub her back until her crying dies down. Next to her I place Bunny, her beloved stuffed animal, and her encyclopaedia. Marley has always adored Bunny. Back then when my mother used to dote over Marley, she gave her Bunny as a 1st birthday gift. The toy is rather simple with its glassy black eyes and its long floppy ears but Mar acts like he's one of a kind. Of course, it sports the standard nose that kids always adopt when drawing animals. You know, that triangular nose that's connected to an obscure smile and a few whiskers. Bunny has gone everywhere with Marley and has managed to stay fairly clean. Though I can assure you that if Bunny did get dirty somehow, Marley would not let you clean him. She has this thing about sentiment and not getting rid of memories. If Bunny gets dropped in a puddle, Marley will want to remember that. I feel like this could be because, like me, Marley has no friends whatsoever. Normal kids make memories together at the park and take cute pictures and all that. We can't do that. Every day is just as the one before; eat, work then work some more and, for me, blood-shedding. Satisfied that she's content, I leave, making sure to close the door behind me.

I decide to explore the confines of the only beautiful room in the house to calm myself down. I tread along the small landing and grab the stick that leans against the wall. Although the ceiling is reasonably high up, it isn't too difficult to elevate the stick and hook the curved end to the tab. I yank the stick and the trapdoor swings open. I latch the stick to the ladder and pull it down. I know I'm not allowed in here but this is a good opportunity to do so. Mother and Cassius are distracted by the tv so they won't hear the creaking noise as I climb the metal ladder. Once I reach the top, my head feels light as it's hit by a gust of cold air. I haul myself onto the floor of the attic. The sight that greets my eyes is something that everyone in Zayathai should be allowed to experience. There's so much contraband that I've barely got through a quarter of it in my eighteen years of living. Dad was a collector, you see. He got a thrill out of owning things that the monarchy didn't want us to have. His obsession started out with buying the odd book from the black market. Only a few years later, we could barely house all of his illegal magazines, films and books.

I am grateful though. It allowed me to understand the outside world. The real world. Information about other countries is scarce in Zayathai unless it's a WW3 book, in which the author invariably gloats about who we managed to destroy and how. Honestly, from what I've read, the people of Zayathai like to take a lot of credit for things that had nothing to do with them. Sure, we were on the winning team, but we didn't win. I've read quite a few banned history books and from what I've gathered this is a recurring theme about world wars. Mind you, Zayathai didn't actually exist during the other major conflicts; we weren't founded until 2036, which is about midway through the war.

I weave in between boxes full of contraband until I reach my all-time favourite: the vintage films. I drop to my knees and start sorting through the box in search of my favourite movie. It must be here somewhere. My hands are coated with dust by the time I tear it out from underneath tens of other disc jackets: The Truman Show. In the movie, Truman's whole life was a lie. Sometimes I feel like that. Zayathai is a fake, horrifying take on reality. I wish I could break free. I blow on the cover and a cloud of dust flies into my face. I sniff and wrinkle my nose, but that doesn't stop an extraordinary sneeze from flying out of my nostrils, as I mutter, "Dammit, Dakota. Shut up." After searching for the old DVD player, I plug it into the so very faulty socket, sit on the floor and let the story consume me. The strange thing is, the concept of a DVD player isn't even that vintage to us. The war was so devastating that all technological advances had to be put on hold. Our world is no more high-tech than the days of the 2020s. If anything, I think technology was more impressive back then. The whole world is impoverished so no one can really afford to own the same technology that they would've had. It's like when a plant isn't watered. Of course, it will still grow somewhat but not early enough as when nourishment was in abundance.

I bring my knees up to my chest and a frown spreads across my lips. Ironically enough, sitting here with a tragic movie and an equally as tragic expression on my face, is my happy place. Even the smallest opportunity to not be grinning is much more therapeutic than you could ever imagine. Of course, we frown around the house but it's discouraged. You never know who's watching you through the window. The snitch culture in this village is astounding and I sure don't fancy being locked up any time soon. Never do I feel more comforted than when I can let my true emotions be released. I guess I'm lucky. This respite is something that every non-malsum craves and will never have.

Later, I throw myself onto my single bed and release a dramatic sigh. My eyes glaze across the almost walls of my box room. I've put up a few paintings and posters but that's about it. I really should decorate around here at some point. Although, it's not like I get the time. If I'm not doing my schoolwork, or Cassius' because he forces me to, I'm blood-shedding in that goddamn chamber. Maybe I should decorate the chamber instead. I spend more time there, sitting bolt upright in that wooden chair than I do in the comfort of my own room.

**3**

"Home by sunset," that's what Mother told us. I'm surprised she has it in her heart to even let us go out in the first place. All we seem to do is work and clean. I sometimes manage to go for a walk alone, but Mother has a special thing about letting Marley go out. Perhaps, on a good day she'll let me take her to the market, but that's about it. I suppose it's protection. The less we're out in public, the less likely we are to expose our demons. So, you can imagine how grateful I was when she allowed us to go to the local park for a little while. She didn't even say anything when I took a pack of grapes for us to share. Granted, her jaw did harden and her eyes squinted at me but I knew I was pushing it. The park is busier than normal. I suppose everyone's decided to get all of their kids tired out for the party. Having your offspring acting up in the presence of the monarchy would not be a good look.

We found a bench under a tall oak tree. It took us a considerable amount of time to flick off all the leaves and foliage, but it was worth it. This gives us quite a nice view of the outstretched field before us. I wouldn't call the park beautiful as such, but it's certainly prettier than the rest of the village. Simply having green grass and a couple of trees already makes it so much more appealing than the bleak, grey housing estate.

"You took all the good grapes," Marley complains, her delicate smile gleaming in the soft glow of the afternoon sun. She sits cross-legged with Bunny planted in her lap.

"I did not!" I protest.

"Did so." Marley sweeps a blonde lock of hair from her face and grabs a grape. Most of the grapes are squishy and bruised, but we are always grateful. Fruit is scarce in our house due to the amount of ration points they cost. The only things that tend to live in our moulding cupboards are rice, soups and lentils.

"I hope the party has good food," Marley quips.

"It will, I'm sure. Dianne will be keen to put on a good show." I pop an overripe grape in my mouth and lean back. "She always does." Marley nods and smooths out a crease in her jeans before looking across the park. At least a hundred little kids litter the field, shadowed by their parents. Groups of teenagers lay on the grass and watch the scarce, grey clouds. This all seems so tranquil, but I can't help but tear my gaze away from the smiling citizens to stare at the tens of guards that roam around. They go by the name of The Royal Guards, but they'll always be thugs to me. A group of men who march around Zayathai with their menacing guns and uniforms and buzzcuts, with the sole intention of scaring the living daylights out of us all.

Nothing in Zayathai ever feels real. It's nearly impossible to tell if these people are happy. They can ride their tandem bikes and play with frisbees all they like, but that doesn't excuse the fact that every single one of them is probably crying inside. No matter how happy the situation, the aching agony of keeping emotions quashed is unbearable. Even as someone who suffers from Malum-sensum, I spend all of my life pretending that I'm happy. At least in privacy I can cry and frown. Normal people can't. Marley presses a particularly bruised grape to Bunny's mouth. Obviously, he doesn't eat it so the flesh smears across his fur.

Marley lays down on the bench, her head resting in my lap. I curl the blonde strands of her hair between my fingers and for a few sacred minutes we just relax. I say sacred because something always ruins any remnants of tranquillity in this damned country. This time it happened to be the silhouette of a man casting over us and blocking the sunlight. I feel Marley shudder as our sun source is blocked by whoever is standing before us. My eyes train up and meet the eyes of a guard. The tips of his dark buzzcut glimmers with tiny beads of sweat that stand proudly on top of each hair like the jewels on a crown. The other thing that I notice to be glimmering is the silver gun in his waistband. I try not to look at it. Being stared in the face by a firearm is only going to make me nervous and confidence is key when trying to fool a guard. I wait patiently for him to speak as his hazel eyes glaze over Marley and me. When encountering a guard, you never speak first. Never.

"Good afternoon, ladies." His voice is gruff and laced with that prideful edge that every guard's voice obtains. It's that edge of superiority. Sure they are still ruled by Dianne but they are just that bit better than us and they take great pleasure in that.

"Good afternoon, sir." I say, dipping my head in a slight bow of respect. Marley doesn't speak. She doesn't even move. He waits for her to speak but her eyes simply train to the floor in disacknowledgement. When it becomes clear that he isn't going to get a greeting from Marley, the guard looks back up to me.

"I trust you'll be attending the gathering tonight." The accusatory tone that glosses over each syllable makes me want to punch every tooth out of his grinning mouth.

"Of course. We'd never pass on the chance to respect our queen." I add a faint, barely noticeable edge of sarcasm into my voice. Enough to give myself satisfaction but not enough that the guard can be certain he even heard it. By the slight kick of his left eyebrow, he definitely noticed.

"Well we're just doing our round of the park to advise everyone to head home and prepare. This is going to be an event that you'll want to be dressed up for." I can't help but notice the way his hand caresses the trigger of the gun as he speaks. We were going to leave soon anyway but now that a guard has told us to, I really don't feel like doing it anymore. It's very difficult being a defiant person who lives in a dictatorship.

"As you wish," I say, moving to get to my feet. With a sigh, Marley lifts her head allowing me to stand. The guard looks down at Marley and my eyes follow his gaze. She's frowning.

"Don't worry," I blurt out. "She's not had her Mixi yet." His face relaxes a little and he nods.

"Understood. I must get on with my duties so…" His hand rises to his forehead in a salute. "By the power of the crown we trust…"

Marley and I return the salute and complete the mandatory phrase, "May the Escobars eternally reign over us."

"Good day," he says before turning and marching off. Marley's small palm falls into mine.

"He's right, we should get back," I tell her. "The sun is starting to set."

# 4

No matter how much I try to convince myself, this dress looks horrible. The satin fabric clings to me in all the wrong places and I can't seem to get it to flow around my waist. I look like I've bought a dress in the wrong size, but this is the closest I could get. My body is extremely thin, making shopping for clothes the most tedious of practises. I do have other coloured dresses that fit me much better, but the dress code is black. Of course, this colour choice is Dianne's way of mocking us for being unable to show our emotions. She only brought in this injection to torture the citizens of Zayathai. Don't ask me why, I have no idea; nor does anyone to be completely honest. Well, I say Dianne brought in the injection. She didn't. I think it was her great grandfather or something. I'm not really sure but it was a long time ago. The Escobars have reigned for an ungodly amount of time. Like I mentioned earlier, it all started after the Great World War. To put it simply there was a huge battle across the planet. The world was in absolute ruins, devastated by weapons and violence. Billions of people died, a third of the population, I think my textbook says. By the time everything settled down, there wasn't much life left. The world was essentially made up of bomb craters and broken cities. The reality of just how long repair would take is what lead to our suffering. Like the rest of the planet, Zayathai was in tatters. People were desperate for any form of relief. That's where the Escobars came in. They rocked up with their false agendas and empty promises and everyone bought it. Soon enough they were elected for the monarchy and still to this day no one can overthrow them. I guess we are living in a dictatorship. I'm not too sure how politics work.

Even though my sheer ugliness is all too real, I can't help but watch myself in the mirror. I take pride in the fact that I'm not vain in the slightest. Mind you there isn't much to be vain about. My hair is jet black, which only serves to accentuate the paleness of my skin. I'll give it to myself; my hair isn't utterly scarce of volume. It's very thick and has the slight hint of a wave pattern and I've never had to deal with it being greasy. I decided to tie it up into a bun plait just to keep it out of my way for the night. My face is this odd shape, sort of long and triangular. Chiselled jaws are supposedly attractive on men, but girls are supposed to be slightly…. squishier. You know, like cuter and daintier and soft. I wouldn't say I have a sharp jawline, I'm just hopelessly skinny. This isn't complemented by my out of proportion limbs. Mother always tells me that I look like a twig. As much as I could deny that, we all know I'd be lying. I wouldn't necessarily say I'm scrawny. I'm of a reasonable height, kind of that awkward middle ground between average and tall. One of my eyes is a tad bigger than the other, but they're both quite small and squinted. Although a lot of people tend to think one of their eyes is bigger so maybe I'm just seeing things like everyone else. Like everyone else…wow I don't say that often. Life for me kind of revolves around the idea that I'm not like everyone else.

When I come downstairs, Mother is making a massive fuss over Marley's dress. Personally, I think she looks fabulous, but everything's a faff when it comes to my mum. Even as Mother is tying the bow on Marley's dress, my sister is still reading her book. I sometimes envy her passion for literature. I do write the occasional line of poetry, though I've never indulged in the pleasure of reading the work of fellow writers. I guess it comes with my dissociation from most of society. Mother forced me and Marley into homeschooling when we found out that I had emotions, because if I were to burst into tears at school, we'd all be burnt at the stake for hiding information from the government.

"Now," Mother begins as she smoothes out the last creases in Marley's dress, "I want all of you to be on your best behaviour. Dakota, if I see you so much as think about frowning, you'll bloodshed for double hours tonight. Understood?"

I nod but the harsh scowl on my face remains. A sharp pain surges through my back, biting and tingling at my flesh. A small gasp escapes my lips but I'm careful not to cry out.

"Stop being stupid," Cassius hisses into my ear.

Rule number one of living in Zayathai: never leave the house without putting your smile on first. My mouth stretches into a painful grin and he pulls his chosen weapon out of my back, a fork. I'd believed the gap in the back of my dress to be quite stylish, but it has seemed to have come back to bite me. Cassius presses a plaster over the wound and pushes me towards the front door. My Mother stretches her grin as wide as possible and parts her lips to speak.

"Now everyone, be happy."

A gentle buzz fills my ears as we leave the house. Every man and his dog are readying themselves for the party. Zayathians tend to be quite reserved. We aren't the kind of people to go outside and chat with our neighbours. I suppose everyone is just trying to get by. Whether you're a Malsum or not, the Escobars are always watching you. Let's say that I become best friends with my next-door neighbour. If, God forbid, I was discovered to be a Malsum my neighbour would be arrested immediately. They'd be rigorously interrogated by guards at the station, and forced to admit that they knew what I was. Even if that wasn't true, the monarchy has a way of making people confess. For every person you decide to associate with, you put yourself at a higher risk of arrest. And nobody returns once they've been put in one of those black vans. No one.

I feel an odd sense of camaraderie as we acknowledge people that I have never seen before. People that I didn't know lived right beside us, until now. My siblings and I repeat the awkward waving thing that everyone along the street seems to be doing. I think it must have something to do with the extra number of guards that seem to be on duty today. I suppose this week is dedicated to Dianne and what does Dianne love more than anything? People smiling. She must revel in seeing everyone happy and jolly, as if it proves to the rest of the world how much better we are than them. In my opinion, it makes us worse because we're so miserable that we need medicine to force smiles upon our lips. At least the scarce number of grins that occur in the destroyed parts of the world are genuine. Mother can't just grin and wave; she has to go the extra mile, yelling 'how's the husband?' and other pleasantries at old ladies across the road. If only she could act so sweet and harmless at home.

It takes a good five minutes before we can finally turn to the safety of Mother's grey four by four. The stench of waterlogged material attacks my nose as I open the door. It takes all my willpower to force myself into the dingy vehicle.

"Something must've died in here," I murmur from the backseat. Mother glares at me through the rearview mirror.

"Don't be ridiculous, child. After a hard day at work, I accidentally left the windows open overnight. It must've rained at some point." Everyone in the car knows that she probably blew off work to go gambling or clothes shopping, but no one dares mention it.

The journey takes a lot longer than anticipated because people from the whole area are streaming to the city centre at the same time. To my luck, Mother has quite profound road rage so I learnt a few new insults on the way. It's quite amusing to watch as she has to do it all with that stupid grin on her face. As we approach the car park, gentle music seeps through the cracks in the windows. The sounds of hundreds of car doors shutting hammers at my ears as we step out of the car. Families and groups of all kinds abandon their cars and make their way to the main event. Guards are situated all over the car park, ordering people to park their cars in specific positions. Dianne does things like this. She's deployed her men and told them that they have to force people to do such a minor task in a particular way. Deciding where to park is a simple task, and it ought to be your decision. She likes to take away simple liberties just to make us feel incompetent.

The party is just as I'd expected. Opulence and sophistication cover every ounce of the town centre. The area consists of a huge green with a towering statue of Dianne at the centre. A stage has been set up, presumably for Dianne to make one of her speeches. Tables made of the finest oak hold platters of various hors d'oeuvres; salmon and cottage cheese, figs with anise and walnuts. She even bothered to get mini jam sandwiches for the children. Dianne is really in the mood for manipulation today. This probably means that she's ramping up to do something horrible to us. Normally, when something good happens in Zayathai it's only to compensate for whatever devilish plans she has in store. Last time she gave every worker in the country a day-off. Not a week later, the number of ration points needed to get sugar quadrupled and sodas were made illegal. Why? I have no idea. There'll be no logical reason. Like I said, taking away our liberties is all a part of the monarchy's sick game.

Of course, every face wears a vivid smile, but I can easily tell who suffers from Malum-sensum. Our smiles just aren't the same as everyone else's. Others can't tell the difference, but the devastating contrast is all too real for me.

The town centre is absolutely huge. The population of Zayathai is two million, rather small, I think. If I've calculated correctly, there are approximately two hundred and fifty thousand people in our Northern town square at this moment. You'd assume that the area is crowded, but we're actually very spaced out. There's room to dance and chat and do all the other social niceties.

Marley's small hand is tightly pressed into mine, so I find it difficult to drink the sauvignon blanc that swishes in my glass. Tied to Marley's small wrist is a black ribbon that is attached to a black balloon, which contains black confetti. Everything at this party is black. Even the podium at which Dianne is about to give her speech is as dark as the coat of a panther. Some strange variation of soft jazz plays in the background of the party. A few old couples attempt to slow-dance but they look ridiculous. See, Dianne doesn't allow many forms of media from outside Zayathai so none of us know much about other cultures. My father used to be a smuggler, so our attic is full to the brim of forbidden items. Mother won't let us go up there but sometimes I do when she's gone out (or even when she's downstairs, if I'm feeling particularly brave). I'm quite privileged to have such a broad knowledge of the outside world. Most people don't get that pleasure. I've seen a few contraband videos of ball dancing from a place called France. From what I've heard it sounds like quite a lovely country to live in. Although they might say the same about us. As far as other countries are concerned, we are the happiest culture on the planet. Access to Zayathai is restricted, but should someone be allowed to visit, they are only shown what Dianne wants them to see: the crystal waterfall in Mavolee Lane, the beautiful art museums containing pieces that they don't know are made by tortured prisoners, that sort of thing. It's all an act. A painful act.

The screeching feedback of Dianne's microphone resonates through the entire square. The congregation falls into a deep silence as the Queen stands up to the podium.

"Good evening, my subjects. I thank you all for attending my birthday celebration. I count myself quite lucky to have been born at such a wonderful time of year. The flowers are blossoming, the wind is blissfully absent but best of all, strawberries are back in season."

The crowd seems to think this crass attempt at humour absolutely hilarious, so I'm forced to laugh along with them. I squeeze Marley's hand encouraging her to join in too. A hysterical cackle escapes from my sister's lips and my whole body cringes. I hate it that she has to feign her happiness. I hope that one day she'll live in a world that values her feelings, instead of quashing them. Dianne continues to drone on for at least ten minutes and by the time she's finished, I have consumed the remainder of my wine. I suppose that being of the tender age of eighteen I should refrain from alcohol, but I doubt I'll make it through this so-called 'party' without it.

As I chat to Marley about the latest chapter of her encyclopaedia, I can't help but notice that the prince keeps trying to catch my eye. Gabriel stands with a group of men around his age as they chuckle and chatter about politics and horses and other 'manly' topics. I can't imagine they're actually enjoying the conversation, but these types of people will do anything to be above everyone else. Even though Gabriel is around quite often, I still never get used to seeing him in the flesh. He's one of those people that just doesn't seem real. I suppose that's because almost every poster, tv show and book is dedicated to him and his dreadful excuse of a family. He continues to look over at me and he's so cocky that when our gazes do meet, he doesn't look away, but prolongs the awkwardness by holding my gaze. He's way too confident for my liking. By the tenth time, I almost scoff at his audacity. As much as I'm angered by his haughty sense of self, I notice something about myself. I can stand here and criticise him all I like for not looking away, but neither did I and I have no idea why.

Before I can make sense of the situation, Gabriel bids farewell to his friends. They all smack him on the back and shake hands in the usual toxic demonstration of their masculinity. I expect him to move towards his mother, his family. Instead, he spins on the heel of his loafers and begins stalking towards us. Mum notices and instructs Marley to stand up straight before he makes our acquaintance. Her hands do these excitable flicks as he moves nearer. My grip tightens on the wine glass and I find that it's near to shattering, but I don't let go. I hope with everything in my heart that he's about to make acquaintance with another poor family, but sure enough his promenade ends when he reaches us.

"Good evening, your majesty," Mother says, before Gabriel has a chance to say anything.

"Good evening to you too, ma'am." He nods his head towards her and I swear she almost faints. I snort not so quietly and Cassius nudges me. I hold the transparent cup to my mouth, trying to hide my giggles. Gabriel's left brow raises at me slightly and I notice him trying to stifle a laugh of his own.

"Why, it is a pleasure to meet you at last." Mother drags his attention back to her, for which I'm quite grateful. "Might I be so presumptuous to say that your speech last night was absolutely invigorating! I have never felt so inspired in my whole life!"

"Thank you, ma'am. That is quite–" Gabriel doesn't even manage to finish his sentence before Mother falls into a curtsy. I fight the urge to physically facepalm. "How very kind of you. Really, I am quite flattered at your… gentility. I don't want to intrude but might I be able to talk to your two daughters?" Mother's eyes darken but she remains calm.

"Those two? Yes, that is…absolutely fine."

She gestures towards us. Gabriel gives her this look. It isn't inviting or polite; rather it's cold and provides a surefire warning that she needs to make her excuses and leave us to it. Due to her horrific case of egotism, Mother ignores this clear signal and stays rooted where she is, as does Cassius.

"Alone." Gabriel's voice is raspy and tainted by faint irritation. Mother's face goes as red as a blood moon. Cassius doesn't look best pleased either.

"Oh, of course your highness. Be my guest." Mother moves off still in the curtsy position with Cassius close behind her. All three of us watch as they retreat into the distance.

"I must say your dress is simply magnificent," Gabriel tells Marley, kneeling down to her level. Her face stays in an unimpressed expression.

"I didn't choose to wear this. Personally, I think it's ugly."

"Marley!" I almost scream, though I'm careful to refrain from frowning.

Any display of anger could end in me being burnt to ashes. Instead of my anticipated reaction, Gabriel's thin lips sport an even brighter smile. He stands back up and straightens his suit. The signature beanie that always remains on his head seems to have been left on the hat stand for the night. I'm sure he wanted to wear it but I don't think even he could pull off a suit and beanie. Instead, he's sporting what normal princes wear: a crown. It's quite a simple design. The metal is of a rich silver and each peak holds a black gem that I couldn't identify. However, I can easily recognise the jewel that forms a regular pattern around the crown: diamond. Pure diamond.

"So, I presume she's yet to get her injection?" He enquires, and I nod. "Well, that'll all change tomorrow." I can't help but notice the venom that laces his words.

"And you…"

"Dakota," I announce without hesitation.

"Dakota. You also look ravishing tonight. I could only imagine having such a fabulous dress sense."

I can't tell whether this is polite conversation or sheer flirting, but I manage to blush all the same. I hope to God that he didn't notice my pale cheeks flush red; it would be stupid to believe he hadn't.

"I'm so sorry but I must go. The balloons are about to be set off and I must stand with Mother. You know what she's like."

I want to tell him that his mother is a stone-cold witch but obviously that would be an abysmal mistake. He offers a gentle bow and we curtsy in response. I don't know if my eyes deceive me but I'm sure I see him wink at me before he leaves. My mouth opens and closes like a goldfish. I find it strange that he didn't make us recite the mandatory phrase. Perhaps he doesn't have to, as the prince of the country, but I could've sworn it was a law. As soon as he is out of eyesight, Mother and Cassius rush back to us.

"What did he say?" Mother squeals.

"He looks so handsome tonight." Cassius ogles.

"Please tell me you were polite. Did you offer him a proper curtsy?" Mother continues. Marley and I remain silent as they hurl an array of questions at us.

"I need a drink," I mutter. Taking Marley's hand, I

turn and head for a nearby table. I take a champagne for me and a juice carton for Marley. She stabs the straw in the silver disk and slurps the drink. I tip my head back and empty the contents of the glass into my mouth in one swell gulp.

"Careful, Kota. That champagne contains at least 12.5% alcohol by volume." Marley reaches up and snatches the cup out of my hand. She taps a nearby butler who gives me a disapproving look and takes the glass from my sister. Does he seriously think I gave my six-year-old sister that alcohol?

"What do you know about alcohol content?"

"More than you, apparently," Marley retorts. I bite the inside of my cheek. "In the attic there was a book on alcohol culture. It's quite a good read, Kota. I really recommend it." She vacuums the rest of the juice out of the box and tosses the container onto the table.

"You shouldn't be going into the attic. If someone finds you up there it's not going to be pretty." She squints her eyes at me.

"Kota, you go up there all the time." Marley makes a very good point, which can only be responded to with the most stupid phrase known to man.

"Do as I say not as I do." She opens her mouth to release another good point but I start walking before she gets the chance. I hear the pattering of her small footsteps as she chases after me. My left palm tingles when her teeny hand slips back into mine.

We move closer to the stage where the Escobars stand. Men dressed in expensive tuxedos hand each person a black balloon. Marley is delighted to get another balloon, even though she already has one. At the sound of a trumpet, the entire town falls into silence. A sudden uptake of wind surges through the square and my body shivers from the cold.

"We fly these balloons to recognise our adoration for our Queen, our inspiration, our reason to live. By the power of the crown we trust..!" Gabriel yells.

"May the Escobars eternally reign over us!" The crowd bellows. The sky is littered with a sea of black as we release our balloons into the atmosphere.

To my surprise, Mother excused me from my blood-shedding session tonight. I suppose she was so crestfallen by her encounter with Gabriel that she forgot about my duty. This is lucky for me, because I don't think I've ever felt more tired in my life. As soon as I fall through the door of my room, I kick off my stilettos, tear off the dress and crawl into bed. My feet ache after all that walking in those stupid high heels, but the pain eases a little when I finally take the weight off them. Combined with all of this exhaustion, I think blood-shedding would've tipped me over the edge. I should probably explain again why I call it blood-shedding. When I sit in that basement, alone, freezing and hungry, I feel like death. Every drop of blood that is sucked from my veins feels like a battle against my own body. It's akin to the sensation of being at war. I'm seldom overcome by a feeling of honour or pride as that machine extracts each ounce of my being. It is bloodshed. Not just giving blood. Not even donating blood. Bloodshed.

**5**

I. Hate. Weed. And, before you jump to any conclusions, I don't mean marijuana. I quite like marijuana actually. Kidding! I tried it once in a park and it made me splutter like there's no tomorrow. What I'm talking about is weed-weeds. The ones that line our entire front garden. The ones that Mother has forced me to pick for the best part of the afternoon. It's tiresome work and it doesn't help that the blaring sun projects its heat on me as I tug at these useless shrubs. I thought it appropriate to wear dungarees in true farmer style but now the summer warmth has come along, I'd do anything for shorts and a t-shirt. The street is quiet. A few grinning families pass me but that's about it. The guards, however, seem to be on the prowl much more often than usual. I'm used to seeing maybe five guards pass down the street per day but now it's becoming an hourly thing. A few of them have knocked on doors and asked stupid questions like 'Have you seen or spoken to anyone whom you believe to be a Malsum?' First of all, if I had I wouldn't snitch. Secondly, if I was the type of rat to dob someone into the authorities, I would've done it by now. For the guards to be so present something must've happened. I don't have time to think about this much as I swear repeatedly under my breath and try to uproot a particularly stubborn weed.

"Just get out you...you stupid weed!" I scream at the plant. I put my foot against a rock for extra stability and tug with all my might. I break before the plant does, losing my footing and ploughing to the floor. My head slams into the ground, throbbing and burning. I lay on my back and let out a deep sigh. As I'm in public view, I'm careful to keep a smile on my face. I'm sure several people must've witnessed my failure. A shadow falls over me. It can't be cloudy already, can it? A gentle face looks down at me.

"Nice day, isn't it?" A deep voice asks. I jump up and dust myself off, heart hammering against my ribcage.

"Good morning, your highness." I curtsy awkwardly in my dungarees. He watches me with a careful glance. I can't help but stare at the dagger in his waistband. The diamond glares back at me. His beanie has made a reappearance on his head, despite the blazing temperature.

"You can call me Gabriel." It takes me a minute to process this. As much as he has a very swarthy composure, normally the prince reserves his first name for people he's well acquainted with. Strange. "Gardening, I see?" He looks past me to all the random tools I took from the garden shed.

"Yep, that's me. Always...doing my bit." Act normal, Dakota! The prince nods with his hands clasped behind his back. "Can I help you or...?" "No, no I was just doing my rounds. I've been made the guard's supervisor of this area, so you'll be seeing me every day for a while," he explains.

It seems Dianne can't trust her guards recently. Their sole purpose is to watch us and enforce the law yet Gabriel is out here helping with the job on a regular basis. Although, Gabriel has always been quite a prominent face on our streets. Rarely do you see Dianne or Malcolm in public, but Gabriel roams the streets like a stray cat. Though he's unlikely to stop for a proper chat, he still likes to wander around, dapping up young men and winking at swooning old ladies. You may think this is incredibly unprofessional, but Gabriel's whole aesthetic is the 'too cool for school' prince. Whether that's his true personality or not, I'm unsure. What I do know is that his strong presence on the streets is no coincidence. If the severity of Dianne's rule starts to become too obvious, all Gabriel has to do is flick his hair and charm some commoners to keep us sweet. It's quite clever really.

"Wait. Do I know you from somewhere?" He studies my appearance, trying to put my face to a name.

"I'm Dakota," I say. Obviously, he's smiling but his face is blank. "From the party?" I remind him.

"Ah yes! What a splendid night that was." As splendid as a terminal illness.

"Indeed." We stand in silence for a few seconds. I can't help but look at how his smile gleams in the sun and I notice him watching me too.

"Well I must be off. Duty calls," he says, breaking the silence.

"Yes, yes of course." I find myself falling into a curtsy again. He chuckles and stalks down the street. Well, done, Dakota. You've made yourself look like a royal idiot. I don't have time to cringe over that because my mind is consumed with something else. Gabriel didn't say the mantra again before he left. That would be illegal for anyone to do but the prince? That is beyond strange.

**6**

I've anticipated this day since the moment Marley took her first breath. Mixi day. Sunlight peeks through my curtains and burns at my eyes. I roll over and throw the duvet over my head. Darkness cuddles me as I attempt to get in a few more minutes of rest. I relish in the abnormal tranquillity of our house. Apparently, everyone has collectively decided to sleep-in this morning. On any normal day, Cassius is up at dawn doing press-ups in his room or something else to prove his masculinity. Mother would be downstairs rewatching one of Gabriel's speeches for the hundredth time. Marley is the type of kid who would just sit there and read but that doesn't mean she doesn't have her crazy moments. She's either silent or screeching her head off, there's no in-between. Small, pattering footsteps grow closer and closer to me as I hide under the covers. Please don't. Please don't. Please don't.

"Kota, wake up! I want you to do my hair!" Marley shakes me as I groan and bury deeper into my bed. She huffs. "Pretty please," my sister says in the softest voice she can muster. I turn to face her and smile.

"Go sit at the desk," I mumble. She grins and runs over to my desk chair, plopping into it. Her small legs swing back and forth as she waits patiently. With an exaggerated stretch, I pull myself out of bed and tug on a big hoodie that I stole from the dry cleaners. Marley watches me in the dirty mirror on my desk as I stumble around my room. I pick up some scissors and an assortment of brushes and combs. A few years ago, while scouring through a skip, I found this strange box. It had a large disk inside of it. Cassius told me that it was a record player. He let me keep it so it's made a residence in my room. There are only three songs on the disc but they're all so beautiful. The record player never leaves my desk. Today I decide to play the second song, a contemporary piano piece that never fails to calm down Marley.

"What can I do for you today, Miss Calaway?" I ask in a mock professional voice. Marley cups her mouth in her hands and giggles.

"Just a trim please!"

"Of course, madam."

I sway to the music as I take my scissors and begin to cut my sister's hair. We've never been granted the privilege of going to the hairdressers because it costs ration points. Mother only spends points on necessities and items to comfort herself. However, in Zayathai you can only pick from a select few hairstyles. Any sort of unnatural colour or extravagant hairstyle is forbidden. My hair is as simple as it comes. The only modification I've ever made to my waist-length locks is the odd cutting of my split ends. Once I coloured a strand of my hair with a pink permanent marker, but Mother went stir crazy. I couldn't leave the house until it had faded.

Dust particles make themselves known under the sharp light of the sun. My room glows golden as I take care in brushing through my sister's blonde mane. Her big, blue eyes watch my every movement with noticeable adoration. Mar holds Bunny in her arms as if he were her child. I smooth out the last few knots in my sister's hair with a detangling brush.

"All done," I say, putting the brush down on the desk. "Do you like it?" Marley nods and jumps up and hugs my leg. I pick her up and she wraps her legs around my waist then buries her head into my shoulder. A lone tear streams down my face and leaves a dark spot on her hair as I cuddle her tighter than I ever have before.

"You'll be okay today, Mar," I whisper.

"I know," she whispers back.

# 7

I find it almost impossible to complete my schoolwork with Marley watching Frozen in the background. I'm not sure why this movie isn't contraband. I think it's because there's a focus on the royal family. To my dismay, humming a sweet melody can't block out the familiar voices of Anna and Elsa. Marley particularly likes the song, Let It Go, so I endure numerous replays of the cheesy ballad.

"Conceal, don't feel, don't let them knowww!" Marley sings, gliding around the living room like a spinning top. I don't ask her to be quiet because it warms my heart to see her happy and to show real emotion. After today her life will completely change. Once the song finally ends, Mother tells me to move to the sofa so she can teach Marley her daily mathematics lesson. I'm quite taken aback because normally that duty falls into my hands. I suppose she's building up to something. My mother taking any form of responsibility usually means that she wants me to handle an even bigger responsibility later. With a sigh, I pack up my things and amble over to the

46

sofa. I open a propagandistic pamphlet about Zayathai that's designed for visitors, and start flicking through it. Pictures of smiling families and beautiful landscapes lay across each page of the shiny printer paper. Even a dog has been edited to have a smile, which I think is a bit of a stretch.

"Now, Marley. We're going to start off with some simple maths," I hear Mother say. Marley looks almost offended at the term 'simple maths'. My sister can do quadratic equations without the aid of a calculator. Mother flicks through a textbook until she finds a certain page, licking her finger excessively each time.

"Right. First question." She looks at the page over the bridge of her reading glasses, attempting to look smart. I find it hard not to break out into hysterical laughter. "If twenty-five dirty Malsums are a threat to Zayathai and then a further ten Malsums are born, how many Malsums deserve to be burnt at the stake?" Mother reads from the textbook. Marley glances at her then proceeds to write out loads of fake calculations in her notepad. She even ponders for a moment, holding a finger to her lips and staring into the distance.

"According to my calculations, precisely zero Malsums deserve to be burnt at the stake," my sister snarls. Mother slams her fist on the table, causing the textbook to fly off the table.

"Thirty-five. It's thirty-five, you dimwitted vermin! In fact, everyone should be burnt at the stake because no one, and I mean no one, can equate to the perfection of the Escobars. Understand?" Marley nods and looks down at the floor. Mother turns to me, realising I'd watched her whole manic episode. She takes a deep breath and wipes her heat-damaged hair from her face.

"Dakota, you'll take Marley to the clinic to get her Mixi dose."

"Oh, but Mother–"

"There'll be no discussion, child. You'll take her or I'll see to it that you regret your callous defiance yet again." I try to contain my anger but find myself slamming the leaflet down and hoisting myself up.

"C'mon then, Mar, let's get this over with." Marley grabs Bunny and her book and we head to my car. It's nothing worth glossing over. A little, red thing with a broken taillight. You have to tug at the doors several times before they inch open.

Marley clambers in the back and slides into her carseat. Bunny rests in her lap as she begins to read. I start the engine and pull out of our tiny driveway. The car trundles through the grey streets, each avenue looking exactly the same as the one before. Us citizens live in the parts that visitors don't get to see. Tourists remain in the South -particularly the city centre- and we reside on the outskirts, the suburbs if you will. In contrast to the urban areas, our villages are rather run-down. I find myself checking on Marley in the mirror every ten seconds. She doesn't seem bothered by the whole ordeal at all. Five minutes into the journey, I find myself offering some rendition of a pep talk. Marley seems so intensely interested in reading her book that she's barely listening to a word I'm saying.

"…and please don't worry, alright? It honestly doesn't hurt an ounce. A prick of a needle is all that it is, and…"

"Kota, please. You sound more scared than I do," Marley says without even looking up from her book. Maybe she's right, I just can't bear the thought of her rejecting the injection. Life will be like a walk-in-the-park compared to mine if her body just complies. She has the brains to get an incredible job and the social skills to carry her through the whole of adulthood. She might even be allowed to go to school. It all depends on her blood. This is all I can think as we pull up at the huge, white building before us. The car park is bigger than any other in the entire of Northern Zayathai. Every single six-year-old in the north has to come to this building today, so they need a lot of space. We have to do several rounds of the parking lot before I can find a free space. Hundreds of parents stream towards the long queue outside the building. Marley readies to take her encyclopaedia and Bunny with her but I suggest she only take the rabbit. A young child reading such an intricate book is bound to draw attention and that's the last thing I need. With a sigh, she picks Bunny up and tucks him into her zipped-up coat so only his head peeps out. The back of the queue takes you right around the back of the facility, so it takes us ages to walk there.

Forty minutes into the waiting line, I wish I'd let Mar bring the book with her after all. She is so immensely bored that she has resorted to finding rocks on the pavement and naming them with Bunny's expert assistance. The hustle and bustle of hundreds of young children and parents is

sending me insane. The only young child in this world
that I can bear is my sister. She's smart, eloquent and easy
to compromise with. These children are nothing short of
feral. They scream and babble and eat dirt. This is why I
didn't want to take her. Kids. I hate kids. My eyes glaze
over as I read the words hanging over the reception area a
few times: "North Zayathai's Perfection Facility." What
a stupid word to use: perfection. Destroying people's
emotional outlet is the complete opposite to perfection.
It's inhumane and disgusting. I sometimes feel as though
I'm the only person that sees through the corruption of
this country. It would make sense to assume that only
Malsums bother to comprehend the disdain that we live
in because we have displayable emotion. If I feel angry
over the situation, I can scream and cry to my heart's
content (in private of course). The most a Malsum could
do is emotionlessly kick a wall, still grinning like mad.
The frustration is something that they're not willing to go
through, so many of them numb themselves to their real
opinions. They push away those thoughts and succumb
to complete denial. It's the only way to survive and that's
partially why everyone is so brainwashed.

By the time we've made it to the front of the line, I
feel like my legs are going to fall off. We've been waiting
for approximately two hours now. Three sets of revolving
doors greet us at the entrance. Every other child is excited
by the prospect of a door that spins but Marley seems
unbothered. She walks straight into the building with a
purposeful air about her. Despite the hundreds of people
milling about, the building is eerily quiet. A low murmur

of conversation hangs in the air. There are numerous desks lining the wall, behind which are men and women in striking white outfits who type on white computers and chat away to families. We walk over to the only available employee, a small man with boxy glasses and a beauty spot below his right eye. He's so small that I almost have to peek over the table, just to see him.

"Name?" He asks, clicking his pen over and over again, without looking up at us. The man's voice is whiny and it makes my head hurt.

"Marley Ellice Calaway," I say. He taps a few buttons on his computer.

"Would that be Marley Ellice Calaway of thirteen artichoke lane?" I hate our street name. Whoever thought of it must've truly been running out of ideas. There are so many magnificent things in this world that our street could've represented, but artichoke? Give me a break.

"Yes, sir." He gives me a short nod. My sister watches him with a firm scowl as she holds onto my hand. I want to tell her to smile but I suppose she doesn't have to. In a few minutes, she won't ever be able to appear sad again. Props to her for making the most of it. The man scribbles away on his paper. He looks up to the shiny, white computer before him and starts typing. A lot, like a lot. He pauses, pondering over something, then continues to clack away at the gleaming keyboard. I'm convinced that he doesn't have anything to note down and this is just some sort of power move. If my suspicions are correct, it's certainly worked. I've worked up quite a sweat waiting for him to finish.

"Down the hall, take a left, up the stairs to floor

twelve, take another left, down the hall and you'll find clinic 149. Got it?" Marley nods and thank goodness she does, because I didn't catch a word of those directions.

"After you," I say. Marley rolls her eyes and strides ahead, still holding my hand. This place is a labyrinth. A white labyrinth. Smiling families and nurses weave around each other through hundreds of identical corridors. The staircase is unnecessarily steep and has me panting when we reach the top. Marley, on the other hand, is right as rain. She seems quite eager to get this over with, thus is walking a lot faster than normal.

"Don't panic, Marley," I tell her as I knock on the door of clinic 149.

"I'm not," she responds. And she's right. The only person panicking here is me. Footsteps approach the door before it's flung open. A slender woman in a white uniform bends down to my sister's level.

"You must be Marley!" She exclaims.

"How did you guess?" Marley mutters with sarcasm etching each syllable. The nurse looks up and gives me a look that is hard to decipher when she's smiling so vividly.

"Well come on in! We'd best get started." The nurse stands aside as we huddle into the small room. I'm sure it's no surprise that absolutely everything is white. The walls are basically whiteboards, complete with that stupid shiny gloss that makes my eyes ache. I help to take my sister's coat off and stand to the side of the room. Marley sits in the big chair in the centre and waits while the nurse busies herself with all the equipment.

"This won't hurt an ounce," the nurse assures Marley as she tugs on disposable latex gloves.

"Yes, Kota has made sure I'm aware of that," Marley responds, holding Bunny in her right hand. Her left arm is propped on the arm rest as the nurse wipes it with an antibacterial cloth. The nurse is what someone might call 'pristine.' She has a pearly-white smile, long eyelashes, platinum blonde hair and immaculate red lipstick. Sometimes, perfection isn't…perfect. A little roughness and the odd zit never hurt a person. Why people strive to be completely flawless is beyond me. I just want to be real.

"So, what have you been up to today, Marley?" the nurse asks.

"Singing, mostly," Marley replies.

"Singing? I imagine you're a beautiful little artist."

"How can you possibly know that? You've known me for about five minutes."

"Just say thank you, Marley," I say, playing it off with forced laughter.

"Thank you," Marley mutters.

The nurse joins me in some awkward chuckling. She then takes the needle out of the packet. I swear I almost throw up just looking at it. I notice Marley takes a big gulp when she observes the length of the metal that's about to be shoved into her arm. The nurse takes note of my sister's apparent nervousness.

"Do you have any pets?" she asks.

"Why does that matter?" Marley asks, her eyes not leaving the needle.

"I was just trying to—"

"Make small talk? Don't. Let's not pretend that either of us want to be here and just get it over with." The nurse gives me a sideways glance. *This nurse is definitely a Malsum,* I think to myself.

The nurse flicks the needle a few times and inserts it into Marley's arm. The liquid is a vibrant blue and I have vivid memories of the day I endured this procedure. I'd been much more worried than Marley is now. Although, I was unaware of the prospect of the injection being rejected. I still remember that feeling afterwards. There was no urge to smile. I was empty. Just as I'd been before.

The nurse injects the Mixi into Marley's arm until the needle is empty. "Now the injection should kick in over the next minute or so," she explains. As the nurse turns away to dispose of the needle, I watch Marley with squinted eyes. Her face turns from a scowl to a glimmering smile. It worked. Oh, thank the sweet lord, it worked! The nurse sorts through cabinets and does various other things. While we wait, I can't help but look at the tray of injections on a table. The table is so painfully near to me, arm's length, I reckon. Am I really about to do this? Well, Marley is concentrating on Bunny and the nurse seems quite busy, so no one will notice. And with that thought in mind, my impulsivity gets the better of me. I reach over and grab an injection, shoving it deep into my pocket. Just as I stand back against the wall, the nurse spins around, holding some paper. She gives them to me and explains that they're important documents for something or other. I'm not really listening to anything she's saying. Surely one missing syringe won't be noticed. She'll peg it down to her poor organisational skills and take a spare from the lab, right? Although by the tidiness of this room it's clear that organisation has never been a problem for this woman. She seems to have stopped talking and opened the door in the time it took for me to panic.

"Thank you very much, nurse," Marley says, standing up from the chair. We exchange our goodbyes and head out into the corridor. It's weird how Mixi works. Marley has always been so blunt but the injection somehow makes her more polite. I've heard that you feel some sort of compulsion to be polite immediately after having the injection. We don't talk at all on the way out of the building. We pass the queue of children and parents on their way in. I feel quite proud as my smiling sister strides alongside me. For the best part of the car journey, we remain silent.

"How do you feel?" I ask, looking back at her for a second.

"Good." That's as much as I can get out of her for the whole car ride. Marley smiles the entire way.

**8**

"**D**id it work?" Mother presses as soon as we make it through the doorway.

"I think so," I say, looking down at my beaming sister. That injection must've been too strong because she seems to be smiling rather oddly. It's like someone's grabbed her face and is literally pulling it into the desired position. Don't get me wrong, the Mixi smile doesn't exactly look natural but Marley looks possessed. Mother takes one look at Marley and a light seems to switch on in her head.

"Cassius, fetch the gun." Oh no. Oh god no. Not again. Cassius stalks off to the cabinet and I chase after him.

"Cassius no. You don't have to do this." I attempt to wrestle the gun from his grasp but to no avail. He shoves me out of the way and by the time I've scrambled back to my feet, Mother has taken hold of Marley and is guiding her outside. Still Marley's face stays in a smile.

Mother orders Marley to stand by the fence and she complies. Marley holds Bunny tightly in her left palm. All I can do is watch as Cassius hands Mother the rubber bullet gun, which she aims at Marley's arm. Still, Marley's face stays in a smile.

It never occurred to me why this was her, and many other parent's, weapon of choice. Why a gun? A sharpened knife to the arm would easily tell you if your child had rejected the Mixi or not. There is absolutely no reason to take a revolver to your own child. But I guess desperation breeds cruelty. Everyone wants to be sure of their child's fate and a bullet will give you instant answers. You could pretend not to be hurt by a knife wound. I would know. I'm a master in the practice of concealing pain.

Suddenly, I'm back there again. Mother holding a gun to me. The congealed mess of breakfast gurgling in my stomach. Heat rising through my face like lava in a volcano. Head heavy and limp as the barrel is pointed to my arm.

BANG.

The bullet soars into Marley and blood splatters on the fence behind her, and all over Bunny, who is dangling by her side. I feel like I'm standing in Marley's place, just as I had long ago. Mother watching me like I'm a parasite. Legs buckling underneath me as I crash to the ground in one hopeless heap. The name calling. The screaming. Please Marley. Please be ok. You can do this. You're strong. You aren't like me.

"Ahhhh!" Marley yells, crumbling to the floor. She screams and wails until her voice is hoarse. I sprint over to her aid, careful not to touch the wound. She writhes and screams so much that my head begins to ring. How the neighbours aren't already outside and peering over our fence is beyond me. I suppose a lot of them are taking their children to get the injection. That's lucky for us because Marley's screaming is louder than anything I've ever heard.

"How could you?" I shriek. Cassius' smile is as wild as ever. Disgusting.

"Another one? Another useless disgusting emotion-filled child!" Mother exclaims. The hypocrisy is almost cringe-worthy. She is literally a non-blood-shedding Malsum and she has the audacity to call us useless?

"Marley will start blood-shedding as soon as possible," Mother announces. She chucks the gun to the floor as if it's not the machine that's destroyed our family.

"Mother, you can't do this! Please let her–"

"I won't hear any more of it. Dakota, take that insolent child to the infirmary immediately." I cradle my distraught little sister and hurry back to the car.

"I tried, Kota," Marley whispers. "I really did try."

# 9

Marley lays across the backseat, clutching a blood-splattered Bunny. She's too weak to even sit in her carseat. For a child of such intelligence, I struggle to understand why she chose the name 'Bunny' for her toy rabbit. It's so basic. Every time we make contact with a speed bump, I try my best to go slow. That doesn't stop Marley from crying out each time. I've never seen her like this and I never want to again.

"I know it hurts but you must smile in the hospital. If you frown, bad things could happen. We don't want that, do we?" Marley only conjures enough strength to shake her head.

"Ok, so I need you to smile." With her hand pressed over her wound and tears brimming in her eyes, Marley musters a placid grin. I give up trying to go slow and step on the gas. It may be the most uncomfortable car ride Marley will ever endure but at least she'll get medical attention as soon as possible. The hospital is ridiculously far away because we live so far out in the suburbs. There are only four of such facilities in the country. Yes. Four.

They're always overcrowded and they smell of stale pee but at least the doctors are reasonably trained. That's another tactic of Dianne's. Give us horrific facilities with one outstanding factor to keep us from complaining. How could we possibly be unsatisfied with the hospitals? Every doctor there is a certified phD holder and proud servant under the Escobar crown. That's all good and well but if you can catch chlamydia just by touching the front desk, I think things need to be reviewed. I try to remain calm for Marley's sake but when a man cuts me off, my limit is officially reached.

"Who the hell taught you to drive? A blind nascar driver?!" I shriek, my smile wavering, as I barely miss hitting his cheap, yellow bumper. I thank my lucky stars that these cars are soundproof or I'd be toast. Escobar-shaped toast. The traffic comes to a slow, causing me to tap my fingers impatiently on the steering wheel.

"Kota?" Marley whispers slash squeaks.

"What?!" I almost shriek.

"Please...relax...y-you...making arm h-hurt more." There is absolutely no correlation to my road rage and her bullet wound but I take a deep breath and swipe black hair from my sweaty forehead.

"Sorry I'm just– yeah. Sorry." I slump back into my seat and look into the mirror.

After what feels like sixty-thousand decades, we get off the highway and I swerve into the bleak car park of the tiny hospital at the top of Acacia Avenue. The rotten wood sign above the door reads 'North Zayathai medical facility' in wonky, printed letters. Slamming my door, I rush over to Marley and scoop her out of the backseat.

Her arm dangles out of my arms, so that it doesn't press against my torso and worsen the pain. Though I vowed to calm down, the nerves build up in my throat as I tug the dirty, glass door open with one hand and hurry inside.

"She's been shot. She needs a doctor. Please get a doctor." My words are rushed and tumble from my mouth in a mess. This is the first time in a while where I've truly struggled to keep a smile on my face. If I want to keep out of handcuffs, I need to keep my composure. Just smile, Dakota.

"We're very busy today. Just take a seat and we'll get her taken care of soon," the receptionist tells me. My eyes widen. Just smile, Dakota.

"I'm not sure if you heard me correctly. She's been shot. What if she–" The word gets caught on my tongue. It slips off and splats on the cheap, carpeted floor. The receptionist looks around at her colleagues to make sure no one's looking. Her face softens and that's when I see it. It's not much but it's enough. A frown. A Malsum. It calms me that she understands our situation. She knows the pain of keeping these smiles upon our faces.

"She will be ok, my love. Please just sit down and I'll get someone down here." I bite my lip and nod. "Thank you. Can I take a name?"

"Marley. Marley Calaway." She takes some notes then reaches out to touch Marley's hand.

My instincts tell me to jump back before she can get near my sister. Rule number two of living in Zayathai: don't let anyone touch you. If they've noticed you're a Malsum, they may be trying to take you into citizen's arrest until the guards arrive. The receptionist gives me this look that somehow draws me back toward the desk, back to her. She takes one of Marley's hands, the one that's dangling from the bounds of my arms. The one with the ghastly wound in it. She barely seems to acknowledge the wound as her thumb caresses the outside of Marley's hand.

"Fight it, darling. You can do this," she murmurs. Marley manages to nod but it's weak and I can tell it causes pain to soar through her body.

"By the power of the crown we trust…" she begins.

"May the Escobars eternally reign over us," I reply. The woman nods at me and I do the same back before turning to walk to the waiting room.

The waiting room is disturbingly quiet. I've always been quite creeped out by the hospital because people have obtained such dire injuries yet they're still smiling. The sound of screeching wheels approaches the room. Everyone watches as a woman is wheeled in on a trolley. Her body is completely singed. Every inch of her skin is shrivelled and flaky. Parts of her body have turned completely white, others a deep shade of crimson. Blood oozes from a deep gash in her leg and for some reason the wound is occupied by an infestation of almost minuscule maggots. And the most terrifying part? Her smile is so vivid that one might assume it was her birthday.

"Marley Ellice Calaway?"

The doctor flicks his little torch on and inspects the wound. He looks over the top of his rectangular glasses, muttering things under his breath and squinting at the bullet. Marley watches every move he makes, as if she doesn't trust him not to tear the slug out right there and then.

"You were smart not to take the bullet out before you got here. That could've made it so much worse," he says without looking at me.

I'm unsure if he wants me to dignify that with a response so I decide not to. Instead, I turn to shifting from side to side on the chair he'd provided. I curse myself for wearing shorts as the cheap wool irritates my skin. The doctor, no older than forty, flicks the light off and turns to me.

"So how exactly did she obtain such an injury? Only guards are allowed guns, so I can only assume that she was shot by the royal force. Of course, if that were the case, we'd be best off pretending this never happened."

I almost snort at the double standards of this society. If someone who is supposed to be protecting the country shoots an innocent child it's excusable, but no one else can do the same without prosecution? Ridiculous.

"It was a guard, sir. She tapped him to ask for assistance, but he assumed the worst, spun around and shot her. He was only protecting himself." Marley lifts her head and looks at me like I've gone crazy. I know it's a terrible lie, but I couldn't think of anything else. The doctor looks between us several times. I'm conscious that he doesn't believe me a single bit.

"Right. Well, we should never question the credibility of Dianne's forces. If he shot her then it is clearly her fault and her fault only. I urge you not to take legal action."

He doesn't have to tell me twice. There are reality tv shows about people that tried to speak out against the royal guards. Within days of putting in a complaint, each one of them coincidentally committed suicide. Coincidentally.

"It would be in Marley's best interest for me to remove the bullet immediately. It is made of rubber so it wouldn't have made such a dangerous wound if she hadn't been shot in such close range. The bullet only grazed the surface so the best course of action would be to dig it out with a pair of forceps." He moves across the room towards a drawer. When his back is turned, Marley mouths something to me, which I can't quite make out. Whatever she said, all I know is that she's panicking. One of the contraband books that I read was about this substance called anaesthetic. I think it stops you from hurting, so the doctor can perform painful procedures on you. That absolutely amazed me. In fact, I read the page over and over again just to check that my eyes weren't deceiving me. We don't have anaesthetic. Zayathians have no emotional outlet, non-Malsums that is, so there's supposedly no need for it. Someone could be in gut-wrenching agony but the doctor can easily miss that because they'll be smiling. Although I'm sure the southern hospital will have some anaesthetics stored away for when foreigners come to visit.

The doctor returns to Marley's bedside, bearing a pair of forceps that makes my stomach plunge. The instrument is fairly long with two pincers at the tip. If the pliers unnerve me, I dread to think how Marley must be feeling. As the metal braces the wound, Marley looks towards the wall and away from the doctor, so he won't notice the wince that she fails to stifle and the single tear that rolls down her face. Yet again, Marley manages to astound me. If it was me on that table, I would be screeching. In fact, when Mother shot me, they didn't even bother to take me to the hospital. The bullet was ripped from my body right in the confines of the chamber. As soon as they were done, I was tied to the chair, still screaming and reeling from the wound.

He bandages her up, lowers her sleeve and puts the forceps away.

"Make sure to clean the wound on a regular basis and it should heal just fine." I scoop Marley off the bed and nod.

"By the power of the crown we trust…" I begin.

"May the Escobars eternally reign over us," the doctor responds, nodding. As I walk through the corridors, down the stairs, through the reception and into the carpark, I don't dare look at Marley's face. The sight of my little sister grinning after just bearing a shot wound from her own mother is too much for me to handle. I slide her into the backseat and put a blanket over her.

"Kota, I really should have my seatbelt on," she says with a scratchy voice that had been choked with tears.

"Mar, for once in your life just act like a little kid. Be reckless."

"Reckless never kept anyone safe, Kota."

# 10

When we arrive home, Mother is waiting for us at the front door, grinning like a madman. I can barely bring myself to step out of the car because my gut tells me that something isn't right.

"We have guests!" she beams. Suspicions confirmed. Cradling Marley in my arms, I look behind Mother. Down the hallway I can see someone sitting on the sofa. Three people, in fact. A woman around the age of my mother has a young child sitting in her lap and a teenage boy beside her. The older boy seemed engrossed in his phone but he put it down as soon as he saw me. They wave and grin at me, so I have to release a hand from Marley to reciprocate the action.

"Are they–"

"No. No, they're not," Mother interrupts, her smile deepening even more. Non-Malsums in the house. What on Earth is going on here? "Melissa is a work friend," Mother says through a tightly pressed together set of teeth. "We planned on a coffee morning at her house like we do every week, but she suggested that we go to our house for once and I thought that was a wonderful idea. She even decided to bring her lovely sons, Jacob and Kristopher."

She speaks a lot louder than normal so they can hear our conversation. The tone of her face would seem like that of someone happy to the untrained eye. Not to me. The burning rage inside of my mother is all too apparent.

"That's…well that's delightful! I am eager to make their acquaintance," I respond, matching her volume. She gives me this nod that suggests I haven't failed her for once and steps aside. We exchange the usual pleasantries and all sit down on our small, grubby sofas. Marley, Mother and I obtain one chair, while Melissa's family occupies the other. My little sister can barely hold herself up but she manages. The older son, Jacob, keeps smiling at me as we delve into polite conversation. I can't work out what colour his eyes are. They're a mixture of all the worst shades: a dull brown, a weak blue and a tiny fleck of yellow. Not gold. Yellow. His hair is spiked with gel, in a style that I've only seen in those contraband American 1990s movies. He's reasonably tall, I'll give him that, but in the wrong way. He kind of reminds me of those floppy, balloon men that you see outside of car dealerships. Not a good look.

"Well, aren't you just cute as a button!" Melissa says. She reaches over to tap Marley's nose and explodes into the type of laughter that would usually be triggered by only the funniest of jokes. Everyone joins her in awkward laughter. I can tell that Marley wants to bite her head off so I discreetly cup her hand in mine. The room falls into complete silence. Mother's left eye starts to twitch like a faulty lightbulb.

"So!" She beams. "Dakota, why don't you show Jacob around our village? He isn't familiar with this area." As much as she poses this as a question, I know I have no choice.

"Sure." My deadpan tone shows that I have no interest in doing anything with this guy and I think everyone realises. Except Jacob that is. He still seems eager as ever.

"Can I go with them?" Marley pipes up.

"No," Mother responds quickly. "You and Kristopher can play in the garden while Melissa and I catch up." My sister can barely fend off the anger that tries to write itself across her face. I'm surprised that they had the chance to clean the blood off the fence before they all arrived. She must've borrowed next door's jet washer. I rise to my feet and stalk off towards the door.

"Let's go," I instruct without looking behind me. Enthusiastic footsteps bound behind me. Lord have mercy.

"I haven't seen you at school before," Jacob tells me. There's only one school in the whole of Northern Zayathai. It's an immense building made of, you guessed it, stone. Children get their fill of propaganda in the institution ten hours per day, six days a week. Borderline torture, if you ask me.

"I'm sure you haven't," I murmur. Our footsteps fall into unison against the grey tarmac. Jacob rubs his fingers against his blonde bush of hair and nods at a slow, measured pace. "Homeschooled, Jacob. I'm homeschooled."

"Oh!" he exclaims. "That makes more sense." I want to kill Mother for putting me in this situation. Keeping me locked up in that ghastly house has really limited my social skills. Interactions, particularly with people my own age, have and never will be my strong suit. She knows that.

"Do you…have a boyfriend?" Poor kid. I'm sure his mum told him that they were going to meet a lovely girl who just so happens to be single. There can't be any other reason why he'd tag along on a coffee morning.

"I do not." A whirl of warm wind swishes around us and flings my hair upwards. I tug a clump of hair from my mouth. A slight shudder that courses through my body is apparently a signal to Jacob that he needs to wrap his arm around me. It wasn't a signal in any way shape or form. He squeezes me tighter as we traipse down the road. All I want to do is shove him off of me but I'd feel bad. Jacob starts blabbing to me about something that I don't care about but all I can pay attention to is the scene unfolding down the street.

"…and then my guitar went completely out of tune, but I didn't panic and I managed to…"

"Jacob…Jacob shut up and look!" Finally, the kid stops talking. One glance across the road and he takes my hand. We sprint across the street, not bothering to check for cars. A young girl, twelve at best, is cowering beneath the barrel of a gun. *Who's holding the gun?* I hear you ask. A man around 5'8 in height. His tight, black jacket is done up with blue buttons, each imprinted with a curly E. Atop of his head is a black buzz cut with defined, trimmed edges. His shiny black boots reflect his gleaming, silver and turquoise gun. A guard.

"Whatever she's done, I'm sure she didn't mean it," I

say, careful not to sound or look afraid. His eyes don't leave the situation of the small girl. Her fawn hair hangs over her face, casting a shadow across her youthful features.

"So, you mean to tell me that she accidentally stole from Mrs Webber's house?" the guard fires back.

Mrs Webber. The old bat that lives a few doors down from us. She's always mumbling and grumbling about something or other, with a smile of course. She's the kind of old bat to go snitching to the guards about anything and everything. Zayathians have a code. We don't grass. If someone is a Malsum, that is none of your damn business. People that break this code, and there's a considerable number of them, are scum. No one likes them and once you prove yourself to be a grass, there's no going back. Mrs Webber demonstrated her disgusting excuse of a personality long ago and now seeks revenge on us all by sucking up to the authorities like a wrinkled, old suction cup.

"I only picked a flower," she whispers. He can't be serious.

"Are you kidding?" Jacob says, which takes me by surprise. That's no way to speak to a guard. Not unless you want to have your tongue cut out. This startles and angers the guard. Grinning, the gun-bearer turns on his heel and presses the barrel into Jacob's head. I swear I stop breathing for a moment.

"What was that?" The guard growls. "Say that again, son." Jacob doesn't falter. He doesn't even seem rattled. I may have underestimated this kid; he isn't as feeble as I thought. I take this opportunity to run to the girl and haul her to her feet. She trembles under my grasp, still smiling like she's on vacation.

"Marcos, what are you doing?" a startlingly low voice asks. All eyes dart up. A stout figure with dark hair spilling from beneath a grey beanie. A similar uniform to the guard, except that he obtains polished medals and a black cloak. Prince Luther.

What was previously a confident, proud guard is now a quivering man. His gun drops from Jacob's head. Jacob's shoulders relax and he moves to stand beside me and the girl.

"Prince Gabriel, I was just arresting this girl and–"

"Threatening. You were threatening her," Gabriel spits at Marcos. The man melts into a blubbering puddle of nerves.

"Y-you don't understand. She–" Gabriel steps closer to his colleague, causing his words to drift off in the wind. He squints his eyes and plucks one of the many badges from Marcos' uniform. He holds it up to the guard's face.

"Read that out to me," Gabriel orders.

"Protector of the Zayathian citizens," Marcos almost whispers.

"Louder!" Gabriel barks, his smile reflecting off the metal. The girl shrinks back into my embrace.

"Protector of the Zayathian citizens, sir." Marcos' voice is certainly louder but he is terrifically afraid. Gabriel drops the badge on the floor and stamps on it, twisting his heel for dramatic effect.

"By the look of things, Marcos, you don't seem to be doing much protecting. Remind me what the arrest protocol is?" Every word Gabriel utters is threatening and harsh.

"Handcuff the perpetrator, call for a black van and take them for questioning," Marcos recites like he's had to say this a million times over.

"Now where in that protocol does it say to threaten them with your firearm?" Gabriel asks, condescendence etching each letter. Marcos takes a discreet gulp.

"Well, your highness, the use of our firearms is permitted if the perpetrator is endangering anyone." That was bold of him. Jacob takes my hand, the one that isn't wrapped around the girl, and squeezes it tight. Whether he thinks I'm scared or thinks this is an opportunity to get me to like him, it annoys me all the same. Gabriel looks past Marcos and to us, to the girl.

"What did you do, kid?" Obviously, she remains smiling, but her eyes say it all. My grip tightens around her, which seems to help her relax.

"A flower, Prince Luther. I stole a flower." Her voice is so hushed that I'm surprised Gabriel hears her. He knocks past Marcos and kneels to her level.

"Listen." His voice is rough and aggressive while his smile looks as welcoming as ever. "I'm going to let you go. But if you ever steal again, whether it be a flower or a car, I'll see to it that you face the full wrath of the law. Got it?" She nods hurriedly beneath my grasp. "Good. Now get out of here before I change my mind." The poor girl breaks from my embrace and sprints down the road. She doesn't look back. Gabriel looks down at his shoes and chuckles before standing back up. A few stray hairs have escaped from beneath his signature grey beanie and drape across his eyes like curtains. The sharp of his jaw flexes with a gentle vein.

He turns back to Marcos and snatches the gun from his hand. With his free hand he grabs Marcos' collar and pulls him closer, whispering to the guard. His soft lips curl and twist against the cool, evening air as words slither from his mouth and into Marcos' ear. I can't make out what he's saying but, by the way Marcos' knees are weakening, I can't imagine it's very kind.

"...and you won't get this gun back until I decide you aren't a threat to the village anymore. Am I understood?" Gabriel says. Marcos nods over and over again.

"Sir, yes sir." Gabriel drops his collar and Marcos salutes. A smirk kicks at the corner of Gabriel's mouth.

"Good." Gabriel stretches out the word as the gun twirls around his hand. "Get out of my sight, Marcos." With no instruction to say the mandatory phrase, Marcos nods and marches into the distance. Gabriel looks Jacob up and down. The smirk flickers on the prince's face.

"Are you two...?" He waves the gun between us. I find myself snatching my hand away from Jacob's.

"No! No, we are not," I almost scream. Jacob looks to the ground and tenses a little. Oops. Gabriel holsters the firearm besides his own diamond-encrusted shotgun.

"Right. Well, uhm...I'll be on my way. By the power of the crown we trust..." he says. That aggressive edge to his voice has dissipated. Now he's soft and regal all over again.

"May the Escobars eternally reign over us," we say in

73

unison. Gabriel nods and stalks past us, his black cloak swishing behind him. Jacob and I turn around and walk home in silence. I can imagine Jacob is quite stunned by our encounter with the prince. Not many people get to speak to the royal family in their lifetime. Even if Gabriel is the supervisor of guards for our area, he rarely stops to properly talk to people. Perhaps you might be lucky enough to get reprimanded by him. That is all. When we get home, Marley looks exhausted from all the playing. Kristopher seems like a very excitable boy, which must've been torture for my sister. That bullet wound can't have made the playdate any easier.

For some reason, Mother granted me the small privilege of having an old tv with me in the basement, while I do my nightly bloodshed. Maybe, she felt a pang of guilt after putting me through hell these past few days. I doubt it. This tv is so far from high definition that there's only about five pixels on the screen. Even still, I can make out the familiar face of Gabriel on the tiny screen.

"I'd personally like to congratulate any and all six-year-olds who had their injection today. This is our next generation of warriors and I can hardly wait for the bright future that we will share with them." Lies.

"On that note, I'd like to remind you all that if you do suspect someone of being a Malsum you must report them immediately. Failure to do so will result in dire consequences. That'll be all. From me and everyone at the Escobar Estate, we wish…"

Unwilling to listen to that nonsense of a closing line again, I turn the tv off. I look up at the machine beside me. Three tubes carry my blood into pouches at the top of the contraption. It's quite mesmerising to watch but it's painful all the same.

"I guess it's just you and me, bud," I whisper to the machine. It doesn't respond.

**11**

"Marley, pass the remote please."

Without looking up from her book, my sister chucks the remote directly at my head. I inhale sharply to refrain from screaming. *Why not just scream?* I hear you ask. Sitting at the kitchen table, scratching his head like the idiot he is, is my brother's friend. Rio is absolutely braindead. He has this stupid fluffy silver hair and a cross tattoo under his eye. This getup can only be to deflect attention from his sheer stupidity. Rio is a non-Malsum so he shouldn't be in the house but Mother is always out. He doesn't know that he's not allowed to be here because he doesn't know what we are. Even though I can't stand Rio, I'm jealous that Cassius got the chance to become his friend. He's allowed to waltz around playing the non-Malsum life whilst me and my sister suffer. I flick onto some dumb cartoon just to drown out the noise of the two idiots in the kitchen, both of which are retaking their final year of school.

"What did you get for question 7?" Cassius stares at

his notebook, tapping his temple with a pen. His friend looks down at his paper.

"I got nothing." Rio sighs and drops his pen. Marley looks up from her book and makes eye contact with me in desperation. I shake my head at her. I know what she wants to do but she can't.

"Maths is dumb," Cassius says. His voice is muffled as he rests his face on the table.

"Right! I mean who can even do algebra anyway?" Rio asks, rolling his eyes.

"Anyone with half a brain cell," Marley mutters to herself. Both of the boys look over at my sister.

"Marley…" I warn. She huffs with a forced smile and continues reading.

"I say we give up and skip to the next question," Rio suggests. Cassius nods and turns over the page.

"State the equation of a straight line," Cassius reads out.

"Ladies and gentleman, we have another impossible question," Rio announces. Cassius chuckles.

"Y equals mx plus c," Marley mutters.

"Excuse me?" Rio asks.

"Y equals mx plus c," Marley repeats. "It's not rocket science."

"Mar, stop," I murmur. She closes her book.

"You're telling me you aren't losing hope for humanity listening to these halfwits?" She asks, turning to me.

"Well yeah but–."

"I rest my case."

"You're six. Go play dollies or something," Rio says.

"I'm six yet I'm smarter than you'll ever be." My

brother turns and shoots lasers through her soul with his eyes.

"Good god, Marley, will you just–."

"I'm going, I'm going," Marley says. She hauls herself up from the sofa and trudges upstairs.

# 12

Again, I find myself in this stupid, satin dress. I'll only have to take it off in about ten minutes time, but we have to look smart upon arrival at the ritual centre. One Thursday per month we are obliged to attend the ritual centre to perform…you guessed it! A ritual. A horrifying, blood-curdling ritual. The centre is located a few miles away from our house so we took the car. Normally I prefer to take the easy way and get in Mother's ugly four by four, but not when it comes to the ritual. I always feel sick afterwards, so the various speed bumps that we fly over never help with the gurgling in my stomach.

In the whole area, the ritual building is the only colourful architecture to be seen. Striking, rainbow pillars protrude from the building and tower into the sky. Exotic shades of red and orange and purple brighten up stained glass windows, showing illustrations of the royal family in all its glory. Thousands of people will attend this building today to pay their 'respects.' There's a number of large halls that can hold hundreds of people at a time. The Escobars go around each room, one at a time to perform the ritual. My family and I always attend ritual room 1. The extravagance of this building is a testament to what our priority should be in life: worshipping the Escobars. This may just be a tale but I've heard of people going to prison for saying 'God.' Even the implication of a higher power that isn't Dianne and her sad excuse of a family can get you put behind bars.

~

"Good evening! Please take a blade and head inside."

As we head into the glistening building, we each take a sharp-edged piece of metal from a woven basket. The woman holding the basket is already dressed in her worship clothes and is obviously one of Dianne's slaves. I wonder how many more years of service she has to do before Dianne will consider releasing her and what she might've done to land that ghastly job in the first place.

I enter the preparation room with my family. It's quite large and is carpeted with this odd red substance. It's fluffy and itchy, but we have to remove our shoes in places of worship so it irritates the soles of my feet. I help Marley slip on her worship cloak. It's very difficult to get the hang of putting on because it's simply a piece of black cloth. It takes years to work out how to wrap it around one's body and where to tuck it in and where to let it flow. Brandishing our blades, we head into our worship room, silently in single file.

Rows of people are already sitting on the floor and are ready for the ritual. I guess we should've arrived earlier because risking punctuality can get you in a lot of trouble if Dianne finds out. Just ask Mrs. Tappeldora next door. Her husband arrived during the ritual and he now only has seven fingers to count on. We sit down beside a young family and place our blades in front of us. The silence is forced on us, not only by fear but by the fact that the large room has the potential to provide a mighty echo, even if you were to whisper. Hundreds of people line this hall and yet there isn't a sound to be heard.

Seeming as Marley has only just had her injection, this is her first time performing the Ritual. I suppose getting Mixi is a coming-of-age. You become immersed in all the torturous aspects of non-Malum life. Before you're injected, you are neither a Malsum nor a non-Malsum, you're just there. I'm anxious to see how Marley will cope with this. We practised at home last night and she seemed to be ok but that was without the pressure. Now she's in a room of strangers and she has to make her strength known. She cannot cry, no matter how she's feeling.

"All hail the Escobars!" A man calls from the front.

We all stand and recite his words. One by one the Escobars enter the room, waving at their subjects. We cheer and whoop as loud as possible, so they know our apparent appreciation. Guards amble around the room ready to catch anyone who doesn't yell loud enough. The congregation continues to scream and whistle. My voice goes hoarse from the screeching as a particularly intimidating guard makes himself known right beside me. He holds his gun as if he's ready to kill at any moment. I look over and Mother and Cassius are genuinely having the time of their lives. Why they love these people so much, I will never understand.

"Thank you! Thank you, all!" Dianne beams. The cheers die down as we take a seat on the floor. The Escobars sit on their thrones on the stage.

"It is so lovely to have you all here to worship us. You are our subjects, our property, our pets." Strange word choice, Gabriel.

"Now I invite you all to take your blades and slice in adoration for us, as your worthy leaders."

In a moment of silence, everyone takes up their blade and presses it into their skin. The room is so quiet that you could almost hear the piercing of each individual body. I'm barely concentrating on my own blade because I need to supervise Marley. A million thoughts race through my mind: *Press gently then…ah there we go! She's got a nice stream of blood. Oh god is she going to cry? Now like we practised. Oh man.*

A large vase is passed round the room and each person squeezes their arm to empty some blood into it. The vase is black, of course. It has intricate carvings of the royal family's faces on it. Creepy, I know. The one thing I made clear to Marley was that not a single drop of her blood was to go in that vase. I didn't tell her why, because she doesn't truly understand what being a Malsum means for her. All she had to do was pretend to give blood and wipe it up discreetly. But she didn't. And now the vase continues to go around the room with a splatter of her Malsum blood in it. Why is this a problem? I hear you shout. Well, my friend, you're about to find out.

Once the vase meets the front of the room, a guard approaches the stage. The woman that greeted us at the front door arrives on the stage and gently slices each of the Escobars. They each add a droplet of their own blood to the vase. Taking a gracious bow, the woman retreats from the stage and leaves the room. The room stays in complete silence. I make sure I'm sitting in the correct position, legs crossed and hands on either side of my body. Even sitting in a different way than you're told can get you in deep trouble. God, how I hate the next part of the ritual. Gabriel nods and we all begin chanting. Palms slam against the floor as the chanting gets louder:

"Sacer Sanguis!"

"Sacer Sanguis!"

"Sacer Sanguis!"

"Sacer Sanguis!"

"Sacer Sanguis!"

"Sacer Sanguis!"

If only I had the words to describe the sheer terror in my sister's eyes. However, being the good actor that she is, Marley keeps smiling and starts chanting. The chanting becomes even more satanic and they dim the lights to add to the craze. Guards begin circulating the room, handing people shot glasses of the blood concoction. I stare down into my cup. The mixture is an odd brown colour and the odour...I can't even describe it. Have you ever smelt a rotting carcass?

"Ad Victoriam!" Gabriel yells, raising his glass in the air.

"Ad Victoriam!" The congregation echoes.

Everyone downs their shots in one go. The taste is absolutely vile. It sort of burns my throat and the odour sticks to your taste buds like honey to a jumper. Before you ask why we're doing this, I have no idea. I think Mother said it's something to do with our blood all being equal and Zayathai being one. I think fusing our blood and drinking it makes us all a part of each other. I guess adding the royal family's blood makes it seem like we're equal to them. It's all manipulation.

Okay so far, so good. Everyone has drunk and...oh no. First a woman, then a man, then another woman and another and another. Soon the entire room is in a fit of hysterical tears. All composure is lost. It must be Marley's blood. She's set them off. Mother and I join in with the crying because, if we didn't, they'd know we were Malsums. Marley just sits there, staring around with bloodshot eyes. Still crying, Cassius snatches up his blade and drives it straight through her leg. She bursts into hysterics and is now fitting with the rest of the room.

"Stop it! Stop it at once!" Dianne yells but nobody can obey. Once someone's consumed Malsum blood, it's game-over. At first, I think we're safe. Nobody knows it was Marley's blood, right? It could have been given by anyone. Just as a soft reassurance settles in my stomach, I look up. Through a screen of fake cloudy tears, I can see Gabriel. And he's staring directly at Marley.

# 13

We are awoken by the blaring of a siren. The sound is so high frequency, I'm surprised my old mother can actually hear it. Oh god, I know what this siren's for. This hasn't happened in about four years and the last time was terrifying. I run downstairs and everyone is already dressed and preparing themselves. Cassius has told Marley menacing stories about this event when I told him to read her a bedtime story, so my sister is all too aware of the situation. She picks up Bunny, but I tell her she won't be allowed to have him with her. With great reluctance, she places him on the sofa and covers him with a blanket, whispering, "I'll be back soon, Bunny." As we head to the front door, Cassius grabs Marley by the shoulder. "No matter what, do not cry, frown or speak."

Every resident for miles lines up along their street. We stand at the top of our tiny driveway, joining the line with our neighbours. Mrs Tappeldora leans against her walking stick and shudders in her t-shirt. It takes everything in me not to rush over and take her inside. Someone of her age should never be forced to stand in the cold like this. No one should. I look up and make a pointed smile at the family across the street. The parents notice and nod at me warmly but the two teenagers stare at their feet (they're still smiling, of course). A biting wind swirls through the air and flings my hair about my head. A tornado of leaves whirls at my feet then settles down. As I inhale, icy air slides down my nostrils and cools my insides down. It is absolutely freezing out here but we all know that the strict dress for this event is a t-shirt. The wind dies down and all around is silence. I take a quick glance to my right to see the royal family approaching. One person at a time, they make a harsh incision on their arm to see if they react. This is what's known as slicing. While it's easy to cut yourself with a small blade and not react, this is different to the ritual centre. Here they might as well cut your whole arm open. Mother has made us practice slicing at home numerous times to prepare for this event. Personally, I think it's a futile practice because if you train yourself enough you can refrain from reacting. They only ever conduct this practice if they suspect specific Malsums are present and want to publicly arrest them. Well, if they suspect me, they're going to have to do more than cut me. I've endured much worse at home.

A scream echoes through the valley. They've found one. A woman not too far from us is dragged by guards into a van, kicking and screaming. The doors are slammed shut but we can still hear her distressed wailing from outside. Dianne and her husband are slicing people on the other side of the street and Gabriel has taken charge of our side. We are ridiculously lucky that they decided to start on our street. Once they've sliced our entire street, we can all go inside. People on the other streets will have to wait for hours before the Escobars reach them. Gabriel makes his way down the line until he reaches us. With a firm grip on the blade, he makes a harsh incision on Mother then Cassius. Neither of them shows any emotion. Next, he comes to Marley. I curse myself for not going before Marley but it's too late now. He takes her hand and leans into her ear.

"Take a deep breath, ok?" he whispers. She nods. The blade is of the most beautiful diamond. An intricate pattern of a lion is engraved on the handle and a big letter "E" for Escobar is carved on the blade.

Gabriel lightly presses the blade into Marley's skin, barely making a cut. She takes a sharp intake of breath and momentarily closes her eyes but apart from that she manages to stay calm.

"Good girl. Now cover up the cut so no one can see how small it is." She folds her arm so that the wound is pressed against her body. A small wince escapes her lips but she keeps it under control. He pats her on the shoulder and advances to me, wiping off Marley's blood from the blade with a deeply stained cloth. Gabriel knows she's a Malsum and he didn't snitch? The prince takes my hand and slices my arm a little more harshly than Marley's, but he shows evident sympathy. I mouth "thank you" to which he nods. I feel a pang of guilt for being so rude to him the other day. Before letting go of me, he gives me this look. I'm not sure what to make of it. His eyes have lightened somehow, his smile stretching slightly bigger. It's a smile that brims with excitement and cunning. As he continues down the line, I stand frozen, unsure as to whether I should be curious, terrified or a bit of both.

After the whole ordeal, Mother and Cassius find better things to do outside of the house. By now it's heading towards evening so they should be home soon. Of course, the one day that I wanted to just sit alone and relax while Mother and Cassius are out, Marley insists we make cookies. Well, I call them cookies. Mother doesn't exactly buy luxurious food, so it's kind of a cookie without the sugar. It looks and tastes as gross as it sounds, but Marley enjoys baking them and parading them around the house, showing off to any unfortunate onlooker. And if Marley's happy, I'm happy.

"Kota, that's not enough flour. You've clearly never learnt ratios before," she huffs. Marley snatches the bag and throws some more in. A great, white cloud flies from the bowl and showers me in grainy ash. I sigh and take the bag from her, slamming it down on the counter, which only forms another cloud. Marley stifles her fake little giggles in her hands but stops immediately when I offer a cold glare. My hair may look dandruff-ridden, but at least my 'Mummy's little helper' apron caught most of the dust.

"We should do this every week!" Marley exclaims.

"Make a mess?" I look up at my hair, trying to pull out clumps of self-raising flour.

"No, silly! Baking." Marley stirs the mixture with

enthusiasm, reading the encyclopaedia that sits in her other hand.

"Yeah, no thanks." A shrill sound goes off. Our broken doorbell. The doorbell I'd been casually hinting that mother should get fixed for about five years now. Marley puts her book down and climbs off her stool. She's made it her duty to answer the door because she loves to make snarky remarks at any door-seller or guard who dares to make a visit. I suppose she can't do that now that she's reached the Mixi age. She waddles to the front door with a light dusting of flour lining each of her otherwise pristine pigtails. I hear Marley do her routine of straining to go on her tippy-toes to unlatch the door and swing it open.

"Is Dakota in?" I hear a familiar, rather deep voice ask.

"Yeah, why?" Marley's tone is harsh and uninviting.

"I need to speak to her." Harsh and uninviting... She hates cold-callers but she's never this blunt. My sister would only talk to someone like this if they'd hurt her. If they'd...hurt her.

"Kota, crazy psycho-man is here!" she yells, though I'm already trying to flick flour off me as I run to the front door. I almost shove Marley aside as I force a smile on my lips. I'm met by the face of a smirking Prince Luther.

"Marley! You can't call people that. Especially not Prince Luther." I grin like mad and check to make sure Marley is smiling too. To my luck, she is. I don't know why she bothers, seeming as he made it clear earlier that he knows she's a Malsum. Precaution, I suppose. He looks between the two of us and adjusts the beanie on his head.

"Please. Like I said before, call me Gabriel." His eyes search mine and I find for a minute I feel like I'm completely alone with him. It's almost as though our hearts are bonded somehow. I just feel this connection. I don't see an authority figure before me. I see a peer. A friend.

I clear my throat in an attempt to gain some control of the situation.

"Okay uhm… Gabriel. Might I ask why we have the pleasure to make your acquaintance?" Gabriel squints his eyes, trying to figure me out. He wants informality, I'm not sure why, but he's not getting it. There's no other reason for the prince of the country to want to be chummy with me than if he wants something.

"May I come in? I have something to ask of you." All I can do is blink. Did Gabriel just…did Gabriel Escobar just ask to come into our house? My mind scans all of the rooms, trying to think of anything illegal we might have in the house. I hope I didn't leave any blood bags in the fridge. What do I do if he asks to go to the basement? Help me. HELP. ME.

"Sure. Come on in." I swing the door open further and he slides past me. I notice a few of our neighbours watching us from cracks in their curtains. Gabriel looks around the hallway, inspecting it casually. Instead of asking for somewhere he could talk to me, the prince heads for the staircase with calm, measured footsteps. Marley seems interested in keeping her distance because she hates him for cutting her. She saunters off towards the kitchen, probably intending to continue reading and baking.

I practically sprint after Gabriel. At one point on the staircase, I almost fall over my own feet. When I finally catch up, he's in my room, looking around. If you didn't know him, you might assume he was a sniffer dog. His small eyes scour every inch of my tiny room, drinking in the detail. He moves towards my desk. Within seconds he's looked through the pile of books and decided on my modern politics textbook. It's sheerly propaganda and I'm one of the few people that can see that. He opens it and flicks through the pages with purpose, as if he's seen the book a million times and is looking for a specific section. He lands on the page about the Escobars.

"Awful picture they chose of us. My nose looks so shiny, don't you think?" He holds the book up and shows it to me. All I can do is nod as I stay rooted to my place in the doorway. Gabriel chuckles and drops the book on the table. It lands with a thud that almost shakes the entire house. Gabriel sits on my bed and glides his fingertips over the rough material. He looks up at me then points to my sans-a-wheel, rolling desk chair.

"Please do sit," he prompts, as if I'm a guest in his home and not vice versa. I find myself struggling to drag out the faulty chair and perch on the edge of it.

"What do you want, Gabriel?" I spit my words out, tired of his stalling.

"Well, that's no way to talk to a royal, is it?" I slump back into my chair and look at the ceiling.

"I just wanted to give you this." I hear the ruffling

of lots of paper in his pocket. After several painstaking seconds, he grabs a specific piece of crumpled paper and holds it out. I go to take it but he snatches it away.

"Ah ah! Before I give you this, I want you to promise you won't read it out loud. Just peruse, put it in your pocket and do as it says." I nod. He raises a condescending left brow at me.

"Okay, fine. I promise." He hands me the note, which I practically snatch in desperation to rid of the suspense. I unfold it and my eyes scan over text I never thought I'd read:

> *I know what you are and I want to get you and Marley to safety. Meet me at the West woods edge on Wednesday at 11pm. Don't let anyone see you.*
> *Gabriel C.E.*

I read it once, then again, then another twenty times. My eyes flick crazily over the paper until they're tired. I look up to see that Gabriel is watching me carefully, trying to anticipate my reaction. He takes his beanie off, fluffs his hair and puts it back on. A wave of his hair remains free from the beanie, as per usual.

"Run away with me."

"Gabriel, that's crazy!" is all I can stutter out.

"Is it?"

"Yes! Yes, it is!"

"I thought we were just perusing and pocketing like you promised," he observes, the hint of a laugh swirling around his tongue.

"This isn't funny, Gabriel…"

"You're a Malsum, as is Marley. The country doesn't want you, I'm tired of my mother. It's perfect!" An excited fleck glimmers in his eyes. It's almost like his soul is burning with passion and the ignition is showing in his iris. He really wants this. All I can do is stare.

"So? What do you think?"

"I *think* this is all a trick. How would we even escape?"

"That's for me to worry about. Now, is that a yes or a no?" I squint my eyes at him in utter disbelief.

"Gabriel, you've barely given me time to think. This is…I can't…" My voice trails off as he stands up and moves closer to me.

"Just imagine, Dakota. You, me and Marley against the odds. Travelling through the unknown, living off berries and hiding from the authorities." He twirls my chair and I find myself squealing in a moment of sheer delight. I quickly quieten and mentally shame myself for giving in to his charm. I hold tight onto the note, as if it gives me some sort of stability. Blowing a hair from my face, I look up at Gabriel.

"It's Monday now. That gives you a whole two days to think about it."

"A whole two days? Gosh, you are generous!" I mock. A slither of anger seems to make its way into his eyes when I say that. I guess, as his loyal subject, Gabriel had expected me to come quietly. Well, as he would learn if I did decide to go on this ridiculous journey with him, I'm not the sheepish type. He stands up, brushes off his uniform and heads for the door.

"So that's it, you're leaving? How do you even know

I'm a Malsum anyway? You saw that Marley is but where's the evidence that I am too?" It's a stupid question to ask. Obviously, I'm a Malsum. From the slicing to me asking how we'd escape, I couldn't have been more obvious. The real question I should be asking is why I'm so stupid. I'd sold myself out without a second thought.

Before I can comprehend the situation, Gabriel spins on his heel, takes a pair of scissors from my stationery jar and sticks them through my hand, which is laid flat on my desk. A coil of sharp pain torpedoes through my fingers. The latter part of a scream is muffled as he presses his hand over my mouth. My whole body trembles. He leans in closer to my ear, dark hair draping over his eyes Warm, minty breath smothers my face.

"That's how I know," he whispers. I stare straight forward as tears brim in my eyes and spill over. He straightens and leaves the room. His shoes click clack against the wooden floorboards as he goes across the corridor, down the stairs and through the downstairs corridor. I continue to stare at the wall until I hear the front door slam. Sucking in breath, I gently ease the blade from my hand. He did a good job of stabbing me, even managing to get the blade right through to the desk. Two questions swirl through my confused brain as I sit by the contraband medicine cabinet and dress my fresh wound. What the hell just happened, and more importantly, what am I supposed to do about it? Before I even think about his offer, I need to make sure that getting rid of my Malsum curse isn't a possibility. I need to do what I've been holding off for days.

**14**

"What happened to your hand?" Mother asks from across the table, through a mouthful of whatever we're eating. It's some weird brown substance, mixed with burnt rice. Yummy! Throughout dinnertime, I've found myself readjusting the bandage numerous times. It's itchy and the wound aches like nothing I've ever felt before. At least we've managed to smuggle medicine to help with the pain. It's strictly illegal to use medicine because Dianne wants us to be in pain. Bandages and dressings are fine but that's about it.

"I snagged it on a razor when I was shaving," I respond a little too quickly.

She nods, clearly unconvinced. We're actually sitting at the kitchen table for dinner, which is an uncommon occurrence in our household. Mother normally likes to watch Escobar Daily, but today she'd said something about us needing more family time. I'm not sure what sick kind of emotional manipulation she's trying to pull on us, but it's certainly not working on me. We can play happy families all she wants, but that won't deflect from the titanium chamber waiting for me downstairs.

"You should be more careful. I wouldn't want you to get seriously hurt," she continues. If that was true, she wouldn't force me to extract blood from my system every twenty-four hours.

Instead of blurting that out, I just nod. Cassius is scrolling through his phone and Marley is unbothered by our conversation. She's too busy mixing up her food into a mushy mess and trying to spoon-feed her toy rabbit. Of course, Bunny doesn't consume the brown concoction because…well because he's a toy. The mess goes all down his front and into a splatter on the floor. It's quite amusing watching Mother bite her lip as my sister wastes copious amounts of food. I know that Marley isn't stupid enough to think that feeding Bunny would work. She's simply testing Mother's patience and I love her for it. Marley readies herself to offer the toy another spoonful, but Mother slams her fist onto the table before she gets the chance.

"Enough!" she screeches. "You can't get off your phone, you won't stop fiddling with that stupid bandage and you can't stop messing about with that mangled toy of yours. Is it too much to ask you to just be normal, for once?" Her voice is ragged and raw as she points at each of us. I internally scream at the ounce of sympathy that creeps into my body. Cassius puts his phone down and Marley starts eating the mush. I stare down at my plate and we complete the meal in utter silence.

By the time we've gone through the silent ordeal of cleaning the kitchen and doing homework, I'm mentally drained. I just need to take a walk before blood-shedding and I'll be fine. I make my excuses and leave before anyone can tell me otherwise. The sun smiles down on the gloomy streets as I tread down the path. I hum a soft tune and head pointedly in the direction of the dry cleaners. Our village is quite simple. Grey houses are the only buildings to line each street, except for a small shop, a post office and a dry cleaner. I don't have any laundry with me because that isn't my reason for heading there. It takes me about ten minutes before I make it there. I make pointed nods towards several smiling old ladies as I pass them on the narrow path. The wonky green sign, reading 'Matty's Laundromat' comes into view as I head down a final street. Checking around to make sure no one's watching, I slip around the back of the building. This is where all the teenagers tend to hang out, but that just makes it all the safer. Sure enough, there's a group of five girls sitting on kegs, chatting away. I'm their own kind so they won't question my presence. In the contraband films, the teenagers are all moody and never smile. Of course, that isn't an occurrence in Zayathai, but I know I do remember feeling angrier with the world when I hit my fourteenth birthday. I'm not sure if it's true for all teenagers because they're all smiling. Zayathian teenagers do tend to be a bit blunt with their words, but that's the best they can do with Mixi in their blood. I slide down against the brick wall until I hit the floor. My hand reaches into my pocket and pulls out the Mixi. Vibrant blue liquid stares at me from the barrel of the syringe. My thumb catches on the needle and blood draws.

"Dammit," I mutter, sucking on my thumb to ease

the bleeding. When the liquid continues to flow from my hand, I give up and wipe it on my jeans. A red smear smothers across the blue denim.

Now am I really going to do this or am I just kidding myself? If I rejected the injection the first time, it's quite a stupid idea that I could somehow retake it and become a non-Malsum. But anything is possible. I'd be stupid not to take up the chance. Funnily enough I've never injected anything into myself before, so I'm not sure how to do this correctly. I know you have to find a vein. Now just like the nurse did...flick the needle a few times, hold it above the skin and...

"This area is forbidden and by the looks on your faces it seems you already know that. I'm going to give you five seconds to get out of here before I arrest you all," a familiar voice growls. I look up, needle still poised above my skin. He holds his left hand up and knocks his fingers down, singing out, "Five...four...three..." The girls scramble to their feet and hurry away, mumbling their apologies. He drops his hand and rubs it together with the other, making his veins and knuckles stand out more so than they already do. I don't know why I didn't just hide the needle but it's too late now. He treads over the weeds and nettles until his shadow towers over me. His extravagant cloak contradicts that stupid beanie that seems to be superglued to his head.

"Is that–"

"Heroin? No." A surprised laugh soars from his lips.

"That's not what I was going to say and I think you know that." A wave of courage seems to be flowing through me today. I don't feel nearly as intimidated by a guard as I normally do, never mind Prince Gabriel. I'll peg down my bolshiness to the fact that I know he won't do anything to me. He's made it quite clear that my welfare is of the utmost importance. Although I can't help thinking that me and Marley are just toys for him to get himself out of this oppressive kingdom. I wouldn't put it past him. With a careless shrug, I stab the needle into my vein and empty the needle. I make deliberate eye contact with him as I do so. He looks towards his shoes and shakes his head with pity.

"I could get you in serious trouble for that, you know?" He rocks back and forth between his heels and toes before taking off his beanie, fluffing that goddamn perfect hair and putting it back on. So maybe it's not glued to his head. In that case, I can't think, for the life of me, why he allows that monstrosity to cover up such flawless curls.

"Oh yeah?" I clamber to my feet and hold my wrists out. "Come on then. Cuff me."

"Excuse me?" He looks down at my wrists before his eyes trace slowly up my body, pausing in very precarious places. I could criticise him for that but I find myself staring at those eerie, dark eyes of his.

"You heard what I said. Arrest me Prince Luther. Tell me how disgusting I am and whisk me away in one of those big scary vans."

"Dakota—"

"We both know you won't." The confidence surges even stronger through my body. I don't know why I'm challenging him. Is this the Mixi kicking in? It's not supposed to do this.

"And why's that?" he asks. His left hand moves down

to the hilt of the dagger and caresses it. I hope he doesn't think that intimidates me. If he does, he's really going to have to up his game.

"Because for some reason, which I haven't quite worked out yet, you care about me." I poke him as I say this. I'm not sure why but I think that makes him really angry. His jaw hardens, confirming my suspicions to be correct. Gabriel looks about us before he speaks again. He steps closer so that the space between us is basically non-existent. I don't move but my breath catches in my throat.

"I care about you enough to drive scissors through your hand." I can't help but squint at him when he says this.

"I'll admit that was a weird way to convince me that I should trust you." He shrugs, smiling down at me with those perfectly pink lips.

"I have my ways."

"I'm sure you do."

He stands up straighter and shifts his beanie a little to the right.

"But so do I," I continue. "I don't need some damaged prince to swoop in and save my sister and I." This makes Gabriel smile properly. Not the Mixi smile but one that comes from the soul. He holds his hand to his heart and sucks in a sharp breath.

"Damaged? That hurt."

"I'm a force to be reckoned with, Gabriel. You don't scare me anymore."

The bravery swirls through me like a tornado and I can't control it. I sigh and walk straight past him.

"Don't mess with me, Dakota."

"I wouldn't dream of it, your highness."

**15**

So, it turns out that my confidence was not down to the injection, it was simple arrogance. The dose did nothing. Now I know my options. And I find that no matter which one I choose, the outcome seems to be just as bad.

# 16

Tonight's blood-shedding is particularly horrific. For some reason Cassius managed to shove all three of the needles into my vein with such carelessness that blood squirted out of me like a water jet each time. Of course, my brother blamed me for staining his new shirt with blood, even though it was his own bloody fault (pun intended). Despite the burning pain in my arm, I found it rather amusing. That is until he decided that I will bloodshed for an extra hour again tonight. Trust me when I tell you that I protested. If I wasn't tied to this damn chair, I genuinely would've had an all-out brawl with my narcissistic twit of a brother. Well, I guess this extra alone-time will finally give me a chance to read the note from Gabriel properly. After contorting my body in ways that I didn't know were possible, I manage to move my cuffs in a way that lets me reach into my pocket. I pull out the now very crumpled note and manage to open it with one hand.

*I know what you are and I want to get you and Marley to safety. Meet me at the West woods edge on Wednesday at 11pm. Don't let anyone see you.*
*Gabriel C.E.*

I can't trust him. This is just his way of luring us in. We'll arrive at the woods and he'll be there with a flock of guards, ready to take us away. I can't trust him. This is all a setup. Just a stupid setup…right? But it might not be. I couldn't bear to live with the guilt of keeping Marley here if there's safety waiting for her. Not to mention the fact that denying Gabriel's offer could anger him. What if he decides to hand me in as an act of retaliation? My options are so simple yet so mind-bogglingly big. I can either spend the rest of my days watching Marley suffer at the hands of my tortuous family…or I can risk it all. I can take her with me and get the hell out of here.

**17**

"Good heavens child, will you put that paper down? You've been staring at it all day," Mother demands, lunging at me to snatch the note. Like a ninja, I whip the paper out of her reach before my cover is broken.

"What *is* that note, Dakota?" Cassius asks with narrow eyes and a mouth full of cereal.

"What it is, is none of your goddamn business," I mutter just loud enough that Marley hears me but Cassius doesn't. She covers her mouth and tries to stifle her laughter.

"What did she…Marley, what did she just say?!" He grabs her collar and puts his face close to hers. Let me tell you I have never seen my little sister's eyes widen so much in my life.

"Get off her, you rat!" I yell, trying to prize her out of his hands. I'm quick enough that Cassius doesn't get a chance to backhand me into next week.

Knock, knock, knock.

Three raps on the back gate.

"Dakota, go and answer the gate. It'll be Mister Warren after his weekly supplement."

Sure enough, Mother was right. The creepy man from down the road is here to drink some of my blood. I must say I do feel for him. You can tell he isn't exactly well kept. Though the sweet grin still plays on his face, the dried egg on his shirt and the dark circles under his eyes tell a different story.

"Morning, Mister Warren." I make sure to keep my voice low and to stay vigilant of our surroundings. Even though my gate backs onto a quiet alleyway, you never know who's listening.

"Ah, young Dakota, it's been quite a while since I've seen you. Aren't you looking lovely today!" Now this would be a compliment if this man wasn't at least fifty years old and most definitely a paedophile. Not that I want to stereotype, but he just has that look that screams 'creep'. You know, when they just constantly look on the prowl and ready to pounce. Like a lion, I guess. A very perverted lion.

"Now have you got my Kota juice?" When I was younger, I used to call my blood 'Kota juice' to make myself feel better. Obviously, he caught on the name and is yet to realise how unnerving he sounds when he says it.

"As always, sir." I hand him the pouch and he snatches it out of my clutch as if he's been craving it for some time. Normally customers are courteous enough to wait until they're out of sight to drink my blood; not Mister Warren. He goes right in for the kill, slurping like a child with no manners. He drinks the pouch all in one go, leaving a blood moustache on his upper lip. It really isn't safe

105

to consume that much blood in one go. Not only could he catch diseases, it'll really overwhelm his emotions. Sure enough, his face crumples into a messy heap and he falls to the ground, wailing like an infant. I would try to quieten him so the neighbours don't hear, but there's truly no point. A soul with Malsum blood in their system is truly unconsolable. His crying lasts at least ten minutes, probably more. It is quite a delight to my ears to hear someone crying. As you can imagine, I don't hear it often. If I do it's either my own cries or one of those scary "report the Malsums' adverts on tv. At last, his cries die down and he stands back up straight. His withered eyes are bloodshot and wet and his face is red.

"Wow, that was…truly amazing. I haven't had such a good cry in quite a while. Kota juice really does do the trick." Again, I know he's trying to be kind, but good god does it make me uncomfortable. He shakes my hand, pressing a few Zayathian ration points into my palm. I pocket them, smiling. I'll have to take them to the bank and get them put onto our card soon.

"Now I best be off, my wife wants me to do the laundry. Farewell, Dakota."

"Goodbye, Mister Warren. Oh, and before you go…" The middle-aged man spins around as if I'm about to offer for him to come inside.

"You've got a bit of…" I motion to my lip.

"Oh yes uh…thank you," the man says, wiping off the blood with his shirt sleeve as he makes a brisk exit. I couldn't help but notice the disappointment in his voice. What was he expecting me to say? I dread to think about it.

When I return inside, Mother is helping Marley put her little boots on. She's shoving the shoes onto Marley's feet with such force that I worry she'll snap the poor kid's ankles.

"Mother, allow me," I race over and take her place. "What is Marley getting ready for exactly?" Mother wipes the sweat off her brow and stands back up.

"I want you to take her shopping for food." I don't bother trying to argue against her because there's quite literally no way I can win. Mother has genuinely threatened to rat me out to the authorities before, after disputes over small things, like the dishes. Yes, you heard me right. My own mother. Though by the way she acts, I can't imagine you're surprised.

We speed through the streets, away from our village and to the centre of North Zayathai. Dark strands of hair fly around my face as we soar down the road, windows rolled down and radio on full blast. As much as I don't want to go shopping, I'll ensure to make this an enjoyable excursion. I like to make an occasion out of any time that I take Marley out of the house. She needs a chance to live a little and she certainly can't do that cooped up in our sad excuse of a house. We sing along to the national anthem, as it's the only song with lyrics that's allowed on car radios.

*"Our heroes, our heroes, our leaders! We will love them forever! We owe them, we owe them our freedom! All hail the Escobar crown!"*

There is an element of sarcasm to our voices as we shriek to the sickeningly jingoistic tune but no one would be able to decipher it. There is something therapeutic about this journey and I almost feel sad when we pull up to our destination. I can already hear the hollers of marketers and customers as we clamber out of the car.

The market is incredibly busy. Families of all sorts are bustling around, trying to get their weekly groceries. Shopping for food is such a chore but I do love the chaosity of the place. Something about the atmosphere is just so soothing. I guess it's because I don't get to interact with society that often. Most of my time is spent in that god awful chamber or doing chores for Mother. We weave in between wooden stalls, selling all different types of goods. There's everything from lentils and beans to things that we can't afford like chocolate and rum. Oh how I'd kill for some rum right now.

"Isn't this just wonderful?" Marley says with a dreamy sigh. "There's just so many colours! The deep purple of the beetroots, the rich red of dozens of ripe apples. Oh, and the dragon fruits! Aren't they simply the most exquisite things you've ever seen?"

It really warms my heart to watch Marley with a genuine smile on her face. On the way from the car, I'd instructed her to maintain a convincing grin but it looks like I didn't need to. My sister isn't interested in the things that matter to a normal six-year-old. She doesn't indulge in ludicrous children's tv (except Frozen) and she doesn't enjoy alphabetti spaghetti. This child is excited by things like fruit and words and poetry. She truly is a genius. But don't get me wrong, my little sister is still a six-year-old by nature. She still has tantrums, she's still scared of the dark and she still believes in fairies. She may be smart but my sister is a child. An oh so intelligent child.

"Can we get some cherries? Oh, I do love their flavour. Especially the candied ones. Dakota, pretty please can we get candied cherries?"

"Well, how can I say no to that cute little face?" I respond. Marley literally does an air punch and grabs a pot of cherries. The woman manning the stall is tall and thin. Her lips are small and puckered and they glisten with red lip gloss.

"That'll be twelve ration points," she says. I almost faint. That's enough points to buy a whole turkey.

"Ooo that's a little steep, don't you think? How about eight—"

"That'll be twelve ration points, ma'am," she repeats. The monotony in her voice makes me want to shove her ration points where the sun doesn't shine. Marley looks between the woman and I, a hint of disappointment creeping into her eyes. I hesitate before taking out our ration card and allowing her to scan it with a device. The scanner beeps a few times before flashing green. Cherries are a luxury so Mother won't be happy that I've spent so much. Not that I care though. Marley's happiness is worth it. My sister thanks the shopkeeper and breaks open the packet. She pops one in her mouth and I swear my sister almost melts.

"Goodness gracious, they are incredible. My taste buds really are being treated well today." Listening to Marley speak with such grand words does make me feel inferior sometimes. And when you feel less intelligent than a six-year-old there's definitely something abnormal.

As we navigate the bustling isles of the market, Marley skips along and eats her cherries. Before I can make sense of the situation, Marley stops dead in her tracks and keels over.

"Mar? Mar! Oh my god!" Her face has turned the same colour as the cherry that's lodged in her throat. I have to keep smiling so as not to raise any suspicion from the rude onlookers. Tens of beaming faces watch as I heimlich my sister. I hope to God that no one notices how much I'm trembling. That's a dead giveaway that I'm a Malsum.

"C'mon Marley," I hiss, anger starting to build up in my throat. "You need to breathe…"

Her body starts to go limp in my arms.

"Just breathe!" With a final push, the cherry soars out of her throat, through the air and rolls into a puddle. Marley cuddles into me, though she's careful to keep a smile on her face. I wish I'd been that careful. I look up and everyone is staring at my red-hot and very angered face.

"It's a dirty Malsum! Get her!"

Believe me when I tell you I've never sprinted so fast in my life. I scooped up Marley so she wouldn't trail behind me and raced to the car. I only managed to close the door by a margin before some crazed old man tried to prize it back open. I'm pretty sure I heard a crunch as I drove over his foot and sped down the street. A few cars followed us but I managed to lose the mob of smiling people at the top of our village. Though, when we reached the driveway, that didn't stop me from yanking Marley out of the car and flying through the front door. Mother almost falls out of her chair when we storm through the living room door.

"What in the name of…" She only has to take one look at us to know what's happened. "You showed your emotions in public, didn't you? Cassius take 'em to the chamber!" Strategically, he only has to grab Marley so I follow right after them, screaming till my lungs give out. He keeps hold of Marley's hair even as he storms down the steps to the chamber.

"Cassius! No no no no. Please not Marley! Anyone but her!" I screech. He holds Marley in one hand and types in the key code with the other. I tug on his arm, desperate to prize his grasp from my sister. His elbow flies back and connects with my face, knocking me to the floor. I scramble to my feet and run after him, ignoring the burning sensation in my nose. When we arrive, a sickening sight greets my eyes. A second chair. A chair for Marley. That's why they wanted us out of the house. So, they could surprise us with this new torture device. Sickos. Marley stands in a far corner, watching in horror as he grabs me and I scream bloody murder. I kick my legs fiercely and struggle to get away. My shrieks bounce off the wall and pierce my eardrums. I don't know what my plan is but I have to try. When thrashing around fails to work, I drop to the floor and try to scramble away. He grabs me by the waist and practically throws me into the chair.

"I'll give double my normal amount of blood if you just let her go. She won't survive this." He ignores my pleas and proceeds to tie me to my chair. "Cassius, remember when we used to play with dolls in my room? You always wanted the purple-haired one but you let me have it." He stops for a split second. An empty blood bag trembles in his grasp. He looks at me with cold eyes and for a moment I believe he'll let her be. To my despair, he scoffs and continues readying the machine. My tear-stricken face remains sullen as he finishes up.

"You. Over here." Clutching the hem of her sleeves, Marley shuffles towards him. Her whole body quivers as she makes her way across the room. He shoves Marley into her chair and puts the handcuffs tight around her wrists. I can see the metal digging into her tender skin. She looks at me for reassurance but I find myself looking away. I'm too ashamed to be her support net. I am the reason she is going to be strung up to that machine.

"Cassius, you don't have to do this," I whisper.

"But I do. You could've gotten us all killed, Dakota. It's unbelievable how stupid you are!"

"Ditto," I mutter, earning a deadly glare from my brother. Once he's strung Marley up to the machine, he stands back to admire his work.

"Now you better show her the ropes because, after that ghastly performance, you're going to be in here a long time." With that he steps out of the room and slams the chunky metal door shut.

After just five minutes, I don't even think Marley is going to make it. Her face has washed a deep shade of grey and every vein in her body is bulging through her skin. I remember having this exact reaction the first time I did blood-shedding. I'll never forget that one thought that kept crossing my young mind: 'Are these four walls the last thing I'll ever see?' Marley hasn't stopped crying since Cassius shut the door. I'm surprised her tear ducts have anything left inside of them.

"Everything will be alright, Mar. Look what I managed to sneak in." I reach behind me and pull out Bunny. I try to edge my chair closer to her, so I can hand her the stuffed animal. She holds him tight but it isn't enough to stop her wailing.

"You need to stay strong, Mar. Let's sing your favourite song, ok?" She musters enough energy to nod.

"Don't let them in, don't let them see," we begin. "Be the good girl you always have to be. Conceal, don't feel, don't let them know..." I find myself choking up on my own tears now.

"Well now they know," Marley finishes the lyric in a whisper. Her sobs are gone but the pain is still there. She stares straight forwards at nothing in particular, her mouth slightly agape.

"Why don't we just end it?" she mutters. My eyes dart over to her.

"End what?" She doesn't respond. Her body trembles in the seat. "End what, Mar?!" I find myself raising my voice. Silence. "What should we end, Marley?!"

"EVERYTHING!" she yells. "This pain. This anguish. And for what?" She scoffs, her eyes momentarily rolling into her head as her body starts to weaken. "Quality of life over sanctity of life, right?" Marley retches and projectile vomits across the room. Her eyes roll again and she falls unconscious. Oh my god. My sister. My six-year-old sister...was contemplating death.

113

Two hours later, my brother returns.

"What's up, losers," Cassius says as he observes our obvious suffering. Marley jolts awake, as if his menacing voice had yanked her back into consciousness.

"Wow you look rough." He tears the needles out of Marley like she's a rag doll. She winces every time. I watch him with glowing eyes as he unties me. My brother's Mixi smile twists into a small smirk before he turns his back on me. He busies himself, bustling around the room as he chucks away the used needles and turns off the machine.

"Do you get a kick out of this?" I ask through malicious, gritted teeth. He stops dead in his tracks.

"Seeing you in pain? Yeah, I suppose I do," he says with a shrug. He spins to face us and, oh the temptation to wipe that grin off his face is overbearing. Mind you, I suppose scientifically that's impossible.

"You should get her to bed. She looks pretty err… tired." Cassius points to our half-conscious little sister. Chuckling to himself, he shoves past me and saunters up the stairs. Mar is still very weak so I carry her limp body to bed.

I make sure Marley drinks enough water to get her strength back up or I fear she won't survive the night. As I tuck her in, she lays there trembling and clutching Bunny for dear life. He seems to have obtained another blood splatter in the chamber, making him look even more creepy. After I'm certain that Marley will be ok alone, I make my way to the door.

"Kota," Marley says, just as I put my hand on the door knob. I turn around to face her.

"Why doesn't Cassius and Mummy love me?" My mouth opens and closes a few times but I find I have no answer. I walk back over and climb into bed beside her. She nestles into my arms and releases a relieved sigh. Marley doesn't even wait for me to respond; within seconds she's fast asleep. She's right. Mother and Cassius don't love us. Maybe it's worth the risk. At this point, putting our lives on the line seems more appetising than spending one more minute in this house. I reach into my pocket and pull out the note again.

> *I know what you are and I want to get you and Marley to safety. Meet me at the West woods edge on Wednesday at 11pm. Don't let anyone see you.*
> *Gabriel C.E.*

Safety. It's what we want. It's what we need. Gabriel Reese Escobar could get us out of here. We'd be safe, we'd be away from here but most importantly…we'd be happy. I haven't felt true happiness in a very long time.

# 18

For the best part of the day, the house is normally stone-cold silent. If she can be bothered, Mother drags herself to the factory and Cassius makes himself scarce at school or with friends. That leaves me and Marley home alone. As much as I'd like to pretend that I sit with my sister downstairs, doing arts and crafts, and all the things you should do with a six-year-old, I don't. She likes her reading and I like being alone and that's the perfect combination, in my opinion. My room is my sacred space. No people. No noise. No pretending. I don't have to smile in here. I can just be myself. On any other day, that's what I'd be doing. Lying on my bed, reading some trashy contraband magazine that I found in a park and eating carrot sticks. But today I can't. It's very difficult to enjoy being home alone when you're not actually home alone. Not even my headphones can block out the giggles coming from downstairs.

"What do you want?" Cassius says, as soon as I make my presence in the kitchen. He and his girlfriend are sitting at the table, flirting and chatting like young couples do. Somehow, despite his looks, Cassius gets a lot of girls. As far as the contraband movies tell me, girls like bad boys. Despite the constant smiling, Cassius certainly fits the description of 'bad' so I guess they find attraction in that. He hasn't got much else going for him so I'm assuming that's why he has a new girl on his arm every week. This new one looks like an absolute nightmare.

"Just getting some water." I make sure to keep a smile plastered on my face as an outsider is present. I can't help but notice this girl's eyes are following me as I head to the cupboard then the tap. I take a sip of my water, leaning against the counter.

"Hi! I'm Maya," the girl says, sticking out her hand. Every inch of this girl's body is covered in something pink. From her pink stilettos to her dreadful sequin jacket, my eyes almost can't stand to look at her. She must be from a rich part of Zayathai because no one around here can afford all these accessories. I trudge over and take her hand, offering a gentle shake before dropping it again.

"Maya, huh? So, Cassius, does Mother know you have someone in the house?" God this girl is creepy. Her eyes seemed to have turned black, if that's even possible. She's watching me as if I'm about to make a sudden move.

"No, she doesn't. But that's none of your business, is it?" Cassius' lips are twitching in his broad smile. I take a short glance under the table and my brother has his hand resting on Maya's thigh. Gross.

"Well, it would be my business if I were to tell her."

"But you won't do that, will you?" Is that a challenge, Maya? I've only known this woman for two minutes and

117

I already know she's crazy. Ladies and gentlemen, this is a pure example of how even people who aren't Malsums can still find ways to make their anger known. Her lips may be pressed in a tight smile but she literally owns the saying, 'if looks could kill'. Clearly, she's not one for good first impressions. Mind you, neither am I. I offer a nonchalant shrug that clearly indicates to Maya that I'm going to tell on Cassius. I very much doubt that she knows why we can't have outsiders in the house, but I bet she doesn't fancy having to be dragged into our family drama if Mother were to find out.

"Babe, I think I'm gonna head off," Maya says, picking up her diamante-studded handbag.

"Oh of course. I'll…I'll see you out." As Maya passes me, she stops and gets disturbingly close to my face.

"I'll see you soon…Dakota." With that she heads straight to the front door and slams it behind her, without even saying a proper goodbye to Cassius. How does she even know my name? It's not like I told her and I doubt Cassius has bothered to talk about me. If Cassius wasn't an utter rat, I may have felt a bit bad for scaring off his sad excuse of a partner.

"What the hell did you do that for?" Cassius advances on me.

"Ah ah. Keep your distance, bud. I've already had your psycho girlfriend all up in my face."

"Well thanks to you I doubt she's my girlfriend anymore."

"I did you a favour. She was a creep anyway." I grab my water and head back upstairs.

I stalk across the landing and attempt to pass the mirror but I find it pulling me back. I sigh and start reversing until my dull reflection looks back at me from the tall, pine-framed glass. For someone so displeasing to look at, I find myself looking in a mirror much more than I imagine the average person must do. This has been on my mind a lot recently: beauty. What is it? There's no real explanation for why people associate blonde hair with perfection, yet everyone seems to be attracted to brunettes. There's no real explanation for why short girls are deemed cuter than their taller counterparts. There's no real explanation for why my brown eyes are a curse and my siblings' blue eyes are a blessing. There's no real explanation for why I'm so 'ugly'. Of course, I could probably put in more effort and stop wearing hoodies every day, but why can we only be pretty when we try? Surely it would make more sense that our pure, natural state is the most beautiful thing in the world. In that condition we are unscathed by the ravenous claws of ludicrous expectations. We are free. My thick, black hair never used to scream 'ugly' at me. It never did until I realised that every smiling model has blonde hair and now that's all I see. Ugliness. I'd thought about this earlier and decided to do some research. Here's how the Official Dictionary of Zayathai describes ugly: 'Something unpleasant or repulsive, especially in appearance.' When you think about it, there is nothing unpleasant or repulsive about an abundance of melanin in my features. The darkness in my hair and eyes is only ugly because society tells me it's ugly. We're an intelligent species. We have robots, cars, planes, fifty-storey buildings. Science has governed how we see the

119

world for decades, so why do we let nonsensical social constructs govern how we see ourselves? So maybe that's why I look in the mirror so often. Because I know that I am not unpleasant or repulsive. What I am is a girl who is drowning. I am drowning in the toxic whirlpools of the societal ocean. But I refuse. This toxicity will not flush out my lungs. I won't let it.

I set the cup and myself on my windowsill. I fling the window open and dangle my legs outside. A sea of stone buildings glares back at me. I ignore it, turning my eyes to the area above all the drab colour. I love to watch the sunset from here. I love to see the sun spreading its largess into the darkening sky. A soft glow of amber, violet and a fierce scarlet all blending to make a concoction of beauty. It's beyond me why we're ruining such a beautiful existence. The seas, the forests, the wildlife. They're all gifts. Wondrous, spectacular gifts. Yet we're destroying them. We'd never tear up a present in front of the gift-giver's eyes so why are we destroying our home? We are wrecking this present, whilst Mother Nature watches. Sometimes, just sometimes, I really wish I'd never been born so that I don't have to be a part of the wrecking ball that is tearing through the planet, inch by inch.

I don't look as a pattering of feet become closer and closer to me. Marley lowers herself beside me and looks out at the landscape. Despite the lifelessness and dull houses, you could never guess just how oppressed the people of Zayathai truly are. Marley leans her head against my shoulder and we sit in silence for a few minutes before she speaks.

"Zayathai," she says. "A perfect kalopsia." I look down at her as pained tears spring into my eyes.

"What's kalopsia?" I ask, my voice barely audible. She looks up at me and wipes a lone tear from my cheek with a small, delicate finger.

"It's when things seem so, so beautiful but it's all an illusion. Our happiness…it will always be an illusion." The spring of tears in my eyes are just about to morph into waterfalls when we hear it. Another siren. This one is slightly different, more pitchy and painful. A thousand possibilities of what the event could be race through my mind. Surely, they can't be slicing again. That'd be excessive, even for Dianne. But it's not impossible. I suppose that's the most unnerving aspect of living in Zayathai: nothing is predictable. One day might be as tranquil as an undisturbed lake but the following morning you might find a dagger being torn along your arm. You just never know. I fly out of my room and Marley has seemed to have disappeared to her room. She reappears, throwing on a pair of worn-out oxbloods and running over to me to take my hand. I have to admit, it's quite sad that Marley is getting used to all of this now. I'd held onto the hope that maybe Dianne would be overthrown by the time Marley could make sense of the world. That hope has long since perished. We run down the stairs so quickly that my legs can barely keep up with themselves. I have to put my shoes on with one hand because Marley is too afraid to let go. After a quick check to make sure we all look smart and presentable, my siblings and I head into the street.

On my way out, I'd been silently praying that they weren't conducting a slicing. When I found out what they were really doing, I would've paid good money to be cut by that dagger. It became apparent that it wasn't in fact a slicing when we followed the stream of people into the city centre. If they wanted to slice us, we'd just stand outside of our houses. All the glamorous smiling we'd done before Dianne's party was all a thing of the past. Each face is grey. Smiling but grey. There'll be some in the crowd that know exactly what's about to happen, others will be clueless. Either way, everybody is terrified. Rule number three of living in Zayathai: if you hear a siren, assume the worst. Normally we'd drive to the city centre but I know it'll be packed with traffic and people trying to walk in the streets. Without our car, we're left to follow the stream of people a good few miles across town. Families and lone citizens trickle into the stream as we make our way towards the centre.

The first thing to catch my eye is the pole. About eight foot high, I'd say. It's on a pop-up stage in the middle of the centre. There's only one pole this time. Thank God. I couldn't bear to see anymore. Just tell us what's going on, Dakota, is what you're probably thinking. You want me to stop stalling and just reveal the situation. Well, here you are. A Malsum is going to be burnt at the stake in public. I've only ever seen this happen once and I was only two years old, thus the memory is quite vague. Although one thing will remain emblazoned in my mind: the smell. That odour of burning flesh took days to wash out of my clothes, Mother had told me. She said I didn't even cry. I just watched as the Malsum went up in flames. She used to tell me this as a bedtime story. Disgusting, I know. I think she is particularly fond of that time because I hadn't cried. Every time she tells that story she is so proud to say that two-year-old me didn't shed a tear. I am not proud of that. The fact that I didn't cry doesn't paint a picture of strength or willpower. All it shows is numbness. The numbness I've succumbed myself to in order to survive the dark cavern that is Zayathian society.

The crowd waits in deathly silence to find out which unlucky Malsum will meet their fate. A winching noise echoes through the town as the person is drawn up higher on the pole. Staring down at the crowd is the face of a woman. I wouldn't say she's any older than forty. Her raw green eyes stare hopelessly over the city centre. She doesn't seem to be hysterical. In fact, she doesn't seem to be showing any emotion at all. Her lips are nothing but a straight line. Her head lolls from side to side in a state of half-consciousness. Just as I'm starting to wonder if they'll actually appear, the Escobar family make their presence. They stand by the pole, greeting us with hungry eyes.

Dianne's royal blue cloak swishes gently around her as she looks over us. Her crown glistens and reflects off a puddle on the ground beneath her. She readjusts it a little then begins to speak. "We gather here today to rid some scum from our community. Normally we'd send her to the burning chambers. However, little Miss Cocky over here deserves a public show. She, and everyone here, needs to learn their place. We are here to love you, to care for you. We cannot do that with snakes among us." Venom drips from every syllable she utters. She turns, shaking the pole with vigour.

The woman squeezes her eyes shut, as if she's trying to refrain from either crying or vomiting. Probably both. Dianne and Malcolm must've driven miles to be here. Gabriel spends a lot of time around here, seeming as he's been stationed in our area, but his parents spend most of their time at the Escobar Estate. Their grand, stately home resides in the middle of Southern Zayathai, far from us. Whatever this woman has done, it must've been bad for them to bother with the whole ordeal. Gabriel stands at the edge of the stage, hands clasped behind his back. Beside him is a particularly small woman who is holding a torch. Their personal servant. You really have to mess up to be sentenced to being at their beck and call, all hours of the day and night. I've seen some personal servants work for them for years, others for days. It's just a case of getting unlucky. Whoever the Escobars hate most at that moment gets tasked with trailing after them.

At first it had seemed strange to see Gabriel standing so far from his parents. But then it dawned on me. They want to dissociate Gabriel from any negative connotations that surround the monarchy. He is the calm one. The one that only hurts people if he really has to. He has to be at these events but he doesn't really have to *be* here.

"State your name for the crowd," Malcolm orders. His frail voice bounces off every surface in the area.

"Lib…" Her voice trails off as it's caught by a gust of wind. The pole shakes some more. Her face crumbles, and a sharp wail flies from her mouth. The crowd gasps and bursts into a fit of booing and screaming. Of course, do remember that each and every person is smiling. There's something quite strange and rather amusing about watching someone smile as they yell vulgar insults at a woman. Amusing? Dakota, a woman is about to die. Have some compassion.

"Louder," Dianne snarls. The woman's sniffling is audible as the crowd falls back into silence.

"Libby," she finally screeches. "My name is Libby Carolthrope! Don't ever forget it!" she shrieks. The broken woman that I thought I was witnessing has now turned into an animal. A hungry animal.

"Now as you can see…" Dianne begins.

"They want to silence us," Libby screams between hard, ragged breaths. The three faces of the Escobars shoot up to look at her. Even though they are smiling, I have a certain gift in deciphering people's true emotions. Dianne looks furious, Malcolm displeased and Gabriel… he looks amused. "They want us to submit but we won't. We will destroy them!" I'm surprised her vocal cords haven't broken yet. They sound like they're on the end of their tether. Not a single sound resonates from the crowd. Everyone stands in a state of total awe.

"That's enough," Dianne snaps. Libby barely spares a glance at Dianne before she continues.

"You don't want this! You want freedom and you all know it! If not for yourselves, then for your children!" My grip tightens on Marley. "Save yourselves! Please!"

125

She's reached a level of hysteria that I don't think anyone in Zayathai has ever witnessed. Not the non-malsums, anyway.

Gabriel looks across the crowd, a single bundle of dark hair hanging over his left eye. He's not wearing his normal beanie. This one is grey but it's darker and smaller. He makes eye contact with me and offers an almost invisible nod. But I notice it. The audacity of this man will never fail to astound me. I don't return the action. Instead, I make a point of turning to watch Libby.

"That is quite enough. The torch, Gabriel," Malcolm says. The prince takes the elegant torch from the servant and walks across the stage, handing it to his father. Gabriel whispers something in Malcolm's ear which causes him to laugh. I wonder what he said. The handle of the torch is a rustic diamond and of course has the Escobar symbol engraved into it. Marley cuddles me tight, burying her face into my jumper. Cassius reaches out to prize her away from me, but I offer him a glare that soon has him backing off. I don't care what he wants, my little sister is not witnessing a Malsum being burnt at the stake. Not today. Not ever.

"Now, my loyal subjects, chant with me! Burn the scum, burn the scum…"

"Burn the scum!"

"Burn the scum!"

"Burn the scum!"

Soon the centre is filled with the cheers of 'loyal subjects', the stamping of feet and the sudden wailing of Libby. She'd been able to remain strong, even though she was screaming, but now all I see is desperation. I know that all she wants is to get down from that pole. She's probably kicking herself right now. Maybe if she'd been sheepish, they may have shown some mercy. Unlikely. There's no time to think about this as Dianne lights the torch and sets the woman on fire. The chanting stays as vivid as the flame that scorches her flesh. I chant along too, but make a point of chanting quieter than everyone else. I want a discreet way of showing my distaste for such a display. Libby's expression is consumed by the flames as her body is shattered to ashes. In the end, I find myself forcing Marley to look at the woman. I realised that if anyone sees her hiding, they'd most likely suspect that she has emotions. The reflection of the flames swim in a mixture of tears in my sister's eyes. Just like I did, she doesn't cry. She just watches. I make sure to hold onto her shoulders because I can feel her body becoming limp. That smell fills the air. The scorched flesh, the ashes, the smoke. They all combine and slither down my throat. Just as I begin to think my sister is going to collapse, the burning ends. Every essence of what makes Libby a human is gone. She is nothing but a pile of sizzling ash. With a final few words, Gabriel dismisses the crowd. I swing my sister onto my shoulders and walk home briskly. I don't even check to see if Cassius is beside us.

Sure enough when we make it through the door, Marley collapses. I don't panic too much as I know she'll come around in a minute or so. When her eyes do finally reopen, she submits to an overflow of emotion. My sister wails like I've never seen her wail before. Nothing I can do or say can help her relax. She lays there, hauled up in a ball on the sofa, crying to her heart's content. Cassius doesn't tell her to stop crying nor does he say anything. With a single glance at our devastated sister, he turns and ambles up the stairs.

"They always did say that death is the only escape," Marley whispers. Buffeted by the wings of slumber, my sister falls into a soft comatose. Really, I should keep her awake because her day is far from over. However, I decide to let her rest. She's going to need all the energy she can get to make it through tonight.

Much to Cassius' dismay, I decide to take a quick stroll before we bloodshed. Too much is crossing my mind and I need to relax. I can't be fretting when Marley and I are in that chamber. One of us needs to have some composure. The dark of night cuddles me as I amble along the broken cement path. I observe the houses, each as bleak as the next. Few people roam the streets at this time for the simple reason there's a Zayathian curfew. *So why are you outside?* I hear you shout. Well, my friend, here's the simple answer. I don't care. My village has gained the trust of the guards because we've only had a handful of curfew violations in the past month. Dianne has halved the amount of security in our village at night so she can use them in more high-risk areas. The only reason we have a curfew is that it's easier to escape at night. Flashlights and night vision equipment would be needed to spot people running through the woods or hopping in a getaway car. There's no way Dianne would spend that kind of money on this stuff when she could just threaten us with a curfew. Besides, if Gabriel is really serious about his proposal, I'd be spared if the guards arrested me. Right?

As I turn the corner, I notice a change. My street was quieter, silent almost. I think I heard a distant motorbike engine at one point but besides that, complete tranquility. I must've taken a wrong turn. I look up to the street sign and pray that I'm not where I think I am. But there it is, written across a graffiti-ridden sign: Darkness Grove. Darkness Grove is different. It's right on the edge of the village, the sketchy area if you will. Everyone in my village knows Darkness Grove. You may laugh at how cliché the name is but honestly there's no better way to describe it. Everywhere is dark and gloomy. The houses are terribly looked after. To put it into perspective, my house looks like a luxury condo compared to the so-called 'homes' that people reside in on this street. It's strange because the rest of our village is so peaceful, to Zayathian standards. I wonder where it all went wrong with Darkness Grove.

Normally I would actively avoid this street but I'm here now. I could turn back but I'm not going to. The rest of the village is boring. I need a taste of adventure in my life. I kick at pebbles with my vintage trainers. The sky closes in on me with it's eerie abyss. In the distance, a cat shrieks in distress. Probably being tormented by teenagers, I decide. My mind settles on a few things, the note mainly. I pull it out of my pocket, reading it over and over again. Putting my trust in the son of a dictator could quite possibly be the most stupid decision I could ever make. It could also be my smartest.

As my head is bowed and I stalk down the lonely street, my head collides with something hard and sturdy, yet very much alive. My eyes train up to another pair of eyes. Dammit. Staring down at me, smile glistening and eyes gleaming, is a guard. And not just any guard.

"Your highness, I was just…"

"Sneaking out?" Gabriel interrupts. His arms are folded on his chest as he stares down at me with condescendence.

"Yes," I mutter. I can't even bear to keep looking into his eyes. Intense fear worms through my veins as I anticipate my arrest. That strange wave of courage I had last time I encountered the prince? Gone. I fiddle with the note, my hands clammy and shaking.

"First the dry cleaners and now here? Is finding you breaking the law going to become a common occurrence for me?" he scolds. The smugness in his voice makes me want to kick out every one of those pearly whites but I fight the urge. I know he's testing me. I look down and away from him, unsure of what the smart thing to say would be. I decide to just shake my head. He takes my chin and lifts it so my eyes are forced to look directly into his.

"Look at me when I'm talking to you." Gabriel's voice is so deep that it seems to vibrate right through to my core.

A breath catches in my throat. He studies my face

then drops his hand and clears his throat. I look away again.

"What you did to Libby was cruel. Marley was distraught. She still is," I tell him.

"If you expected me to decide not to attend her execution, you're clearly not as smart as I'd thought. You could easily not attend and go unnoticed. I, on the other hand, would be missed. Because I'm important." Wow. Real classy. "But don't try to deflect from the matter at hand. You know the curfew and here you are. It's like you are actively trying to get yourself caught."

"So, where's the van then?" The words that come from my mouth are sharp and mean. They don't even feel like mine.

"Excuse me?"

"Instead of standing around and discussing my misdeed, would you spare me the lecture and just hand me in? I've made it quite clear that I don't like you. As you said, I've given you multiple reasons to arrest me but here I am!" There's that sparkling confidence I had at the dry cleaners. This bout of bolshiness isn't a coincidence. Something about the presence of the prince feels like a challenge. A 'how far can I push the boundaries' type of challenge. Before I'd feared him but I fear no longer.

"I'm not going to rat you out, Dakota." He chuckles, almost as if I was the stupid one for assuming he'd take his job seriously.

"You're not?" I move my eyes back to his.

"No. If anything, I admire your daredevilry. You'll need it when we take a break for freedom."

131

"Who says I'm leaving with you?" He takes the note from my hand. The prince waves the paper in my face.

"By the looks of things, you're really considering it."

"Emphasis on 'considering'," I retort, snatching back the paper. Instant regret of my snappiness settles in my throat. Though I do not fear him anymore, I'm not stupid. I know what he can do to me. What he can do to Marley. I turn on my heel to walk away but Gabriel grabs my wrist. The feeling of his hand on me makes my stomach curl. I'm not sure if that curl feels good or not but I like when it happens.

"Wait." He turns me to face him. "You can trust me."

"How can I trust you? Your mother would want me and my family dead if she knew what we were. Chances are, you're exactly like mummy dearest." The Escobar family crest on his uniform glistens under the soft light of a flickering lamp post. I notice a speck of mud on his usually spotless army boots. Each button on his uniform is done up with the Escobar symbol imprinted on each one. That ridiculous, regal cape of his flicks gently against the curls of soft wind. His hair pokes out from under his grey beanie, which I'm sure he's only allowed to wear so he can pertain to the relatable young prince aesthetic.

Gabriel looks deep into my soul. He pulls my wrist which makes me stumble closer to him. He leans into my ear and, with a sudden drop in pitch, utters a final sentence.

"You can trust me because you have no other choice." With that he drops my wrist and walks straight past me. I stay completely still as the thud of his shoes softens into the distance, leaving me alone in the depths of Darkness Grove.

Blood-shedding tonight is sickening. Now that Marley knows what to expect she is even more terrified than last night. At least yesterday she didn't have time to ponder over the pain because she didn't know what it would feel like. Well now she does and even the mention of it sends her dizzy. I don't blame her. It is truly traumatic, particularly when you're not used to it. This isn't the sort of blood extraction that may occur at the hospital. This machine was put together by Cassius. It's not exactly like they could go and buy a machine off the internet so we had to rely on my brother's DIY skills. The pain is excruciating. I know that word is overused but there's no other way to describe the feeling of a vacuum drawing blood from your veins.

"Do you love anyone?" Marley asks out of the blue. She doesn't make eye contact, choosing instead to watch the shiny wall before her. Her gaze is soft and unfocused.

"Of course, I do. I love you, silly." I laugh in an attempt to lighten the mood but her face stays stone cold.

"I mean *really* do you love anyone?" Her voice is weaker than usual, croaky and blunt, almost as if each syllable is scratching at her throat as it's torn from her diaphragm.

"I don't know what you want me to say, Mar. I love you. I always have."

"But if you loved me, you'd get me out of here," she whispers.

"It's not that simple."

"If you loved me, I wouldn't be in this chair."

"You know I can't change that." A desperate anger courses through my arteries.

"Dakota, if you loved me, and I mean *really* loved me," she says, "you'd find a way." Her eyes roll over to me.

There's clearly an attempt on her part to make eye contact with me but she struggles; even the muscles in her eyes are suffering. Even though I've never felt more guilt in my entire life, out of respect for my sister, I make eye contact with her. My mouth fumbles and only manages to produce a few feeble, unintelligible attempts at words. A single tear falls from my sister's tilted face. The room is so silent that I swear I almost hear the sound resonate when the tear hits the metal floor.

Before I can respond, once again my sister blacks out. Call me the worst person in the world, but I'm glad she's unconscious. I'm glad because she was telling the truth. The raw, painful truth. If I loved her as much as I claim to, I'd find a way. It's just this night, this blood-shedding, my encounter with Gabriel and that god awful burning, that helps me to make the biggest decision of my life.

# 19

"**M**ar? Mar, wake up."

I've decided we're going. All night I spent deciding if the escape was worth the risk of getting caught. If we do get found out, our lives would end at the hands of the Escobars. This was the main reason why I didn't think we should go. But then I thought about it. My argument was based upon the fact that our lives would be compromised. But we aren't living, are we? This pain isn't temporary. It's constant and it's torturous and Marley shouldn't have to go through it. A life isn't spending hour upon hour in a titanium chamber. Our lives, our proper lives, belong outside the walls of this country. Based on what I've been taught about our planet, there isn't a whole lot left of it. Each country may be full of broken battlefields and poverty but we can cope with that. I am more than willing to sacrifice running water and my own bed if it means we're truly liberated. Because that's all we've ever wanted: freedom.

Marley sure didn't go with a fight. With one whisper of comfort from me she practically leapt out of that bed.

All I had to say was that a lovely man was going to help us and she was all for it. I didn't mention who this man was because that's not important. I told her to only grab things that are important; she took Bunny and her encyclopaedia. I decided to bring one thing and one thing only. A locket. I know it's horrifically sentimental of me but there's a picture inside the locket of me and Marley. This journey could go wrong and it will definitely be challenging. I need an incentive. I need this picture to remind me why we're doing this. I want a better life for Marley. Nothing else matters.

While Marley brushes her hair, I look out of her window. The front-facing view gives me the chance to check for guards. Two minutes go by before a man with a gun and the distinct buzzcut marches past our house. Perfect. If my approximations are correct, it'll be ten minutes before another guard checks our side of the village. That's just enough time for us to get onto the motorway. Even if a neighbour rats on us, we'll be long gone by then.

With Marley's hand tight in my left palm, we tiptoe down the inconveniently creaky stairs and towards the front door. I swear every floorboard moans as we make a light-footed escape from the house. Lucky for us, Mother and Cassius are deep sleepers. Extremely deep sleepers. Even if they did hear a noise, they'd never suspect it was us. We're too scared of them to dare to leave. We wouldn't even make it that far before we were found. Or so they think. Rule number four of living in Zayathai:

never break the law. You'll emerge from the penal system either broken or dead.

"Going somewhere?"

Oh God. We spin around and the dull face of my brother meets my eye. He thinks he's foiled our plan, though I doubt he knows what it actually is. The victorious smile dancing on his face tells me he really thinks he's got us. Poor sod.

"We're leaving. For good," Marley says. He scoffs.

"Oh yeah? And how do you suppose you're going to do that?"

"A man is going to help us." Oh Marley. I should've told her not to tip anyone off. I would've just told Cassius we were going for a walk, if Marley hadn't spoken first. A little spiral of anger whirls in my stomach for just a split second but I make sure to get rid of it. She had no way of knowing who she can and can't tell. Cassius' eyes narrow and he manages to smile even more. He kneels down to her level, taking her hand out of mine and putting both in his palms.

"Your silly sister has been filling your head with tales, I'm afraid. No decent man would help you. They would know that Malsums deserve to die—"

"Cassius stop." Marley's mouth is hanging open slightly, her eyes just a bit wider than before. The bright spot of hope in her pupils has long since passed.

"She needs to know, Dakota. You're both dirty dirty Malsums."

"And you aren't?" I blurt out. Cassius stops dead in his

137

tracks. His head starts to tremble. Never mind that, his whole body starts to tremble. My brother stands back up and gets right in my face, still shaking. And for the first time in years, my brother frowns.

"You said you wouldn't tell anyone. You said…"

"I know what I said, Cassius. But that was before everything. You used to care for me when Mother didn't but something switched inside of you. Now you mean nothing to me. Nothing! You're so damn lucky that Mother didn't do the bullet test on you. Because if she did, your life would've meant just as much as mine." Cassius recoils back in a sharp instance, as if I'd punched him square in the jaw. He knows I'm right. He knows that he turned on me and left me for dust. My brother's body is still shaking like a telephone line in the wind.

"Alright. You got me. You win, Dakota. Go ahead. Let's see how far you get. You take Marley and you escape. But just know we will find you. I will see to it that you never get a chance to undermine me again." He swings the front door open and stands aside. We walk past him and I make sure to knock into him as we go. Maybe that was a tad petty? No. Petty is seeing to it that your sister is slaughtered by the government. Petty is torturing someone of your own kind to deflect the attention off of yourself.

On a normal day, Marley would sit in the backseat. She's always told me that it's a safer position to be, in the event of a car crash. Today she climbs into the front passenger seat. Bunny sits tight in her lap, secured by the seat belt. Cassius watches from the front door as I slide into the driver's seat and slam the door shut.

"It's not like you to sit upfront." The little light in the ceiling illuminates my sister's smiling face. Marley shrugs.

"I wanted to be close to you." A little spark of warmth ignites inside of my heart and I fight the urge to pull her into a hug. She opens the glovebox and takes out the emergency blanket that we leave in the car, in case we get stuck in traffic. Fanning it out, my sister places it over herself and Bunny. Of course, she makes sure Bunny's face is uncovered, so as not to smother him. You'd expect me to be in a hurry in such a situation as this but I feel the need to drag it out. Mother won't wake up because she is the deepest sleeper known to man. We have plenty of time before we're due to meet Gabriel. All I want to do is taunt my brother, just as he has done to me for the better part of a decade. My hands reach up and flick down the overhead mirror. A tired girl meets my gaze. Dark rings encircle my brown, almost black eyes. One thing I've always been proud of is my thick eyelashes but even they seem to be thinning. Jet black hair drapes either side of my shoulders. Most people smile a little more than usual upon looking in a mirror to accentuate their features. I make a point of frowning. Not only am I frowning outside of the house but we are breaking curfew. However, guards are unlikely to stop us. They'll assume we are of some importance if we drive past fast enough for them to not see our faces. No one dares to overtly break the rules so they'd have no reason to assume otherwise. Sure, there may be neighbours watching out of their windows but at this very late hour I really doubt that. Even if there is, that is no longer my problem. The Malsum life is about to become a thing of the past.

"Are you going to drive or just stare at your own reflection?" Despite Marley's rudeness, I do feel relieved. She is ready for this journey. She is dedicated and I'm glad. Something tells me that this is not going to be easy so her enthusiasm relaxes me. Slamming the mirror shut, I take a dramatic breath and place my hands on the steering wheel.

"Ready?" I crane my neck to face her. Each of her hands holds the corresponding rabbit's forefoot. She purses her tiny lips together then releases them.

"Ready as I'll ever be." I turn the keys and the car spurs into action. I flick on the heating and take a final glance at the grey house. My eyes glaze over the cracked exterior and grubby garden. I can't help but break into a broad smile when I look at my brother, who looks so small in the doorframe.

"Wave goodbye, Marley." I offer a small, patronising wave then begin to drive. As we pull out of the driveway, Marley makes a gesture that I'd rather not describe. We both giggle as his face goes grave with anger. And with that we're gone, soaring through the streets of the village.

Within minutes, Marley is fast asleep. Her head rests against the window and strands of blonde hair cling to the glass. She doesn't snore but a slight noise escapes her lips as she inhales and exhales. My hands hang loosely on the steering wheel, freedom tingling through my palms. Though the drive is only about an hour, I find myself stepping harder on the gas, trying to speed up the process. Excited doesn't even begin to cover how I'm feeling. This could all be a huge mistake. Gabriel is probably waiting for us now with a sea of guards. If that's the case then I am a fool. But at least we tried. Adventure is a word that has barely braced my vocabulary. All of my life the idea of travelling any further than to the opposite side of Zayathai was a mere dream. Now it's a reality that I'm barely managing to fathom. This is the longest drive I've ever made. Once we hit the edge of northern Zayathai, all that greets my vision is bumpy country roads and fields of sheep. Not that I'm complaining. I've never been this far out so it's nice to admit the scenery as we twist and turn down the valley. I can't see a single person or car in sight so I step on the gas and fly over the hilltops. I can't tell if the funny feeling in my stomach is from the thrill of speeding or the anticipation of our escape. Marley is still sleeping when we take a turn and are greeted with a distant mass of trees that I hadn't been expecting. Miles of winding roads are afoot, which lead into the eerily dark forest. Intimidation settles into my veins as we draw closer. That's when I see him. We've made it.

I can already see Gabriel's smile from here. He's waiting by what looks like a van. When we pull up beside him, I feel a pang of excitement. The prospect of leaving Zayathai behind seems unreal. The adrenaline is building up inside of me faster than I can handle. By the time we actually arrive by Gabriel, I'm trying to avoid dancing in my seat. But then my heart falls. It plunges out of the dark night skies and lands in a deep pile of dog poo. Because

Gabriel isn't alone. I nudge Marley and her eyes flutter open. Her short arms stretch and the blanket falls to the floor.

"Let's go say hi," I urge, even though that's the last thing I want to do. For a moment I even consider making a u-turn and getting the hell out of here. But I don't. I fight every instinct in my body as I shove my door open and step out. My feet hit a blanket of crunchy leaves. I fix my hoodie and in doing so my hand brushes across the locket. Confidence leaks from the necklace and flows through my veins. It helps me to remember why I'm doing this as we walk towards them. Marley. I'm doing this for Marley.

"Hey," Gabriel says. I must admit I'm still taken aback by his informality. When we met him at the party he was all "good evening, ma'am" and "aren't you just looking ravishing tonight". I knew that can't have been his real personality. He's only a few years older than me and I don't know any young adult who talks like that. I have to admit, he looks especially good tonight. He's ditched that stupid cloak (thank god) and donned black jeans, a black shirt and a black leather jacket. I could take a good guess at what his favourite colour is.

"Hi," I reply. Marley doesn't say a single thing but I pin it down to timidity. Although Marley isn't exactly the shy type. Her small left hand is pressed tight into mine with no intent of letting go. In my other hand is the encyclopaedia that she'd asked me to carry.

"I'm glad you decided to trust me. We're getting the hell out of here." I'm still struggling to come to terms with the fact that all of Gabriel's speeches were fake. You could see the passion brimming in his eyes when he spoke. Maybe he's like Cassius. I guess they both live by the motto, 'if you can't beat 'em, join 'em.'

Gabriel looks over at the stout man standing next to him.

"Oh, and this is my friend, Enzo." It's obvious that this Enzo guy is a Malsum. He has a deep-set frown plastered to his face. Gabriel is quite tall but Enzo puts his height to shame. One of his shoulders is probably as wide as my waist and he owns a huge set of biceps. I wouldn't exactly call them impressive. They're all veiny and bumpy like his skin can barely keep the muscle from exploding. Not a good look. His hair is fashioned exactly like that of the royal guards: that stupid buzzcut. My eyes are drawn to a scar that stretches across his right eye. Everything about Enzo screams intimidating. That isn't helped by the fact that he doesn't even greet us. With small eyes and furrowed brows, he offers a small wave. Not exactly the social butterfly then.

"*He's* the one helping us?" Marley finally speaks. All eyes dart over to her. "The evil prince who cut me!" I notice her grip on Bunny intensifies and she drops my hand. Gabriel's smile doesn't falter. Of course it doesn't. He's not a malsum like us.

"He's helping us, Mar. Don't be so confrontational."

She scoffs in disbelief. "Confrontational? Oh, that's rich!"

"Marley!"

"He literally took a knife to my arm, Kota." Her eyes

look up at me and I don't see anger. I just see helplessness. She doesn't feel safe and I've put her in that situation. Without me needing to ask, Gabriel sweeps into action. He moves closer to my sister and kneels to her level. She takes an indiscreet step back which causes him to draw a deep sigh.

"You have no reason to trust me Marley, I understand that. You associate me with danger, with pain." My sister moves Bunny behind her back, as if she's trying to protect him. "It is obvious that I do not have your trust and that is something I will have to earn. But let me promise you this: as long as I walk this earth, you will never come in harm's way again." A gasp gets caught in my throat.

"That's a big promise." I thought I'd said that in my head but apparently not. He stands up and turns to me.

"I mean it, Dakota. You're both safe with me." Marley's face hasn't softened. Enzo checks the time with the imaginary watch on his wrist.

"I don't mean to intrude on this clearly very heartfelt moment but might I point out that we don't have all night." Every word he speaks is sharp and I'm surprised they don't draw blood from his bitter tongue.

"You're right. We must head off now if we're to be on time," Gabriel states. He looks down at Marley. "We have sweets in the van." At that, Marley's expression does relax. Just a little bit.

"Whatever. Just don't sit too close to me." She tries to appear composed but her legs practically fly to the vehicle. As I've mentioned, sugar was a scarce product in my house. We lived off mainly rice and soups. Mar yanks on the door handle and swings it open. A weak source of light spills from the van. Four bean bags- green, red, blue and pink- are placed in the back. Four huge bags and some blankets are pushed to the rear wall. Sure, enough a box of candied goods rests on the floor. Marley plops into the green bean bag on the far side and takes a lolly. Enzo tsks and traipses to the passenger seat of the van.

"After you, m'lady." Gabriel drops into a deep, comical bow. I find myself giggling as I head to the van. I climb in and slide the door shut. I hand Marley the encyclopaedia and she digs right in. Gabriel follows after us, hopping into the driver's seat. He turns around and peeks through the gap between his and Enzo's chair.

"Before we set off, I need to ask if you have your phones with you," he says. I check my pockets only to realise my phone was with me. I had intended to leave it at home.

"I brought mine but Marley doesn't have one." Even though Marley is perfectly responsible enough to have her own mobile, she never wanted one. Besides there isn't a whole lot you can do on them. There are five games that can be downloaded and your messages are monitored by the monarchy, so not many people bother with them. I, however, love my phone. Those five games have been an absolute saviour when the tv is occupied by my family. It took five years' worth of my savings to get the cheapest model there is, but it was well worth it.

"I need you to hand it over," Gabriel begins, holding his hand out. "We don't need any devices on our person that could be used to track us." It makes sense, so I take my phone out of my pocket and give it to Gabriel without hesitation. He drops it in the footwell of the driver's seat and stamps on it. I know this is all for the best, but that doesn't make the sound of crunching glass any easier to hear. Marley watches him like he's a madman and Enzo seems to be enjoying the sight of my decimated device a little too much. Once the evisceration of my beloved cell phone is complete, the van falls silent. Leaving the shattered remains on the floor, Gabriel places his hands on the steering wheel.

"Perfect. Let's head off, shall we?" Not even ten seconds later, we're back on the road.

Gabriel is going over the plan but I keep finding myself losing concentration. He explained that we'd be less likely to be spotted if we sat in the back with no windows. There is however a tinted ceiling window, which gives me the perfect opportunity to stargaze. The sky is particularly clear tonight, as if Mother Nature has decided to give me a departing gift. A sprinkle of iridescent stars litters the sky, undisturbed by clouds or fog. I find a certain beauty in the fact that each star is completely different. We always celebrate the originality of each blazing rock that floats around space. That being said, why can't the same go for humans? I don't understand why we can't all just be allowed to show our emotions. I suppose our emotions shape who you are and without them you are exactly what Dianne wants you to be. Robots.

"Sorry. Can you repeat the plan again? I wasn't listening." Gabriel breaks his concentration from driving to give me a sideways smile as we bump along the country road towards the West woods. I respond with a meek grin.

"Alright, but this is the last time I'm saying it. There

are four forbidden areas that landlock Zayathai. North, East, South and West. We are going to escape through the forbidden West. It's the area with the least security because it has so many biomes to cross. We have enough equipment to cross the four biomes: snow, sand, forest and water. At the end of our journey, a boat will be waiting to take us across the ocean and to safety in a neighbouring country. Understood?"

Wow this is a daring decision. I don't know if I have the physical capability to cross so many obstacles, never mind Marley. Well, no matter how I feel about this plan, there's no turning back now. I made this decision on Marley's behalf and I must see to it that she makes it safely out of Zayathai.

"Yes. I understand."

**20**

"So how exactly do you plan to get past the guards?" Marley asks, sucking on a lollipop. Her eyes train over the words in her book and she flips the page every twenty seconds or so. "Well, I'm the prince so if they don't see you, they'll let me drive right through the gates to the West." His voice seems to soften when he mentions his status. It's almost as if he doesn't like owning the title. Gabriel doesn't take his eyes off the road for a single moment. I must hand it to him, he's a very smooth driver. You'd assume that the royals don't know how to drive because they're chauffeured everywhere, but apparently not. I guess that's the strange thing about public figures. Their lives are all over the news and we seem to think we know every aspect of their existence. The truth is we don't know the half of it.

"Where are we going first?" Marley asks. She decides she's had enough of the lollipop and drops it beside her beanbag, while continuing to read. The lollipop lands on its head and sticks to the dusty floor for a moment before flopping onto its side. Struggling to move with the combination of sugar and saliva, the sweet rolls to the front of the van and collects various pieces of mud and other crusty, unidentifiable items from the floor.

"The snow biome," Gabriel responds. We come to a halt at an unexpected set of traffic. These other vehicles must be driven by guards, food transporters and other workers. Those are the only types of people that are allowed out during curfew. The van falls silent. The only noise to be heard is Enzo tapping away at his phone and the low hum of the engine. For someone who doesn't like to talk to anyone he sure has a lot of texts.

"Cool...so is there going to be—"

"Do you ever stop talking?" Enzo interrupts, turning to glare into the soul of my sister. Somehow, he still manages to type.

"Do you ever stop texting?" Marley fires back, slamming her book closed and placing it in her lap.

"When I was your age, kids were seen and not heard."

"Well, that's because you had nothing worth saying," Marley explains, condescendence worming through her words.

"God you are something else—"

"Can we just...! Listen. To get through this journey we can't be at each other's throats, alright?" Gabriel interrupts.

"Agreed," I speak up for the first time in a while. Marley and Enzo have been tearing into each other like wild animals, so I thought it in my best interest to keep quiet. I'd thought Marley would've maintained her timidity for longer than ten minutes but apparently not. They seem to be making snipes and jabs at each other whenever its possible. I can't work out why they dislike each other so much already, considering they just met. I'm sure they'll grow to like each other.

I have this ill feeling in the base of my stomach. It feels kind of icky like when you sniff too hard and mucus slithers down your throat. There's a possibility that this sensation is the result of a dodgy milkshake I drank earlier but my suspicions suggest otherwise. We've only been on the road for twenty minutes and already Marley and Enzo want to slaughter one another. Maybe this is all a mistake. There's no way we'll get past the guards and into the forbidden West, never mind get through all four biomes. The journey aside, something about Gabriel is unnerving. He keeps watching me in the rearview mirror with an intense gaze, as if he's waiting for me to make a break for it and run away. Every time he looks at me, I stare down at the floor, pretending I hadn't noticed. We repeat this process at least seven times before I decide enough is enough. He takes a final glance at me and I stare straight back at him through the mirror. His eyes tilt back to the road in one smooth motion.

The air seems to darken as we head into a mass of trees. The van suddenly seems less stable, as if we're not on flat ground. The forest. We must be nearing the forbidden West. Twigs and foliage snap and rustle under the wheels as we trundle down what I'm assuming is a dirt path. If I stood up and moved closer to the gap between the upfront chairs, I'd be able to see the scenery through the windscreen. However, we're driving at an immense speed and through such rocky land that I don't fancy the risk of flying through said windscreen. Somehow the distinct scent of pine and oak manages to seep through the van walls. I inhale and drink in the mellow scent. My head relaxes and my body sinks further into the beanbag. The van comes to an abrupt halt. We've arrived at the gates to the forbidden West. If my stomach was churning before, it's now like a cement mixer.

"Girls, stay quiet, ok?" Gabriel stares straight forward as a guard approaches the van.

"Tell that to Enzo. He's the gobby one," Marley says with a proud smile.

"God you are so funny," Enzo mutters, eyes still fixed to his mobile.

"Do you want to stop tearing chunks out of my sister?" I chime in, sitting up straighter. No response. Just an aggravating smirk as he continues to flick through his phone.

"Hide," Gabriel instructs. Marley and I dive behind our beanbags. My sister is clutching Bunny like her little life depends on it.

The guard raps his knuckles on the blacked-out window. Gabriel's wearing this dumb pair of sunglasses that make him look like a mafia boss. He rolls down the window and lolls his head to face the guard. This attempt at swagger almost sends me cackling.

"ID," the guard orders, monotonous and dry. Gabriel hands him a card and he practically snatches it out of his hand. I feel second hand embarrassment for the soldier when he realises who he's just sassed. Gabriel tears his sunglasses off, revealing a menacing glint in his eye. He tucks the left temple of the glasses into his shirt and bites his lip, chuckling. He takes his beanie off, combs his fingers through each glorious strand of hair and replaces it. A condescending brow raises on Gabriel's face as the guard looks on in disbelief.

"Your highness, I didn't realise it was y–"

"Are you going to open the gates or not?" Enzo asks, pausing from his phone for the first time since we set off.

"I...of course, sir. Right away." He scurries off to the control room beside the road and starts talking to one of his colleagues. I'm assuming Enzo is of some importance because he's allowed to leave Zayathai. Though I've never seen him before. Strange. Two guards, one being the one who greeted Gabriel, march to the gate. At each step they kick their legs so high that they almost make it to ninety degrees. Zayathian guards have always done this and we've found it the epicentre of our amusement over the years. Both me and Marley have to bury our faces in the beanbags to stifle our laughter. The gates are tall and of a rich silver. At the centre, is a connector in the shape of a curly 'E'. With a slight struggle, the guards etch the gate open. I swear I hear every person in the van let out a sigh of relief as the engine starts up and we sail through the first of many barriers.

The van jolts as the terrain turns from solid to uneven. Snow. I haven't seen snow in a long, long time. In fact, I sometimes forget about the last time. Probably because humans are programmed to block out trauma. These things always start out so innocently. We'd been building a snowman. He was small and his body parts were obscure, but I thought it a masterpiece. Cassius had managed to find some carrots in the fridge so all of the snowman's features were a dull orange. For once my smile was genuine. It slid across my face like a pebble on a frozen lake. We were dancing in circles around the snowman, singing dumb melodies and opening our mouths so snowflakes could melt on our tongues. It was only a small fall. I tumbled onto the ground, landing safely on my back. The fall wasn't the issue. The lone stick protruding out of the earth was the issue. Being only seven, naturally I hadn't thought about the fact that I was out in the front garden, in public view. My mouth fell open and the tears began to flow. And so did the blood. Mother had darted into the garden, ignoring the fact she was shoe-less. Cassius did try to prize her fingers from my ponytail as she shoved my face into the bitter snow, attempting to stifle my yells. I think that's the last time he ever cared for me. She told him that night, 'Your sister could've gotten us killed with that wailing. She's a danger to us, Cassius.' She assumed I was asleep but I could hear her from my bed. It had been at least five hours since the incident, but still the skin on my face felt like it was burning with cold. I didn't sleep that night. I didn't sleep for many more nights after that. Up until then she'd loved me. They'd both loved me. To this day I still believe that if she hadn't found out about the concept of blood-shedding she would've gotten rid of me. So much for blood is thicker than water.

"We're going to have to sleep in the van for the night."

Gabriel turns off the engine. Marley opens her mouth to protest but he cuts in before she gets the chance. "I know it's not ideal but I have accommodation sorted for tomorrow." It's difficult to imagine what kind of 'accommodation' you could find in the middle of an expanse of abandoned snow, but I guess I'll just have to trust him. Trust. That's a word that I'm really going to have to bring close to my heart if I'm going to survive this. If I don't wholly trust in Gabriel's ability to break us free then we really won't make it out. You could call me stupid for blindly walking into what could be certain death, but put yourself in my shoes. This has and will never be easy.

"But it's so cold in here," Marley mumbles. She shudders as she says this, though it's evident that it was clearly a theatrical move. The van isn't that cold. Sure, it's a little on the uncomfortable side but we knew this wasn't going to be a walk in the park. Maybe Marley thought it would be. She may be smart but she is still six. Little kids don't always think things through. They just see the pot of gold waiting for them at the end.

"Listen, kid. If you want to whinge about it then go ahead. You can cry to your heart's content, but that will not change the fact that we're spending the remainder of the night in this very van." Enzo's snappiness makes me want to tear his head from his huge shoulders. I have never met someone who is willing to speak to a young child like that. Whether she's annoying or not, she is six. No doubt Enzo would retort to that statement with the fact that she doesn't act six. And I suppose he's right. I've never felt like I've had a little sister. If anything, Marley feels like a superior. Marley doesn't respond to Enzo but lays down on her bean bag and stares at the silver wall of the van. Enzo lets out a pleased exhale before returning to texting. Gabriel shrugs and comes to sit with me in the back of the van. For the small moment that he opens the back door, I steal a look at the outside world. The snow looks more akin to glitter than anything else as it rests under the soft moonlight. Icy air temporarily soars into the van before Gabriel shoves the door closed. He grabs the blankets and distributes them to each of us. Marley made no reply when Gabriel offered her the cover so he spread it over her. She didn't move. Enzo decided that he was okay sleeping in the passenger seat, despite Gabriel's best efforts to get him to join us in the back. He'd scoffed at the idea and spat that he didn't want to be anywhere near 'her'. His distaste for Marley is starting to become comical if anything. Gabriel takes out another blanket from behind the bags and sets it beside mine. I begin to lay on my bean bag when Gabriel puts his hand on my arm, causing me to jump a little. He takes note of this and his palm slivers from my body.

"We should sleep together." I squint at him, confusion worming across my face.

"Excuse me?"

"Not like that," he interjects, rolling his eyes, as if I was making a wild assumption. "I meant to preserve body heat." When I fall silent, he pipes up again. "Like penguins."

"Penguins?" That makes me giggle. Gabriel shakes his head and his smile seems as genuine as ever.

"They huddle together to keep warm."

"Right. Well then, your highness, I suppose tonight we will assume the role of penguins."

"I suppose we will." I push my bean bag closer to his. Gabriel flicks off the dodgy van light and we both lay down on our double beanbag creation. As the van falls silent, I notice Gabriel roll over and put his arm over me. I smirk in the darkness, removing it to place it back by his side.

"That's not what a penguin would do," he whispers. I know he's right behind me but I'm still startled by how close his voice is to my ear. I say nothing but let out a puffy laugh before closing my eyes.

# 21

I'm awoken by the hoot of an owl in the distance. I force one eye open then the other. Everyone else is still asleep. Perfect. That gives me time to adjust to being awake before Enzo and Marley start shrieking at each other. As I'm about to sit up, I notice a weight over my body that hadn't occurred to me before. Gabriel's arm. His chest connects with my back, gentle heat radiating from him. In an almost state of subconsciousness, I sink back into the embrace. No doubt the world waiting for us outside the van will contain a biting wind that I'm not ready to face yet. It's only common sense to make the most of this warmth. I nestle my head into the dip between Gabriel's chin and collarbone. He mumbles in his sleep and draws himself closer to me. A gasp rises inside of me but I push it back down. I close my eyes, ready to indulge in a few more minutes of bliss.

"Comfy?" A raspy but deep voice asks. The sound reverberates in my ear and a shiver travels through my body. I sit bolt upright, knocking his arm off me in the process. "Well, that wasn't very nice," he murmurs. The prince watches me with lazy, half-opened eyes.

"Did you sleep well?" I find myself asking. He closes his eyes for a moment, a small laugh only making it part way up his throat.

"Just fine, thank you. And by the looks of things, so did you." He yawns and rubs his face, an aggravating smirk dancing across his features.

"I was cold." I tug a hair bobble from my wrist and tie up the mass of black strands that hang over my face. With a stretch, Gabriel sits up. His hair is in a fashionable mess all over his head. He swipes it to one side and reaches blindly for his beanie, pulling it atop of his head. "And you put your arm over me, not the other way round."

"Touché." There's that smirk again. Oh, the desire to punch him right now. Before I can put that thought into action, Marley stirs. She rolls over to face us but then turns back again.

"Good morning to you too," Gabriel chides. My sister mumbles something that I don't quite catch but, by the look on Gabriel's face, maybe I don't want to know. Gabriel and I begin to fold up our blankets and tidy up the van. We do so in silence for no other reason than there is nothing to say. Not long after we begin organising, Enzo awakens with a hearty snort. That seems to properly wake up Marley, as she jumps on the chance to laugh at him. Marley huddles in her blanket as she and Enzo engage in their routine shouting match. By the time Gabriel and I have packed all of our sleeping stuff away, Marley and Enzo's rage has subsided. A little.

"Okay," Gabriel says, slapping his palms together.

I sit on my beanbag, cross legged as I had been before. "We need to get a move on if we're to arrive at the accommodation before nightfall." Marley stops stroking Bunny's ears to look up.

"You keep referring to this accommodation. Where exactly are we staying?" She's finally asked the question that I'd been meaning to ask for ages. Gabriel leans forward on his beanbag, clasping his hands together.

"We're staying with a tribe." I almost choke on the air I'm inhaling.

"I'm sorry. For a minute I thought you said a tribe," I spit. By the way that Gabriel isn't laughing, I can only assume that this isn't some sort of sick joke. Enzo's face confirms that he's enjoying the sight of me and Marley's expressions way too much.

"Don't tell me you were expecting to stay at a five-star hotel," Enzo teases. He takes a pack of cigarettes and a lighter out of his pocket, lighting one and holding it to his mouth. My eyes shoot to him.

"Well obviously not but I certainly wasn't expecting to be guests to a group of feral, uncivilised..." The skin around Gabriel's eyes crinkles.

"You're making wild assumptions. The Malafuki Tribe are a group of highly intelligent, well-spoken people. The only thing they lack is the same thing that you do: an ability to accept the injection." Gabriel's voice is careful and eloquent. He makes gentle gestures as he speaks, something he must've been taught to do during public speaking or elocution lessons. I nod, willing myself to agree. These people are just like me. Misunderstood.

Outcast. I remind myself of this over and over again as we ready ourselves to leave.

Enzo takes a long drag of his cigarette before speaking. "We're going to have to abandon the van and walk. It would be way too obvious to guards scouting us in helicopters." He drops the cigarette on the ground and stamps it out. Gabriel gives him a disapproving look to which Enzo completely ignores. God, I forgot that people would be looking for us. Of course they would. We've run away with the prince of the country. For the first time since yesterday, I realise how stupid we are. When in a million years would this be a good idea? They were bound to find us. My concern has never been about my welfare. Whatever happens to me, happens. I can take it. What worries me is the small girl, who is sitting across from me, tugging on her shoes and talking to her toy rabbit. If anything hurts Marley, it is my fault. I am the one who has put her in harm's way. Is her freedom really worth the risk of capture? I guess only time will tell.

Despite the light blaring through the windscreen, the van has remained fairly dark. Therefore, you can imagine the pain that soars through my eyes when Gabriel flings the van door open. Combined with sunlight and the reflection of gleaming snow, my eyesight almost caves in. Multicoloured dots line my vision as I clamber out of the van.

"Watch your step," Gabriel tells me. I reach out to take Gabriel's hand and somehow manage to trip on my way down, but Gabriel's arm curls around my waist and lowers me to the ground. He smiles down at me, still holding onto my torso. "My goodness, Dakota. What am I gonna do with you?" I blush and step away as his arm moves from my body.

Marley follows behind me, though she's more reluctant to take Gabriel's hand. In fact, she looks at it as if he's dipped it in manure. Once we're all outside, Gabriel heads back into the van and pulls out the bags that are pushed right to the back. He gives us one each. They're absolutely huge and I have to help Marley get hers on her back. She looks so unsteady that I worry she'll topple over. The rucksack isn't even that heavy but it's almost as tall as her. Enzo points this out, which only makes her more determined to carry it herself. I notice that Gabriel and Enzo's rucksacks seem a lot fuller than ours, but Gabriel explained that was only because they are carrying our tents. Tents. I shuddered at the thought of spending the night in the wild. My family has never been adventurous and the only kind of holiday you can really take in Zayathai is camping on your local green. Fun, I know. Gabriel pats the van and says goodbye to it. Weirdo. Clutching a map in one hand, Gabriel turns to us all.

"Off we go."

**22**

"Please be cautious around here. This tribe is civilised but they're known to be a bit…aggressive," Gabriel says. I also think about asking him how he managed to communicate with the tribe but I decide against it.

"They are a group of Malum-sensum exiles, who narrowly escaped the death penalty," Enzo explains, another cigarette tucked in the corner of his mouth. Of course, he also says this while staring at his mobile. "Don't attempt to make proper interaction with anyone, except the leader or the head chef. They're dangerous and unpredictable." Gabriel nods along as he speaks. "Although do remember that if they initiate conversation with you, do not walk away. That will only make them angry. Entertain the subject for as long as necessary then get out of there."

"Got it," I say.

"Yes, sir," Marley responds, saluting and smiling at herself. Enzo takes a moment to look up from his phone, scowl and look back down.

We've been walking for God knows how long and

Marley is becoming particularly restless. It doesn't help that we're walking in pitch black because my sister's imagination is way too wild. I see a stick; she sees a deadly scorpion. Gabriel has filled our bags with a variety of things that I haven't bothered to look at. It's rather heavy but I'm just grateful that I don't have to carry the tents too. Marley has loaded up her bag with her book and Bunny. She was holding her stuffed animal but decided he was at risk of hypothermia. Enzo had made a snide comment when she expressed concern for the welfare of her toy rabbit. I don't know what's wrong with him. No one acts like that towards a six-year-old, it's just not right. Unless you count my family but they're deluded. So is Enzo, I suppose.

I hadn't thought to bring strong waterproof shoes so now my socks are soaking wet. No wonder I can no longer feel my toes.

"So, what's this all about then?" I ask, walking beside Gabriel. Marley and Enzo are engaged in another detailed argument about whether you should wear socks in bed or not. As stupid an argument as it is, I'd rather they disputed that than who is going to murder who first.

"What do you mean?" He pulls his jacket tighter to him as a particularly aggressive gust of wind attacks us.

"You're the son of Dianne. Her whole regime is based on the injection. She burns Malsums. *You've* burnt Malsums." His jaw tightens when I say that. His top teeth close over his bottom lip and release it slowly.

"Yes, and people change. It's wrong, Dakota. I can't bring back the Malsums I've killed but I can help the ones who are still alive." He makes a point of not meeting my eyes. We fall silent. I dig my hands deep in my pockets, desperate to try and preserve even an ounce of body heat. I have to take twice the number of steps as Gabriel to keep at his pace. He's made it clear that he doesn't want to talk anymore but I'm a professional at crossing the limits.

"So why us? I mean there's hundreds of Malsums across Zayathai. Why not them?" I blurt out, breaking the uncomfortable silence that settled between us. It feels wrong to interrogate him like this, but the questions are biting at my throat, pining to be released. He looks up to the sky and sighs to himself. A pitiful laugh escapes his lips as he shakes his head.

"You're just like your sister. So many questions."

"No answer? I forget royals are famous for dodging the truth."

"The way you're carrying on, someone would assume that you don't like me."

"Maybe I don't."

"We both know that's a lie." He's right. It is a lie. I don't dislike him. I just don't understand him. The mysterious aspect to his personality does nothing but annoy me. "You seemed to like me a lot when you were cuddling me this morning." I nearly stop dead in my tracks.

"Need I remind you that I was trapped by your arm. You gave me no choice but to lay there." He cocks his head towards me.

"I felt you nestle into me." Of course he did. Well now I look like an idiot. Instead of conjuring up a smart response, I just make this weird scoffing noise and stride ahead. Snow crunches desperately under my sodden footwear. My hair flies around my head as the icy wind circles me.

"You don't know where we're going," he calls after me in a patronising voice that makes me want to tear out his vocal cords.

"I know." His laugh catches on the wind as I continue to charge forwards. And then I see it. Plain as day. A village bursting with life. We've made it.

"Zeus! So good to see you. Thank you so much for letting us stay in your village." Gabriel sticks his hand out for the man to shake but he doesn't take up the offer.

"Come with me." I'm assuming Zeus is the leader of this tribe. He looks like one of those wise old owl stereotypes. A long grey beard drapes from the face of the rather small man. His build is akin to a twig but I can tell this doesn't limit his power. Zeus clings to a cane that seems to be the only thing stopping him from toppling over. He has this sort of sensei-esque vibe to him that really interests me. The man doesn't seem at all interested in a conversation and sets about showing us to our accommodation as soon as possible. He walks at an insane pace so I find myself nearly sprinting after him. The village brims with vibrance. Small kids dressed in brown tunics run all over the place. Elders stand by the fire at the centre of the village, preparing a delicious-looking broth. The smell of chicken drifts from the pots and delights my senses. Men sit on logs, sharpening weapons and laughing together.

We walk right to the end of the village, which is pretty close. So far all I've seen are huts, each quite small but still very impressive. The walls, I'm assuming, are made from animal skins. Each hut could house about three people at best. Right at the foot of the village is a hut, noticeably bigger than the others. Zeus tells us that this is where we'll be staying. Given Zeus' cold glare and sharp way with words, I'm surprised he was willing to give us the best seat in the house.

"There's four of you. The hut is big enough to house all of you. Don't feel flattered." This was his response to us exclaiming profusely at him being kind enough to give us the grandest hut. Within seconds, Zeus disappears into the crowd of villagers.

The hut is just as pretty on the inside as the outside. It's big enough to house two bedrooms. Somehow the tribe has managed to acquire fairy lights that line the walls of both rooms. Though the rooms are simple, each containing two single beds and a wooden dresser, I can't help but adore the cutesy character of the hut. Marley and I share one room, with Gabriel and Enzo in the other. I feel rather unnerved at the prospect of sleeping in a room near Enzo. The only thing protecting my sister from his wrath is a wall made of leather. Marley has already set up camp, placing Bunny on her bed and her book beside him. I don't feel like getting comfy because it isn't like we're staying here for long. Before I know it we'll be setting off into the unknown of the next biome.

"Settling in alright?" I look up to see Gabriel standing in the doorway. Marley makes a point of turning her back to him and playing with Bunny. A pang of guilt bites at my stomach, seeming as he's just trying to help us.

"Just fine, yeah," I reply.

"Have you looked in your backpack yet?" His eyes train over to my sealed bag. Without an answer he picks it up and pulls the drawstring. He empties the contents out onto my bed: a torch; a pocket knife; two outfits, one black and the other camouflage print; walking boots; eating utensils; food wrapped in tin foil and a shotgun.

"What's the clothes for? I've already got stuff to wear."

"Dakota, if we end up getting hunted, we won't stand a chance if you're wearing a tie dye jumper. We need to blend into the darkness." Granted this hoodie wasn't the best choice but it's the most thermal piece of clothing I own. "And the walking boots are important too, you'll need good support for your feet. Leave your other shoes here, they're already wrecked."

"And the gun? You know I'm not using that and neither is my little sister." Though of course Gabriel's face stays etched in a smile, the dark in his eyes gets just that bit scarier. He picks up the gun and twirls it around his hand with an air of nonchalance that irritates me.

"Listen. You will never make a more dangerous journey than this. If you want to ignore my advice and not carry a gun, by all means do that. But when they close in on us, and trust me they will, you will want that trigger by your finger." He tosses the gun on my bed and starts walking out. "I'm going to sit by the fire. You coming?"

~

"All of those speeches about your mother and the injection," I say, "did you mean any of it?" I hold my hands just about the blaze of the campfire and relish in the gentle heat it emits.

"When you're stuck in a situation like that you make yourself mean it," Gabriel responds, taking a sip of his whiskey. His curt answer confirms his disinterest in entertaining my question. Clearly a touchy subject. His small grey eyes seem to watch the fire with such intensity that it seems he's having a staring competition with the inanimate object. I say inanimate. Fires are the most alive things I've ever come across. Their vibrant flames dance like a free spirit, blaring a plethora of distinct colours. All four elements band together to create a blazing flame of colour. It's spurred on by the wind and marvelled at by all. If you ask me, I couldn't think of anything more beautiful.

Marley seems to share my adoration for the wild flames. She's showing Bunny the fire and discussing the science of it. To be honest, I don't know half the stuff she's spewing out. I'm not sure where Enzo has gone but I'm not exactly mourning his presence. I find myself sitting so close to Gabriel that I can't help but breathe in his scent. It's some weird hybrid between a rich citrus fruit, lime maybe, and the unmistakable whiff of strong smoke.

"Why do you always smell like an arson crime scene?" I'd noticed this particular element to his scent when we slept in the van. Gabriel bites the inside of his lip slightly and tilts his head towards me. His smile morphs into a distinguishable smirk. This is the closest a non-malsum can get to not smiling and Gabriel clearly relishes in that power.

"I'm always in the burning chambers where we burn delinquents such as yourself."

"Seriously?" I almost scream.

"No, Dakota. I'm kidding." Gabriel reaches into his side pocket and pulls out two cigars.

"I've noticed the disappointed look you give Enzo when he smokes. Hypocritical much," I say, a thread of smugness weaving between each syllable. Gabriel cocks his left eyebrow and the corner of his mouth kicks into a gentle smirk.

"I'm accustomed to the occasional Belicoso cigar. Enzo, on the other hand, chain-smokes Malboros like some sort of rebellious thirteen-year-old. It's childish of him. Now would you like one or not?"

He holds one out to me. Normally I'd strongly decline, stating how terrible smoking is for your lungs. Today I find myself taking the stick, allowing him to light it for me. I press it between my lips and take a deep drag. I fight the urge to gag so as not to look like a baby in front of Gabriel.

He has this whole bad-boy vibe about him and I feel an obligation to follow suit. My face trembles as I try to hold in one of the most aggressive coughs I've ever acquired. A few painstaking moments later the cough forces itself from my oesophagus and hurls itself from my lips. Gabriel chuckles and moves closer to me. He pats my back while I splutter like the idiot I am.

"First time?" he asks, still laughing. I nod while I try to snub my coughing fit with some water. He eases the cigar out of my hands and takes a drag, still patting my back.

Marley looks up and stares at us in distaste. She puts her small hand over Bunny's mouth and nose to stop her inanimate best friend from inhaling the fumes.

"Smoking kills, you know."

"Exactly," Gabriel says, pressing his own cigar to his lips. I'm inclined to ask what he meant by that but Marley goes straight in for the kill, firing back, "I wasn't talking to you. I was talking to Kota. Bold of you to assume I care if you die."

"Marley, cut it out!" I exclaim.

"No, it's ok. I get it. I'm a stranger, she's bound to hate me." As Gabriel speaks a gentle plume of smoke spills over the top of his bottom lip.

"Don't flatter yourself. It has nothing to do with you being a stranger," Marley snarls.

"What has gotten into you today?" I seriously have to refrain from yelling at this point.

"Hey, Mar," Gabriel interrupts. "How about you go to the food tent over there? I heard the cook makes a mean hot cocoa." She rolls her eyes at him, visible disgust written across her youthful face.

"Only Kota is allowed to call me Mar," my little sister states, but she stands up and walks off all the same.

Marley returns with her drink and plops beside a random young child. I had reinforced earlier how important it is not to interact with the tribal kids, but it's not like she was going to listen.

"Hello," she says plainly, looking the young girl up and down. The villager's hair is in tidy fishtail braids. She can't be any older than Marley and she conforms to that age with cute dimples and an excitable look on her face.

"Me and you play game?" the little girl offers. I'm taken aback by the girl's politeness. By the way Gabriel and

Enzo were going on, I'd imagined we were encountering a group of blood-thirsty animals.

"Sure. I could make us some chess pieces out of sticks," Marley says with a shrug. She glances around her for some stray firewood.

"Chess?"

"Yes, chess. The game...chess?" Marley becomes almost hysterical at the prospect that someone might not know how to play her favourite game. My sister looks over to me in distress but I just laugh and signal for her to stop. She takes a sharp breath.

"Okay then...what do you want to play?"

"What about tag?" the girl suggests. I swear my sister almost buffers in real life.

"I'm sorry, for a moment I thought you said tag?"

"Yes. You run. I catch." I notice the little girl's lack of vocabulary, in comparison to Marley. It's huge.

"I assume there are strategies to this...tag."

"Strategies?" the girl asks, tilting her head in confusion.

"I think I'm just going to read my book," my sister dismisses the girl, opening her encyclopaedia and beginning to read. With a frown, the little girl stands up and disappears into the crowd. My sister seems to have already forgotten the incident. I do sometimes question why Marley is so abnormal. Obviously, everyone is their own type of person and I don't want to discredit her unique personality, but it just seems off. I have never met any six-year-old with this level of intelligence. She is at the point where she could take my exams right now and pass with a higher grade than me. I firmly believe that Marley could work for the intelligence sector of the government right now. She is just that smart.

The whole village is asleep. The only noise to be heard is the faint hoot of an owl and the swish of a calm breeze. I am the only one to remain awake. Something about earlier events really unsettled me. If anyone had offered me a cigar, no matter who they were, I would've said no. I know that for certain. No amount of peer pressure from anyone could make me buckle. Except it has. Gabriel gave me that cigar and I took it. I've known this man for all of about five minutes and yet he holds more power over me than anyone ever has. And that shakes me. It shakes me to the core…

**23**

When I wake up, the first sight to greet my heavy eyes is Marley staring at me. I pull the rather scratchy duvet over my head and groan.

"What do you want?" I mumble. She scoffs.

"Rude. I was only going to ask if you wanted breakfast but I guess I'll go out there alone."

"Is there any grapefruit?" I ask, peeking out from the covers.

"More than you can imagine." I leap from the bed and tug on my shoes. Marley skips beside me, chatting away to Bunny as we head to the food tent. A thousand scents hit me as we head inside. Three long, redwood tables hold hundreds of bowls of different food. I scour each one until I find a bowl of grapefruits. I take a cup of weak-looking tea and some grapefruit, before heading to the campfire with my sister. As we approach, I notice Enzo and Gabriel sipping coffee, while being deep in conversation. Though Enzo doesn't smile, he seems deeply invested in the topic. At one point he even laughs a little. Not much but it's more than I ever expected him to. Enzo says something which prompts Gabriel to slap his knee and double over in laughter.

"You wish," I hear Gabriel say between cackles. Enzo pats him on the back and stands up. He holds a satisfied smirk as he ambles off to a far tent.

"What was that all about?" I ask. Gabriel looks up and wipes a happy tear from his eye.

"Oh nothing," he says, sipping his coffee. I slide onto the log next to him.

"Didn't sound like nothing," I press. He runs the tip of his tongue across his upper teeth and raises a condescending brow at me.

"How was your sleep?" he asks. I try to ignore his unsubtle attempt at changing the subject.

"Not too bad, actually. The duvet was a bit itchy though."

"Oh." He looks to the floor before meeting my eyes. "Well, mine was soft so perhaps you could share my bed." Again? I fight the urge to squint at him. I struggle to decipher whether this is some casual attempt at flirting or pure care for my wellbeing.

"I'm not so sure about that." He shrugs and looks ahead of him, taking another sip of his coffee. While my mind races through a thousand thoughts, I nibble on the grapefruit and steal the occasional glimpse of the man sitting beside me. He seems to make nothing of the offer he made me so I decide it was made out of sheer kindness and kindness only.

On the edge of the village is a wide expanse of trees, barely resembling a forest. Each tree is stripped of colour, except dull shades of brown and the sluggish green of moss patches. At the base of several trees are bushes, which I must admit aren't so ugly. A few even bear a few blossoming flowers, which struggle under the harshness of the snow. We've spent the best part of the morning collecting firewood, which we're doing in exchange for shelter at the village. Gabriel had offered Zeus points but I suppose those are useless if you don't live in mainstream society.

"Kota, can you help me with this wood?" Marley asks, struggling to grapple several logs at once.

"Here, let me help you," Gabriel says, dropping his own pile to come to her aid. Like a ninja, my sister spins in a circle and turns her back to him.

"I said Kota. I don't want your help." With that she struggles to gather her firewood and traipses in the direction of the village. The light in Gabriel's eyes seems to have dimmed. He watches my sister with a gentle gaze as she ambles into the distance. I stand beside him to watch her.

"Don't sweat it. She's...well she's Marley." He bobs his head and starts walking. I have to practically run because his steps are so much larger than mine. I've taken the brunt of my mother's genes and have adopted her irritatingly short legs and long body. We walk in silence, lugging piles of wood that we've collected for the village. The rough bark scratches and bites at my forearms.

"You're really tall, you know," I say, attempting conversation with the angry giant.

"Yes. I do know."

"You're quite the social butterfly."

"What I am is an annoyed butterfly. So if you wouldn't mind kindly shutting up, that would be marvellous." His voice is so calm but the poison drips from his lips.

"Why do you want Marley to like you so much? I mean really. You caused her pain, Gabriel. Don't expect so much of her." My voice is harsher than I expected. I bite the inside of my lip so hard that blood coats my tongue.

"Funny you should say that. I shouldn't expect so much of her yet she's expecting me to get her out of this country. The least she can do is pay an ounce of attention to me."

"We didn't ask you to do this! You chose to."

"But I didn't have to."

"That's not the point, Gabriel!"

"I think it is."

"Ok! Let's just…stop this before it gets too serious. We can't afford to mess this up."

"You're telling me," he scoffs. Gabriel increases his pace so I'm unable to keep up with him. The hair that isn't confined by his beanie, flails around in the harshness of the wind. The footprints left by his shoes are noticeably bigger than mine.

When we arrive back at the village, we search for Zeus. He looks at our wood and comes to the conclusion that it's 'acceptable.' I'm not sure how we could've gotten firewood that was any more acceptable; it's wood. Mind you, I'm quite used to barely being acceptable. My entire life I've been only just good enough. In Mother's eyes, my only redeeming quality is the blood in my veins. Every other aspect of my existence is futile. I've always found this quite ironic, seeming as I'm literally her offspring. When it comes to nature vs nurture, I am most definitely in the nature camp. The likelihood is that you're scrunching your nose as you read this, seeming as nurture has always been the favoured side. Yes, you could argue that gaining all your attributes from sheer nature is a ridiculous idea, but hear me out. Not to be vain but I'm not that bad of a person. My mother, however, could easily be mistaken as Beelzebub himself. There's no way my mother is the reason I'm a mostly pleasant person. She didn't nurture me in the slightest. I think if you're born evil, that's how you'll always be. Evil.

I decide to take some time to myself. Comprehending this situation is difficult enough without the constant noise of my companions. I made sure that Gabriel was keeping an eye on Marley before I wander into the distance. Leaving my sister with someone who is immensely angry at her probably isn't the best idea but it's a risk I'm willing to take for my sanity. Where I'm going, I have no idea, but I just want to get away. I walk in the opposite direction to when we arrived, hoping to find somewhere nice to relax. The manic life of the village fades into the distance as I head deeper and deeper into the snowy abyss. Not long after I set off, maybe ten minutes or so, I find myself at a lake. It stretches for hundreds of metres, casting a gentle blue across the otherwise white expanse. I perch on a lone acacia log. The lake is frozen over, yet still it manages to brim with wondrous life. A family of ducks lay stagnant on the ice, huddled close to one another. One of the chicks wanders off westwards in an enviable state of ignorance.

The mother doesn't run to retrieve her young, but lets it have a gander by itself. At one point it slips. I find myself giggling as the poor duckling scrambles to its tiny legs. Deciding that it had enough, the duck turns and heads back to its loved ones. Call me crazy, but I swear I saw the mother and father smile as their baby returned back to the nest. Though I shiver in the cold, my heart is as warm as it's ever been. The lake holds an obvious fragility with its glazed layer of ice, yet I feel a certain overwhelming power by which the glassy body of water holds. Sometimes we, as humans, forget what came first. Nature is here and it's here to stay. Our lust for permanence is nothing but denial. No matter how much we want to fight reality with ignorance, nature will always win. I stare at the lake and she smiles back. She offers a gentle hug but, before I can take up the offer, I feel a hand on my shoulder.

"Goodness, you scared me!" I exclaim, looking up at the figure beside me. A girl, around my age, sits beside me. Her smile is soft and compliments the dozens of tyrannical freckles that line her cheeks. The clothing she bears is simple, a warm-toned pinafore and t-shirt. Auburn hair is plaited into two neat fishtail braids either side of her head. She makes no reply but stares out at the still lake. We make an unspoken agreement to talk no more. For a few minutes, our silence speaks a thousand words.

"You are lucky," she says, which I have to say startles me once more. The thickness of the local accent trickles from her tongue.

"How so?"

"Chance to escape? One in million."

"Yeah well, you never really escape this kind of power." The words tumble listlessly from my mouth and spill onto the lake, simmering away. At once, she takes my right hand and cusps it between hers. I turn to face her, comfort gliding through my veins.

"Please. I do not know you well, but I ask only one favour of you." I nod, already willing to fulfil whatever this unknown girl asks of me.

Her dark eyes search mine and I feel no inclination to look away. Something about her gaze is so tyrannical, so magical that I cannot help but hold it.

"Please," she says. "Let the whole world know. You? Voice of future. Voice of us. Scream from the rooftop and shout through the megaphone. This country is prison and only you have the key." I nod at an even faster pace, wiping away hopeless tears with my sleeve. In unison, we stand up. Like before, we make an unspoken agreement to head back to the village in silence.

She dives right back into society but, instead of joining in with the hustle and bustle of human life, I decide to take an outsider's perspective. I sit alone and succumb to my senses. The voices disperse from a murmur of random sound to individual conversations. I can hear people talking about tonight's meal, the next festival, all kinds of things. One father sits with his young daughter and shows her how to weave. I notice the admiration on her face as she adopts the skill of her loved one. An icy breeze bites at my face and arms. I wrap my camouflage coat tighter around my torso, hugging myself. I look up to see the sky is nearing completely white, almost as if it's lined with a sheet of ivory or mulberry silk. I move my feet from side to side, taking great delight in the gentle crunch of the snow below them.

From the depths of the village, spawns a creature. A tall and mighty creature. A so very angry, smiling creature. Gabriel grabs my arm but I jump to my feet and shrug him off.

"Get the hell off me, Gabriel," I hiss. He puts two fingers to his temple and takes a deep, drawn-out breath.

"The first thing I told you not to do when we got here was talk to the locals."

"She initiated the conversation and Enzo told us we shouldn't walk away from that. Besides, I'm not a baby, Gabriel. I can fend for myself."

His eyes roll into his head, while his grin continues to glisten. A stray, dark hair flops over his left eye and I cringe at the thought of it going inside his eyeball. He's looking at me funny. Have I been staring?

"You just don't get it, Dakota. You need to listen to me or you and your precious little sister aren't going to make it out of this country in one piece." He folds his arms across his chest. I cross mine too, arching my brows.

"Gabriel, I know you're helping us and all, but if I want to talk to a few harmless villagers then by all means I'm going to."

"No, you're not."

"You can't stop me," I spit. He takes a step forward. My body shudders as his tall stature blocks all sunlight.

He drops a considerable amount and even then, he's barely close to my height.

"See that's where you're so dreadfully wrong," he growls right into my ear. Gabriel straightens and turns on his heel. Despite his height, he merges back into the crowd and all I can do is watch.

I spend the rest of the day stewing over how much I hate Gabriel. When I agreed to go on this journey with him, I assumed I'd be travelling under the capacity of his friend, not his pet. He treats me like I don't have three brain cells to my name. That's one thing that will always get on my nerves. When people underestimate me. The only thing you can possibly gain by acting as if I'm braindead, is an addition to my kill list. Okay maybe I don't have a kill list, but I do have a vendetta against anyone that wants to treat me like I'm any less than them. Whether that's a testament to the emotional trauma of living with a dysfunctional family is up for debate.

We have no other duties but collecting the wood, which leaves me a long time to think about what we're doing. This whole ordeal is crazy. We're fully aware that this could all go terribly wrong. But it's a risk we're willing to take. The days of being Dianne's puppets need to be a thing of the past.

~

Seeing how the tribe has been treating Gabriel has been quite a shock. I'm used to people bowing down at his feet and swooning over anything he says. The villagers have absolutely no interest in him. In fact, it seems they are going out of their way to show how much they consider him nothing more than a normal person. It's respectable, considering his family literally ruined all of these people's lives but it's funny all the same. If anything, he should count himself lucky that they aren't charging at him with sharpened spears and attempting to gouge out his eyeballs at every opportunity. I certainly would try that if he was partially the reason I'd had to evacuate mainstream society. I'm not going to lie, it's been quite satisfying to watch Gabriel being treated as what he truly is: a normal human being. Watching someone get treated like the almighty god that they clearly aren't for the best part of eighteen years is not fun. He needs humbling because if he talks down to me one more time, I think I might just call off the escape and walk home. Anything to get his stupid, grating voice out of my head.

As if on cue to me making that statement in my mind, Gabriel approaches me. I'd been quite happy sitting by the fire, stabbing at a piece of wood with my pen knife. Marley had been sitting beside me but she made herself scarce as soon as Gabriel came into view. I don't blame her. In fact, I wish I'd done the same. I continue to slash at my wood as a pair of black boots appear before me.

"I think we should talk about this." I hate that I like his stupid, grating voice. I hate that I never want it to leave my mind.

"Really? Because I don't." I take a rather hearty stab at the block and my knife goes deep into it, wood splintering either side of the blade. My teeth grate hard against each other as I yank it out and continue hacking away.

"You're going to hurt yourself."

"Don't act like you care about me. You've made it quite clear by the way that you don't listen to *anything* I say." The wood is in tatters now and each stab I take is closer to my fingers than the last but, for some godforsaken reason, I can't stop. My arm flies in the air to take one almighty slash but it doesn't come back down. Cold, strong fingers are wrapped around my wrist, forcing me to look up. Gabriel runs his tongue along the inside of his mouth, a condescending left brow raised at me. The grey of his iris glimmers against the reflection of the snow and attempts to lock eye contact with me. I don't let it.

"With all due respect, Dakota, how can I take you seriously when you're attacking a log?"

"Would you rather I attacked you instead?" I growl, pulling my arm free.

"If it meant you were safe, yes. I suppose I would." Dammit that was smooth. My jaw tenses at that but I don't stop throwing my knife down.

"Well, I don't need your guidance." Slash. "I don't need your pity." Stab. "And I most *certainly* don't need your approval." Slice. The blade goes right through my pinky finger.

"Goodness, Dakota. You're going to kill yourself!" Gabriel exclaims, snatching the dagger. I jump to my feet and step aside.

"At this rate, death would be a treat." It's a weak response but I make it my departing sentence before storming to god knows where. Once I'm a safe few yards

183

from the fire, I yank my handkerchief from my pocket and fan it out. Crimson blood snakes along my hand, highlighting every crease and callus. It hurts like hell as I wrap the cloth around my little finger. The hanky won't stay secure by itself. I'm sure Gabriel had some safety pins but it's a fat chance I'm going to ask him for any help. I pull out the single bobby pin that's holding my hair bun together, causing the dark mane to tumble to my shoulders. The pin doesn't do much but it's better than me bleeding out.

Later, Marley asked me what had happened to my finger. It only took me a split second to conjure up the excuse that I sliced it while helping to prepare food. I wouldn't consider it a farfetched lie by any stretch of the imagination but it was clear that she didn't believe me. There's no fooling a girl like Marley.

Night dawned on us quicker than expected, within a mere few hours. I don't understand the science behind it but apparently the biomes somehow have different time zones and sunlight hours, even if they're in the same part of the earth. I'm no genius but that can't be possible unless it's a manmade occurrence. It must be controlled by the government. Of course, being on the run means sacrificing the privilege of wearing pyjamas to bed. Granted, it's a small trade for our freedom but that doesn't make sleeping in cargo trousers any less annoying. Marley knocked out hours ago. The poor kid is really suffering from all the action. She's used to reading books and sitting around all day. So am I, I suppose, but she's at the age where it's socially acceptable to nap every ten minutes. Despite my best efforts, fluffing up these sad excuses for pillows is futile. In the end, I just clamber into the creaky, wooden bed and hope for some rendition of a good night's sleep.

"Dakota," a rumbling voice murmurs in the dark. For me to say that I jumped out of my skin would be no overstatement.

"God almighty! Would it kill you to make yourself known before you start talking?" I snap. Gabriel's tall stature appears in the doorway. I can't help but notice how he's akin to slenderman, scarce of anything close to normal body proportions. Don't get me wrong though, he still has the definition of very impressive muscles, even through a camo shirt. He's nothing compared to Enzo but that's not necessarily a bad thing. Sometimes I find his best friend's immense muscle mass rather disturbing.

"Sorry," he whispers, even though there isn't an ounce of remorse in his tone. I huff and yank a bobble from my wrist, tying up my unruly locks. The prince's silhouette leans against the doorframe, hand clutching the top. "Your bed does look pretty uncomfortable." Although the hut is relatively dark, I can still see the soft curve of his smile and the curls of his hair. Thank god, the beanie has been taken off his head for bed. He looks so much better without it.

"You'd be correct in that assumption," I say, coincidentally pushing the itchy sheets away from my arms.

"The offer to share mine still stands."

"Even though we hate each other right now?" Gabriel bites his lip and looks to the ground.

185

"Who said I hate you?"

"Well, I assumed you did. I certainly hate you right now." He shrugs.

"Fair enough. I'm not standing here all night. Do with my offer what you will." Gabriel turns and the floorboards creak under his feet as he traipses back to his bed. As an act of protest, I sit in my bed for a few minutes before tiptoeing to the next room and climbing in beside him. The bed is the same size as mine, which is quite small. It's a squeeze but I just about manage to lay down without tumbling to the floor. My head is inches away from the mass of dark hair on the prince's head. I lay still, unsure where to put my arms. I opt for putting them by my side, which is less than comfortable but a much better option than getting any closer to Gabriel. Just as my eyes begin to drift close, a sentence is uttered into the darkness that snaps them back open.

"I knew you couldn't resist the temptation." I don't dignify his comment with a response because I know that's what he wants. Five minutes pass. Then another five. And another. There is absolutely no way I'm going to manage to sleep tonight. Clinging onto the edge of the bed so that I don't fall is bad enough but Gabriel's soft breathing is surprisingly distracting. The fine line between resentment and enticement that I have towards Gabriel makes sleeping beside him no easy feat. I can't tell if he is asleep and I'm inclined to check because if he is, I could really do with him moving over a little. I'll be damned if I'll give him the satisfaction of hearing me face plant onto this solid wood floor. With expert care, I roll over to face the prince's dark curly locks. Releasing one of my arms from the confinement of the duvet, I tap him on the shoulder.

"Yes, Dakota?" There's an amusement to the tone of his voice that both annoys and comforts me.

"Can you move over a little? I'm ten seconds from falling off the bed." The frame creaks in agony as he turns over to face me. A gentle yet arrogant gaze glimmers across his eyes as he looks at me. Despite my precarious position, I inch back a little to put some distance between my face and his.

"I'm afraid I too will fall if I move any further." I crane my neck up to look over him.

"You're lying. There's tons more room on your side!" I scowl at him which he greets with a smug regard.

"Yeah but I need it. I'm bigger." My scowl deepens, almost to the point of no return.

"Gabriel–"

"Okay okay. I'll move over a little but that won't make a lot of difference. You can put your arms around me though, that should help you from plummeting to the ground."

"No chance. Even being in the same room as you is enough." His dark eyes trace every nook of mine before he shrugs.

"Suit yourself." Gabriel turns back over, moving away from me a little. I manage a mere few minutes before I edge closer, audibly sighing as I'm forced to put my arm across him. I can almost feel him smirking into the pitch black of the night.

"Sweet dreams, Dakota."

~

I made sure to wake up way before Gabriel this morning. There was no need for any conversation between us. We're not friends and that's that. The sole purpose of this journey is to gain our freedom, no strings attached. As much as the village is a safe haven, I can't help but be excited to leave. When you imagine a tribe, exotic rituals and practices come to mind. In reality, all we've done is collect wood and eat chicken broth. It pains me to admit it but Gabriel is right. This isn't a group of feral animals; they're just people that society doesn't want. I guess I'm more similar to them than I first thought. Marley and I spend the best part of the morning talking and collecting firewood, while Gabriel and Enzo do lord knows what. Being away from Gabriel for most of the day has helped to calm my anger towards him. I am realising now that maybe I've acted irrationally. Not that I'm going to admit that to him.

Later, Gabriel summons us all into his cramped bedroom to have a 'chat.'

"Get off my bed," Enzo orders as he ducks under the low door frame. I lean against the wall, watching my little sister offer him the coldest of glares.

"But I was just–"

"I said get off my bed." He starts walking, well charging, towards Marley.

"You can sit on my bed, Marley," Gabriel offers, before Enzo manhandles my sister.

With a huff, Marley stands up and sits beside the prince, careful to keep a safe distance between them.

Gabriel launches into this speech about the next stages of our journey. He says how we plan to spend one more night in the village and then set off to the next biome: the desert. Gabriel waves his hands around and nods his head as he speaks. For a moment I think he's reliving the days of making speeches in front of the whole of Zayathai. He seems so captured by his own words, going into meticulous detail about each stage of the plan.

"Sir, I am sent to tell you something," a small child says as he appears in the doorway. He has a ruffle of short blonde hair on top of his seemingly tiny head and scruffy clothes. I can almost smell his fear. I suppose in his mind we are intruders. I doubt this village gets many visitors.

"I'll be with you in a minute. I just need to finish speaking," Gabriel says, barely making eye contact with the poor kid.

"Oh, but sir..."

"Wait," Gabriel snaps, still not looking at him.

"But sir, they're here."

## 24

"Grab your stuff. Now," Gabriel instructs, voice quivering. We jump into action, gathering every of the few belongings we own. The hut trembles with our heavy footsteps. In the distance, I swear I can hear the distinct voices of Zayathian guards. Marley presses a trembling hand into my palm, the other holding Bunny. I had told her that Bunny would be safer in her bag but she wouldn't hear any of it. She believes that if Bunny is hidden away in a backpack, he won't be able to see what's going on around him. The last thing she wants to do is startle her best friend. The one exception to this is if Bunny needs to sleep on the go. At that point she insists he gets a good rest, laying in-between her belongings.

"Right. On three we're going to run to the woods. Whatever you do, don't look back."
"Three…"
"Two…"
"One…"
"GO!"

We hurtle out of the hut, dodging various villagers and objects. Overhead, three matte black helicopters cast spotlights on the ground. They can't seem to spot us but I wonder if that's about to change. After all, we are pegging it at full pace across an open plain of snow. The ground crunches under our shoes as we make our way towards the forest. Marley is lagging behind, but I can't expect much more from a child who's only four foot tall. I try to slow down for her but Enzo yells at me to keep moving. Finally, a shadow casts over us as we enter the mass of trees. The stamping of at least five sets of feet closes in behind us. As long as we just keep moving everything will be ok, I lie to myself.

"BUNNY!" Marley screams. I glance behind me and the stuffed animal has slipped from my sister's grasp. It resides in a brown puddle of murky water. Marley stops dead in her tracks, unfazed by the armed men chasing us.

"Marley, keep running!" Gabriel yells but it's no use; her feet are cemented to the ground. Gabriel's eyes dart around, trying to find a solution.

"Quick! Under that bush!" Enzo shouts. Enzo and I dive under the shrub but Marley still stays stuck to the floor, watching Bunny like he's a fallen soldier. Gabriel scoops her up and ducks under the bush beside us. Marley intakes breath to let out an almighty screech but Gabriel puts his hand over her mouth. The stamping of feet ever increases. I can hear their voices. One of them is particularly familiar but I can't quite place it. It's a rough voice, quite low and scratchy.

They continue in our direction, pausing by the bush. I

feel all four of us simultaneously hold our breath. Through the green of leaves, I can see five sets of heavy black boots. At the hem of each of their trousers is the Escobar's crest: a fancy letter 'E'.

"Where did they go?" one of them says.

"Maybe we didn't see them. It could've been a herd of deer."

"Deer? You can't be serious. Do deer wear clothes?"

"I don't know. Do they?"

"No. No they don't."

Not one of us dares to even move a muscle. If they spot us, we are quite literally dead meat. Marley cranes her neck in the direction of Bunny. Although having Gabriel's hand over her mouth prevents her from talking, the slight movement she made causes the bushes to stir.

"Did you hear that?"

"They aren't here, Greyson. Let's keep moving," the slightly familiar voice responds. Huffing in unison, the armed squad continues walking.

Even after they start walking, we don't move at all. There's still a good chance we could be spotted. I can't even begin to imagine why Marley thought moving would be a good idea. She could've gotten us killed. I shake that thought out of my head because having pent up anger towards my little sister is not a good idea.

"Why would you move? You knew what could've happened," Enzo hisses, echoing my thoughts.

"But Bunny-!"

"Do I look like I give a flying fruit-flavoured f–"

"No! Look at Bunny!" All eyes crane over to the toy. Laying across it is a yellow-bellied sea snake. Marley looks as though she's about to throw up. Her face scrunches up into the unmistakable expression of impending hysteria.

"No, don't cry. I'll get it," Gabriel whispers. I cringe at every syllable that comes from his mouth. The guards' voices are still in earshot and they're already whispering. It's as if they want to get caught. Grabbing a lone stick, Gabriel etches his arm out from under the bush. He jabs at the snake, trying to knock it off Bunny. All he's doing is angering it. The hissing of the snake's tongue gets louder and louder. Soon enough it sounds like the whole forest is resonating with the sound of hundreds of crickets. We all gasp as the snake jolts without warning. One more nudge with the stick and the snake seems to give up, slithering off under a hedge. Immediately, Marley leaps out from under the bush and retrieves her small friend.

"Oh, thank the lord, you're ok!" Marley exclaims, hugging the toy rabbit. She doesn't seem to care that he's dripping with brown water.

"Any louder?" Enzo mutters. "Why don't you just set off a flare?" Marley blatantly ignores Enzo, only offering a middle finger in response. Gabriel and I fight the urge to burst out laughing as Enzo huffs and puffs.

The rest of the treacherous day is spent traipsing through the forest. Our plans have been skewed by the unexpected visitors, so now we have to spend a night in the snow. Everyone is unusually chatty on the forest trek. Of course, Marley and Enzo are getting to know each other in their own way: insults and snide comments. Gabriel and I, on the other hand, are starting to warm up to each other. Granted I never truly hated him, but up until now

I've felt a cold vibe coming from him. You know when you open the fridge and an icy blast hits you? That's how I feel every time Gabriel talks to me. But the cold is starting to fade and the uncomfortable aching in my stomach recedes. Don't get me wrong, I do not intend on becoming friends with Gabriel. Like I said, this is purely business. We'll do what we need to get out of this goddamn country then we'll go our separate ways. It wouldn't hurt to not hate each other's guts for the entire journey so I'm willing to be...acquaintances. Yes. Acquaintances.

At last, we arrive at a clearing in the woodland. We are met by a large open plane of white. And only white. With a substantial amount of bickering and confusion, we manage to put up the two tents. Admittedly, Marley's intelligence was our saving grace with these tents. She's the only one who could make sense of the instructions. Being a prince, Gabriel has never had to do a single thing for himself so I wasn't expecting him to know how to put up a tent. Enzo just stood there, scowling, smoking and occasionally telling Marley she's 'doing it all wrong'. I tried my best and eventually just followed the order of my six-year-old sister. Marley headed to bed hours ago, after we managed to get a fire going, so she could read in peace. Enzo also made his excuses to head to the tent. Probably so he could continue texting like always. This leaves Gabriel and I to sit alone, watching the flames just as we'd done the previous day.

The air is cold with silence. For some reason neither of us start a conversation. I know he isn't as entranced by the flames as he is pretending to be. Cigar smoke swirls around his head and sticks to his hair. That's definitely not coming out without a shower. Well, that explains why his smoky essence is always so overpowering.

"Are you a Malsum?" I find myself asking, startling both me and Gabriel. He lowers the cigar from his lips and turns to face me. I can't quite figure out his glance. Of course, his smile gives nothing away but his pupils... they look so dangerous.

"Cut me."

"Gabriel, I could never–"

"I said cut me. You clearly want to know so bad so why don't you find out?" He reaches into his pocket, pulling out the diamond dagger. Gut-wrenching memories flicker through my head of that god-awful day. I can almost feel the tension in my muscles as he sliced my sister. The sickness in my stomach as I watched that woman being dragged to the van. The sacer sanguis ritual. The note. All of these events swirl through my brain and into my fists to form a myriad of emotions that worms its way into my sacred Malsum blood.

I yank the dagger from his grasp, throwing it as far as possible. Before I know what's happening, my left fist flies through the air and connects with Gabriel's face. He falls off the log and to the ground with an empty thud.

"How could you keep that? You cut me with that! You cut my sister with that!" Gabriel doesn't move. He lays there, staring straight ahead. His breathing is harsh and aggressive. The way he's positioned reminds me of a fallen statue, damaged and futile. Upon looking at him, looking so powerless and weak, my anger dies down. It slithers back from my fists and into my brain, simmering away. I look down at the injured prince. He brings a trembling forefinger to the wound and winces upon touch.

"Gabriel, I…" I reach down to help him, trying to observe the extent of the damage I've caused. He pushes me, not too hard but strong enough to knock me away from him.

"No. Just…just don't." With that he pulls himself to his feet and staggers into his tent. For a moment, I just stand there, watching nothing in particular. Once I feel I can, I turn around and head to my tent.

# 25

" So, you're a Malsum then," I say, sitting beside Gabriel. He's holding a snowball to the developing wound on his face and sipping hot water.

"How did you guess?" A gentle chuckle curls in his chest. Marley appears from our tent, rubbing her eyes and yawning. She shoves her tiny hands into the pockets of her cargo trousers, shuddering at the cold.

The morning sun dawns on us, casting a soft glow over the camp. The open horizon provides an incredible view of the sunrise. The damp of morning dew dances in the air and cools down my lungs.

"What happened to your face?" Marley gestures towards the scarlet bruise.

"Your sister happened," Gabriel responds.

"You punched him?" Marley exclaims, slightly too excited for my liking.

"About time." She picks up a piece of bread and sits on a makeshift chair made from a single log.

"You should never punch people, Mar. What I did

was wrong." Gabriel shakes his head. He winces at the slight movement.

"No, I deserved it. I guess I had it coming." I turn to Gabriel, looking him straight in the eyes.

"I really am sorry."

"For what? The yelling or the sucker punch," he says. "Don't sweat it, Dakota. But seriously can you give me some lessons on self-defence because, good lord, do you pack a powerful punch."

I giggle and he puts his arm around me. Of course, this gesture is sheerly platonic but my heart rate triples.

"I feel like I haven't treated you very well since we set off so I'm going to turn over a new leaf from now on."

"I haven't been the kindest to you either. Truce?" he asks into my hair. I nod and nestle into his grasp. Enzo clambers out of their tent but stops upon seeing Gabriel's face.

"That looks painful. I didn't know spending so much time with her could cause physical pain, as well as mental pain." Enzo shoots a look at Marley to which she ignores (for once).

"It was Dakota, actually," Gabriel clarifies. Enzo arches his brows and shakes his square head.

"I refuse to believe that."

"Believe what you like. She's stronger than she looks." I'm not sure whether that's a compliment or not. It doesn't feel like it.     Enzo scoffs and heads back into their tent. His reason for retreating is that he doesn't want to spend time around someone who is apparently so dangerous. I know he's being arrogant and sarcastic but a powerful feeling still tingles through my veins. Marley sits Bunny on the log opposite her and begins to explain the science behind snow. She leaves gaps in her lecture for him to ask questions and answers them accordingly. Her interactions with her toy rabbit do make me laugh sometimes. It's strange how someone so invested in facts and figures genuinely believes that a stuffed animal is conversing with her. It just goes to show that we'll believe what we want to believe, no matter how outlandish it seems. Gabriel taps his foot against the crunchy snow as I sit beside him, unsure if I should speak or not. It doesn't seem like he wants me to initiate conversation but this silence is bordering on extreme awkwardness.

"Why does Dianne hate Malsums so much? Of course, we threaten her picture-perfect country, but wouldn't that be less suspicious? Other countries are bound to catch on soon." Gabriel seems caught off guard by my question. He looks at his shoes then back at the snow and repeats this process numerous times.

"Dianne hates us because she has her own fair share of issues. She uses this power to hide the fact that she's just as helpless as everyone else."

I want to ask what he means by that but Gabriel stands up before I get the chance. He announces that we need to start making tracks. I'm still trying to get used to moving every time I get comfortable. Up until now I've spent most of my life sitting in the same house, repeating the same tiresome activities. The only time I'd ever been allowed to leave was to do the grocery shopping, rituals, to go for a short walk or to meet with a client. Now we're constantly on the go. I guess it's a small price to pay for the euphoric freedom we'll have outside of Zayathai. As we set off, Marley places her hand in mine.

"He's alright you know. Gabriel," she says, with an air of nonchalance that makes me smile.

"Last time I checked, you hated him." She swipes blonde hair from her face with her free hand and nods.

"Yeah but I changed my mind. You punched him and he didn't go loco-for-coco-pops. I think that's cool of him."

"I'm glad you're accepting him, Mar, but violence is never okay. I'm lucky Gabriel took it as well as he did."

"Yeah yeah." She rolls her eyes and drops her hand from mine. "Gabe, can I have a piggy back!" A surprised Gabriel spins around to look at me. I shrug and smile back. His eyes train down to Marley.

"I uh– sure! That's if Dakota doesn't mind carrying your bag." Marley doesn't even ask before dumping her belongings, including Bunny, on me and running over to him. He takes his own bag off and puts it on his front then kneels down so my sister can climb onto his back. I'm happy that Marley has suddenly decided she likes Gabriel. I'm not so happy about lugging two people's worth of belongings until Marley decides to walk again. I have to speed-walk a little to catch up to the others, which is considerably more difficult with so much luggage.

"You alright up there?" Gabriel cranes his neck to look up at Marley.

"All good. I'm feeling a little tired though." As if on cue, an enormous yawn forces itself from her mouth.

"Rest, kiddo. I gotcha." Marley doesn't have to be told

twice. Within mere minutes, my sister is soundly asleep, bouncing gently with Gabriel's footsteps.

"Isn't she just a little princess," Enzo remarks in a mocking tone, smoke billowing over his bottom lip. He taps the butt of the cigarette and charred ash spills onto the floor.

"Do you have to make a sarcastic comment about anything my sister does?" Enzo looks at me and shrugs.

"I suppose I do. It'd be foolish of me to pass up on such good opportunities."

"What'll be foolish of you is crossing the line with these jokes because I will make you regret it if you do." I'm trying my hardest to seem intimidating but this hunky giant isn't going to cave to me.

"Is that a threat, short stack?" He throws the stub of the cigarette behind him and smirks at me. I divert my gaze, anger whirling in my stomach.

"Enzo, be quiet," Gabriel interjects. "You'll wake the princess."

# 26

This landscape is almost too real. I kinda feel like I'm in that retro game my mother used to play. Minecraft, I think it's called. The border between snow and sand is almost a single straight line. There's no gradual immersion into the change of climate. Biting cold turns to an overbearing warmth as we step into the desert. I'd asked Gabriel why the landscape is so surreal and now that I know the answer, I kind of wish I hadn't. He revealed that the biomes are in fact man-made. The Escobars created them when they took over Zayathai to stop people from running away so easily. If you ask me, spending millions to create fake biomes is a massive waste of money, which could've been used to oppress people even more, if they had thought wisely. I'd make a great evil dictator. The sun blares its rays upon my bare arms. As soon as the sand touched the souls of his shoes, Gabriel removed his beanie. I'm quite glad, really. There's something about the way his hair flips and flops that's quite pleasing to the eye. Ignoring Gabriel's complaining, I decided to wear this black vest that was in my bag, instead of the long sleeved, camouflage top. He'd told me that I was too 'obvious' to the guards because some of my skin was showing. I took delight in pointing out that my skin is closer in colour to the yellow sand than a camouflage top. With great reluctance, he gave in and allowed me to dress how I choose.

Marley seems to be in her own world. After we walked for about an hour, she woke up and is now ambling beside me, singing quietly to herself. At first, I can't work out what she's saying, but I catch on when she murmurs her favourite line: 'Conceal, don't feel, don't let them know.' I'm finding this journey both mentally and physically challenging, so I can only imagine what Marley is going through. One day she's living at home with everything she's familiar with then BOOM. Over. She understands that we need to leave and that we have a better life ahead of us but I took her from her home. As much as Mother despised my existence, Marley was the centre of her world for the first few years of her life. I remember one time when we'd sat down for dinner. For once, Mother actually cooked something. Normally she'd have us eating rice or instant noodles. Not only had she made an actual meal, but it was my favourite: chicken nuggets and fries. Even then the food was still from a packet, but it was better than anything she'd normally make. One sentence, I'd said, to make her angry. I'd been exclaiming about how excited I was to tuck in, whilst we were all settling down in front of our food. 'If only we could have this every day!' That's it. Whilst yelling the odds and calling me an ungrateful cow, Mother picked up my plate and poured the contents onto Marley's. Bear in mind I was fourteen so Marley would've been only about two. I didn't eat that night. I sat in the chamber, empty and in pain. For a few days I resented my sister. I believed that she'd turned Mother against me, even more so than before. She was the devil's incarnate, I decided. But after taking one look at that oh so small child, with her big blue eyes and a smile to melt the nation's heart, I swore to myself that I would protect her at all costs. And look where I am. Walking across an artificial desert with the threat of prosecution looming over me, all so I can get her to safety.

Instead of passively venturing with the prince, I want to contribute to the journey. At the end of all of this I want to feel like I've earned my freedom so I offer to hold the map and guide us for a while. It takes a lot of persuading, but Gabriel finally caves in.

"Are you sure you know what you're doing?" he asks, handing over the crumpled paper and compass with an insulting level of hesitance.

"Don't doubt my intelligence, kind sir. I know how to read a map."

We pace a few hundred metres as I stare at the paper. All I see is squiggles and lines. How he can make sense of such a document I'll never know. I look up to request assistance but he's in a conversation with Enzo. I don't need his help anyway. That's what I tell myself as we amble in most likely the wrong direction. At one point, I'm convinced that this map actually means nothing and he just holds it for dramatic effect. I mean come on, we're in the middle of an empty desert. There's nothing to actually navigate from.

"Okay, I give up." I sigh. Gabriel shakes his head and bites his lip to fight off a smug smile.

"I knew you were clueless so I kept tabs on where we're going. You're only a little bit off. Here let me show you."

He comes over to me and takes my index finger. I can't help but feel a spark of excitement ignite my soul as his skin touches mine. The loose curls of his hair flops over his face as he studies the map then begins to speak.

"First, we take a left." His voice is a soft, regal hum in my ear. He guides my finger across the map and continues explaining. The deep resonance of each syllable makes the hairs on my arms stand on end. We stay there for a few magical minutes, him talking, me drinking in the knowledge. I notice Marley and Enzo staring at us from the corner of my eye but I ignore them. Between every instruction, Gabriel looks up and asks me if I understand. Each time I nod my head, too breathless to respond. Prince Luther straightens up and slaps his hands together.

"Perfect. Yalla habibti." He begins to walk ahead. Marley comes to my side and tugs on my shirt.

"You're not dating Gabe, are you?" she asks, a perplexed expression on her tiny face.

"Uhhh no. What makes you say that?" I almost cackle at the supposed ridiculousness of her question.

"He said 'yalla, habibti.' That means 'let's go, my love' in Arabic." "And you know that how?"

"It doesn't matter," she says. "What matters is that he really likes you." Both of our heads turn to the stark man, laughing with his friend and ambling ahead of us.

**27**

"Why couldn't you have found a cute little desert tribe for us to stay with?" I whine. Gabriel smirks. He reaches for the water bottle in the side pocket of his bag and pulls it out. He readies to take a sip but notices the bottle is empty. He replaces it in the pocket, sighing.

"Because, dear friend, not many tribes want to inhabit one of the most barren and dangerous biomes on the planet." I hate how even him referring to me as a 'friend' makes my stomach knot. Though I can hardly blame myself. He's the first conventionally attractive guy to pay even an ounce of attention to me.

"Dangerous? Dangerous how?" Marley asks, voice heightening as she scans the perimeter with beady eyes.

"Except the blood-sucking snakes and blazing temperatures," Enzo mutters. Marley's eyes have grown so wide I worry that they might roll right out of the sockets.

"Hey, do me a favour and stop scaring the hell out of my sister," I snap, glaring at him. He responds with a smirk and nothing else. I sigh as Marley scrambles to find the chapter on deserts in her encyclopaedia. She won't find much in there. There's no specific knowledge on these biomes because no one ventures into them and Dianne wouldn't let valuable information be released anyway.

I'm overly irritable today. Combined with the piles of itchy sand wedged between my toes and my severe dehydration, I don't think I can cope any longer. The absence of water, or any sign of life, is becoming all too real. Shameless beads of sweat line the foreheads of us all. Each head is aching, each footstep heavy. Although, it comes to my attention that Gabriel has been drinking his water as if there's a well with a fresh spring waiting for us, hence his empty container. Maybe there is. You see, he's been quite secretive about our journey. I know the general direction we're heading in but that's about it. Any question I ask is quenched with a vague, half-hearted response. I'm in no doubt that the prince knows every aspect of the plan with meticulosity; he just doesn't seem to want to let us in. The day offers me plenty of time to ponder over this as we trudge through the dune. Various sand mounds provide even more anguish as we brace our knees for the steep ascent. Thus, when we eventually find ourselves in a safe place to rest, I take deep pleasure in tearing off my shoes and letting the lactic acid simmer away from my aching muscles. Before I can get comfortable, I'm forced to help set up camp, just as we'd done some twenty-four hours previous.

By now, night is starting to set upon us. Cold undertones swish through the air, standing up the hairs on my arms. I didn't think I'd ever end up camping in a desert. I certainly didn't expect it to be this cold. Marley had laughed and told me it's a known fact that the desert drops to record temperatures at night. You could say I feel inferior to my younger sister, based on her brimming brain of knowledge. I don't mind though. Jealousy doesn't even brace my mind. I'm proud. For I know that when I'm gone or too old to do anything, she'll make a difference. Marley will not be reduced to nothing by this world.

We all decide to head to bed early tonight. Today has been…taxing, to say the least. Tomorrow will be a day of replenishing resources and getting enough rest for a lot of walking the next day. This plan is absolutely fine by me. While the prospect of elongating our stay in the desert doesn't exactly appeal to me, I am certainly not opposed to a little relaxation time. Marley is already fast asleep in her dark green sleeping bag and Enzo is sat by the fire, finishing his nightly text-and-smoke before he settles down. I'm not sure what Gabriel is doing but I need some hand sanitiser and I'm pretty sure he has some in the first aid kit. Sure, I could go to the well and wash my hands but that's too much walking for me. I clamber out of our tent and into the semi-darkness, offering a nod of acknowledgment to Enzo as I pass the campfire and zip open their tent door. Despite how small they may look before being set up, the tents are relatively big. Each could comfortably house three people and are tall enough for even Enzo to stand up in. When I step into the tent, I'm not sure how to react to what greets my eyes. Gabriel is facing away from me, his defined shoulders scarce of any shirt to hide them. I've just walked in on Gabriel. A half-naked Gabriel.

"You know it's always polite to knock." He slowly turns around and walks forward. A breath catches in my throat as he leans towards me. Instinctively my eyes close, in anticipation for whatever is about to happen, but they snap back open when I hear a rustle behind me.

"Just grabbing my hairbrush." He straightens and holds the brush up, smirking at me. I can't help but stare at the incredible tattoo that I never knew occupied his left pectoral: two swords crossing over one another with rose vines snaking and twisting around them.

"Yeah I– of course." He cocks an eyebrow and begins to brush his bouncing curls, standing only in his black cargo trousers. "I'm just gonna– " I turn to leave but his radiant voice stops me in my tracks.

"Dakota." I swivel back to face him, as if in a trance. "Did you need something?" I try to prize my eyes from the tattoo but I can't help but marvel at the intricacy of it all.

"Sanitizer. I need hand sanitizer." He nods, still smiling softly, and heads to his bag to retrieve the item. I still find myself looking at the design as he hands me a tiny bottle of antibacterial. My breath catches again as our hands touch for a fleeting moment.

"Forgetting to knock, staring at me and now you don't say thank you? Someone ought to teach you some manners." I know he's trying to be playful and mockingly authoritative but my heart does a- no, multiple- cartwheels.

"Sorry, I'm just so intrigued by your tattoo. If I'll be honest, I really want to trace it with my finger." What compelled me to say that? He's going to think I'm weird now. Gabriel cocks his head at me and his flawless hair flops with it.

"Your wish is my command, habibti." There's that name again. I really should ask about that. Later. I'm too stunned to form full sentences anymore. Gabriel takes my hand and lifts it to his toned chest, guiding my finger along the black lines of the artwork. A puffy laugh escapes him as he watches my fascinated expression. In truth, the tattoo has slipped my mind. All I can think about is how his soft skin glides so perfectly beneath my finger. How every line of his muscles is defined yet gentle, not too much and not too little. I can feel his warm breath on the top of my hair as he looks down on me. Once my finger reaches the end of the tattoo I feel great reluctance in allowing Gabriel to let go of my hand.

"What made you choose that design?" My voice is almost a whisper. I look up at the prince and he moves a strand of hair from my face.

"It's just a reminder to keep strong. Life isn't very forgiving to those who show weakness so the swords help me keep my guard up. To not forget what could happen if I don't fight for what's right."

"I don't suppose you're still in touch with your tattooist?" I joke, in an attempt to dissipate the evident lustful tension in the room (if you can call a tent in a desert a room).

"I'm afraid not. Mother had him executed for drawing, what she described as, 'an atrocity' upon my body." At this point, I can't be shocked.

"That's a shame. I feel I need a reminder to be strong,

more than anyone." Gabriel folds his arms, a tired smile playing across his lips.

"You're stronger than you think, Dakota. It takes guts to be doing what you are, to trust me like you are."

"Or maybe I'm just an idiot," I say, shrugging.

"Maybe." The tent rustles as an unwelcome acquaintance makes an appearance.

"Should I be suspicious of the fact that you're shirtless or…"

"No, you shouldn't, Enzo. I was just lending Dakota some hand sanitizer. She's heading to bed now, aren't you?" I spin to face Enzo, who's watching me from the doorway.

"Yep I was just leaving. Good night, Gabe." I turn to him and, completely on a whim, go in for a hug. If it takes him by surprise, he doesn't show it. Instead, he wraps his long arms around me and gives one of the best hugs I've ever received. I straighten and walk past his best friend.

"Good night to you too," Enzo calls as I head into the darkness. I can't help but feel proud of myself for blanking him. It's the least he deserves for treating Marley as he has. Not even the campfire is lit to offer me any guidance so I'm forced to stumble blindly to our tent. I climb into my sleeping bag and the warmth envelopes me almost immediately. I squeeze some antibacterial into my hands and rub them together, smiling lustily into the darkness. I know I didn't need this hand sanitizer. I washed my hands before and after consuming our nightly vegetable broth. Internally I knew I just needed a reason to go and speak to Gabriel and I ponder over why, as my eyelids become heavy and begin to flutter closed.

**28**

To the surprise of no one, Marley relishes in the chance to sleep through the morning, while we gather resources. Though no one, not even Enzo, can blame her for that. I, myself, am feeling very lethargic and we're barely half way through the journey. I can only imagine the physical toll this is taking on my little sister. Since Marley and I became closer to Gabriel, we've been taking turns to carry her, while we walk. Any excuse to preserve her energy is worthwhile. And, while I love my sister to pieces, it's nice to have her still in bed so that we can talk as adults. Censoring your words around a young child can be quite draining sometimes. I'm not actually involving myself in their conversation, but I'm grateful to be accompanied by people my own age. It's a luxury that I would've died to have, back in the good ol' chamber days.

"I swear to god, try it out. It changed my life for sure," Enzo says before taking a drag of a cigar. Seeming as I'm sitting beside him, the smoke blows in my face and I want more than anything to show him a picture of some black, tar-covered lungs to curb this wretched habit.

You'd think that they'd pack light and leave the nicotine and alcohol at home but clearly it's a necessity for them.

"Vodka…on your face?" I look up to Gabriel, who's sat across the campfire from me, looking as perplexed as ever.

"Bethany told me it tones your face and gets rid of acne and she was right." It's hard to miss the affectionate way in which Enzo's lips curl around the name 'Bethany.'

"Ah there it is. Anything for the girlfriend, huh?" Gabriel teases. I begin to apply sunscreen, in an attempt to save my pale skin from blotchy freckles, while listening to their conversation.

"First of all, she's not my girlfriend–"

"Lies." Gabriel looks at Enzo with a cheeky, boyish smile and I can't help but imagine that these two have been friends for a long time and that that grin is one that Enzo has become accustomed to witnessing over many years. I smooth the cream along my arms and, mixed with the humid haze of desert heat, the delicate scent of summer drifts into my nose.

"I'd believe that if she wasn't all over you for the better part of my last birthday celebration." Enzo scoffs.

"That doesn't make her my girlfriend. We're simply good friends…very good friends." Enzo returns a boyish smile to Gabriel that I still don't quite understand. I feel as if it's code for something that only the male species understand.

"Sure," Gabriel replies, nodding. "So what do you think, Kota? I can't imagine vodka is part of your skincare routine." I look up from frantically rubbing spf into my face that won't seem to absorb.

"I think I'll stick to moisturiser. Besides, I've never even drunk vodka before so I'd have to try it before putting it all over my face."

"You haven't?" There's an element of judgement in Enzo's tone that I don't appreciate at all.

"Of course not. Are you forgetting that I spent most of my childhood locked in a titanium chamber?" Enzo gives an understanding nod and twirls the cigar in his hand.

"You've not told me much about that. Not that we've really spoken." I would give him the full tragic anecdote of my life but Marley appears from our tent, right on cue, weary-eyed and lethargic as ever. Enzo instantly withdraws from the situation by returning to his text-and-smoke ritual.

"Good morning, princess," Gabriel says, holding his arms out. She heads straight for him, barely looking in my direction. I try to hide the hurt on my face as he pulls her onto his lap and she mumbles a greeting to the group. "Would you like some breakfast, love?" Gabriel asks, smoothing down her hair that's been skewed by a clearly very good night's sleep.

"If it's soup or beans again I'll pass," she responds through a soft yawn.

"We could add some wild berries to your beans?" When I say this, Marley looks up and smiles.

"Yes please."

"But first you need sunscreen on. We can't have your delicate skin getting all burnt, can we?" I don't even care when she rolls her eyes at me because I know she's having a tough time. Marley isn't one to show it but I can tell this whole situation could be enough to break her. Gabriel busies himself with cooking Marley's food over the fire, while I help her change from one camo outfit to another and apply copious amounts of sunscreen. If we're going to take such a daring journey, we are not going to be bested by sunburn.

Soon enough, Marley is solitarily munching on her beans-and-berries concoction and speaking to Bunny, while the rest of us get to work with various oddjobs. While I'm washing out the mess tins, I can't help but feel a little annoyed that Marley arrived when she did. That seems like the only chance I had to get Enzo to open up and it was ruined. By no means am I saying that it is Marley's fault but it is irritating all the same. Of course, I don't like Enzo, especially with the way he has treated Marley. But I am fascinated by him. By the sleeves of meticulously drawn tattoos and the constantly angry expression. Not to mention, the chain smoking and texting. I just need to know more and I fear I never will.

Later, Gabriel and I sit in a comfortable silence by the campfire. He seems content with twirling his beanie around his index finger. I feel guilty admitting this but I hope he drops that wretched accessory in the flames. Despite my best efforts, I can't bring myself to find it attractive. He looks so much better without it. I love the sight of his dark floppy hair and the slight curl that meets the end of each strand. Even though I despise the monarchy, I'd prefer to see him in a crown than that grey hat any day of the week. Obviously I'm yet to tell him that because I don't want to hurt his feelings. Maybe I should ask Marley to break the news; Gabriel seems to value her opinion more than mine. It's hurtful, considering she is over a decade younger than me but I understand. We all value her opinion. Even Enzo. Some of us are just better at admitting that she is a genius.

A bout of rustling comes from our tent before my little sister pops out from the entryway. I look up to smile at her before continuing to chop up vegetables. To be honest, there's only so many times you can have broccoli soup before it gets old but it isn't like we have any other choice. Marley smiles back at me and ambles over to Gabriel. He twirls the beanie once more before catching it in the palm of his hand.

"Hey, kiddo." I notice her face lighten up at the use of her favourite nickname. She'd always found it patronising when I said it but she seems to love it when the word is coming from the prince's mouth. Gabriel pats his lap to which Marley climbs onto him and nestles her head into his chest.

"Are you alright?" He moves hair from her face and lifts her chin up to look at him.

"No. It's freezing out here. My encyclopaedia told me it would be chilly but this is ridiculous." Gabriel looks up at me and gives a smile that insinuates laughter, without making a noise. I smile back and shake my head.

"Perhaps you'd like to wear my beanie? It'll keep your head warm." If he'd asked me that I could tell you exactly what my response would be. No. Gabriel holds the beanie out to her and she takes it, grimacing. "Hey! What's that look for?"

"Don't take this personally, Gabe. It's ugly," she explains. His eyes shoot up to mine for reassurance but I look away. I'm staying out of this one.

"Fine. Have cold ears." He gives a blasé shrug and attempts to take the beanie back but she swipes it away from his reach.

"No! I never said I didn't wanna wear it. I can sacrifice my beauty for a few minutes, in the name of not getting hypothermia." Marley tugs the beanie onto her head, which looks huge on her.

"Cheeky," Gabriel mutters but he can't fight the smile off his face. "Alright well, princess, it has been lovely sitting here while you insult me," he continues as she readjusts the beanie. "But I've got some map studying to do." Marley pouts.

"Can't I do it with you?" She nestles into him further, the beanie lifting off of her head a little as it rubs against his shirt.

"Won't that be a bit boring?" Her big blue eyes connect with him and she cocks her head to the side.

"I do differential equations for fun, Gabe. Boring is subjective."

"Touché," he breathes out, picking the map up off of the log beside him. He holds it out in front of Marley with both hands and she relaxes against his chest. "Now you see where I've drawn a red dot?" Marley nods. "That's where we are now. Obviously we want to go to the forest, which is…?" Marley reaches up and points a glove-clad finger at the map. "Exactly! Now…"

I watch mesmerised- and slightly jealous- by their interaction. Marley seems to melt in Gabriel's lap as all of her worries simmer to ashes. It seems the same for Gabriel. He didn't have any younger siblings so it must be nice to have someone to treat as such, even at the expense of my own envy for their relationship. Although, I thank god every minute that Gabriel has taken so well to my sister. It would've been a nightmare if they didn't get along and I was starting to think that's how it would go. It wasn't twenty-four hours ago that Marley wouldn't go within six feet of him but me punching Gabriel somehow gained her respect for him. It's strange but I'm certainly not complaining. Upon first glance, you might assume they were siblings and that's more than I could ever wish for.

"And that, my little genius, is how you read a map." Gabriel rolls up the scroll and puts it beside him. He stands and sets Marley on her feet. Gabriel heads to his tent and I hear him talking to Enzo. Marley tugs on my sleeve and I kneel down so she can whisper in my ear, " I already knew how to map read. I let him teach me so he feels smart." I laugh and shake my head.

"You can be cute sometimes, eh?"

"What do you mean? I'm always cute–!"

"Dakota," Gabriel says, reappearing from his tent. "I wanna show you something. Enzo said he'd watch Marley for me and promised not to start world war four with her."

"I don't need to be watched. Especially not by him."

"Of course not but if an evil monster comes, Enzo is here to fight it off and potentially get eaten while you run away."

"Oh well that's alright then. Have fun!" Marley toddles off to our tent, the huge beanie still pulled tight atop of her small head. Gabriel takes my hand. I fight the butterflies that flutter in my stomach. I will not be one of those girls that melts at a man's touch. That's pathetic. Gabriel leads me across the open plain until we come to a slight incline. The extent of the beauty of our surroundings washes over me when we reach the very top. Dozens of smaller inclines are dotted before us, and are decorated by cacti and small, brown shrubs.

"Wow," is all I can say.

"Beautiful, right?"

We lower ourselves to the ground, me sitting up and Gabriel with his head in my lap. I stroke his long locks gently as we observe the wondrous nature before us.

The sun starts to tumble over the hilltops like a rolling pin on fresh dough, broadening out the wide expanse of gold that now stretches evenly across the horizon. Don't laugh at me for using the word 'horizon.' I know every man and his dog uses it to describe the sunset. But honestly there are no better words to describe what I'm witnessing. It seems I'm not the only one captured by the night that dawns on us.

"This is crazy, isn't it?" I probe, startling my companion. Gabriel looks up at me. I smile down at him.

"The sunset or our escape?"

We end up in some deep conversation about Zayathai but I notice he isn't listening. Well, he's listening, but his eyes seem to be exploring my face. I can imagine that he'll have memorised every inch of my skin by the time we go to bed. His eyes look between each freckle, each pore and slowly down to my lips. In an instance of haste, I turn to look straight forwards. "You're beautiful."

The words that I was about to say get caught in my throat. I force them down, taking a discreet but huge gasp for air. Gabriel seems to be taking great pleasure in watching me blush and fumble.

"Did you just say I'm…"

"Beautiful?"

"Yeah…that."

He sits up, laughing. The kind of laugh that comes right from the heart, travelling right through the aorta, through your body and into your throat. His smile is uncontrollable too, quite literally stretching from ear to ear.

"I'm sorry. I just wanted to see you squirm," Gabriel breathes out between laughs. I giggle, elbowing him. My hands cup my face in a state of embarrassment. He puts his arm around me, pulling me closer. This time I don't feel awkward. I melt into his arms like butter on fresh toast.

We spend a lot of time whispering sweet nothings and watching as the sun's source turns sour. I find myself discreetly studying Gabriel's features, just as he'd done to me. A lone beam of the sun casts its spotlight upon his rusty grey pupils. His lips are pinker than usual, small and thin. Each brown hair on his head seems to be perfectly placed, swished to the side in a perfect boy band-esque nature. Now I know he's a Malsum, I find it odd how he continues to smile all the time. Not once did it cross my mind that maybe he isn't forcing it. Maybe he's just happy.

"So, what are we?" After all he's done, nothing Gabriel says should be able to surprise me anymore but somehow, he really catches me off guard with this question. Mainly because I don't have a good answer. His arm is around my waist, holding me close to his side.

"I don't know. Some might say we're friends—"

"If you say friends with benefits, I'm going to throw you down one of these sand dunes," he interrupts. I smile to myself and look down at the sand.

"I wasn't going to say that but now I really want to." With the hand that's curled around my body, Gabriel jabs at my side, causing me to squirm and cackle.

"Stop! I was kidding!" I howl through painful jolts of elation. At least a minute passes before I can breathe properly again. Gabriel lays back on the sand and I fall down with him. He turns to face me and our eyes fall into line.

"There's no rush to put a label on it. For now, let's just be Gabriel and Dakota," he suggests. I bite the inside of my lip.

"Dakota and Gabriel." Gabriel knits his brows.

"Excuse me?" I move a hair from his face and twirl it around my index finger. He watches my movements, a smile kicking at the corner of his mouth.

"Dakota and Gabriel sounds better," I reason. He squints his eyes at me.

"If you truly believe that then maybe you're not the one for me." I unravel my finger from his hair and push him playfully.

"Shut up," I say, even though that's the last thing I want him to do. Gabriel's eyes drift shut and his face inches

221

towards mine. Are we going to…? I don't know how to do this. I've never done this before. Stop panicking, Dakota. This is completely normal. Just close your eyes and…

His soft lips brush mine like a filbert on a canvas. Somehow it feels as though my heart is smiling as our mouths move in perfect unison. The taste of mango and smoke coats my taste buds and makes my heart do even more unusual things. Gabriel drops his head and I fight the urge to pull him back to me. If I'd known kissing felt this good, I would've tried it long ago. Not that the chance ever presented itself.

"Well, that's the best thing that's happened to me in a while," Gabriel murmurs. Now that's the biggest compliment I've ever had.

"So then why did you stop?" I whisper, a slight anger building up in my throat. Gabriel ignores that. Instead, he bites his lip and sits up. Just as I'm about to repeat my question, an ear-piercing shriek echoes through the valley. Gabriel looks down at me and I look up at him, eyes wide with fear. In a whisper, we both utter the same word.

"Marley."

# 29

When we arrive at the scene, Marley is leaning against her bag, howling like a wolf at full moon. Her face is drenched in sweat and her chest rises and falls rapidly as she fights for air. Every inch of her skin is covered in goosebumps. The most sickening thing I witness isn't my sister clinging on for dear life. No, it's the grown man watching her and letting her slip away.

"What happened?!" I cry, falling beside her. She looks up at me with weary eyes. Despite her best efforts, breathlessness stops her from talking.

"A snake," Gabriel whispers.

"Excuse me!" I hope with all my heart that I've misheard him.

"A rattlesnake…it's bitten her." His eyes glaze over my sister in horror.

"How can you possibly know that?" I yell, hysteria creeping into my throat. Gabriel stands closer to my sister and investigates her symptoms. He puts the back of his hand to my sister's forehead.

"Trouble breathing, sweating…" Marley vomits right into the sand.

"Nausea. They're all symptoms of a rattlesnake bite. Not to mention…" He points to her right shin. Two small, almost inconceivable puncture marks in her trousers.

Barely looking away from my sister, Gabriel says, "Enzo, I'll need my antivenom kit, scissors and a bandage." With a look of distaste cemented on his face, Enzo stays glued to the ground.

"She's fine. Look at her." The audacity of this man never fails to astound me. I look down at my sister then back up at him.

"If I were you, Enzo, I would stop spouting nonsense and get moving," I say through gritted teeth. "Schnell!" I find myself yelling. Letting out a dramatic sigh, Enzo shuffles over to their tent. Marley's eyes keep rolling around her head like a slot machine. It takes all my willpower not to hold her eyes in place. She just needs to hold on.

"Take my hand." Marley lifts a quivering arm and plops her hand into Gabriel's. He closes his fingers over her sweating palm.

"Hold my gaze, Marley. Stay with us." I hate that sentence: 'stay with us.' He's making it seem like we're losing her. We aren't. We can't be. I won't believe it. Her body starts to keel to the side, but Gabriel catches her.

"I know you want to lie down, but the wound needs to remain below heart level." She doesn't seem to take note of this and her body falls the other way. Gabriel rushes to catch her again.

"Mar," he says. It seems that she isn't registering

anything anymore. "Mar, look at me." His tone is assertive yet calm. Marley drags her eyes to his and I notice her body relaxes a little. Gabriel nods and offers her a warming smile.

A few painstaking moments pass before Enzo returns with the kit and the bandages, which Gabriel hastily snatches from him. I wonder if Enzo purposely took his time but I shove that idea out of my head. If I overthink it, I might have to punch Enzo.

"Now Marley, I'm going to need you to stay as still as possible." She's barely able to nod.

I take her other hand and squeeze it tight, but she doesn't return the action. He takes the scissors to her trouser leg, cutting a hole in the shin. The skin surrounding the bite is already starting to swell. My stomach feels like it's developing a swell of its own. Occasionally looking at Marley's face to check that she's ok, Gabriel treats my sister. He seems to know what he's doing, but my sister seems to still be in sheer agony. On any normal day I'd be delighted to have a few respite moments from Marley's constant chatter. Now I'd give anything for her to talk to me.

"She needs a hospital, Gabriel," I say. Her fingers go limp in Gabriel's grasp and a whirl of panic swivels through my stomach.

"I know what I'm doing," he mutters, continuing to work on the bite.

"But look at her! She's—"

"I said...!" His voice rises as quickly as it falls. "I know what I'm doing." He offers me this look, careful yet serious. And I find in this moment, I trust him. I really, really trust him.

With a soft grunt, Gabriel picks up my limp sister and takes her to our tent. I start to follow after them but Gabriel shakes his head.

"I just need some space to do this." Nodding, I step back. He heads inside, zipping the tent door behind him. I turn around to see Enzo has retreated to his tent. No. He's not getting away with it this time.

"What the hell was that?" I practically yell, bursting through the door.

He looks up, brandishing a bottle of whiskey. He takes a swig and hands me the bottle, an irritating smirk dancing on his face. I take the bottle, sitting beside him. By mistake, I take such a big gulp that I shiver like an abandoned dog in the snow.

"She was never in any danger," Enzo chuckles, watching me struggle to handle the copious amount of alcohol.

"And how do you know that?" Enzo cocks his head to the side.

"If I wanted her to be dead, she'd be dead."

"Well, she isn't."

"Don't jinx it." He snatches the whiskey from my grasp, drinking the remaining liquid. It's at least a quarter of the bottle yet he doesn't wince at all.

"You disgust me," I spit. My statement doesn't have the desired effect. If anything, I think all it does is feed his ego. He lolls his head and smiles at the ground. "This hopeless obsession with apathy that you've engrossed yourself in isn't cute or clever. It's ridiculous, Enzo!" That seems to get his attention. With the gaze of a hopelessly drunken sailor, Enzo looks up at me. He's drunk so much that I'm surprised alcohol doesn't leak from his eye sockets.

"Get out," he almost whispers.

"Gladly," I say, storming out.

I can hear things coming from the tent. A cry or the odd, muffled scream from my sister. A sharp exhale or reassurance from Gabriel. I don't know why I didn't convince him to get medical help. Of course, calling for the ambulance would end our escape, but Marley's health is not a risk worth taking. It's all well and good fighting the elements ourselves, but if I don't come out the other side with my sister by my side, I have failed. And I would never let myself forget it. Maybe Gabriel didn't want to call them because he genuinely knows what he's doing. In all fairness, I've never seen anyone look so sure of themselves in my life. Despite having everything handed to him on a silver platter for the best part of his existence, Gabriel is smart. He has more skills than I'll ever be able to acquire. Maybe, at some point in his stuck-up private school they had 'how to survive a snakebite' lessons.

Hours pass and no longer caring about Gabriel's request, I come to check up on them. Marley is sat on Gabriel's lap, her head resting on his chest, whilst he fixes her up. She looks better and brighter. The smile has returned to my sister's face as she reads out an excerpt from her encyclopaedia.

"Isn't that cool?" Marley says, looking up at Gabriel.

"So cool," he says, smiling down at her. He holds an ice pack over the bruise on her leg. The fusion of yellow and purple that spills from the wound draws my attention, but I try to ignore it. If I think about how much pain she must be in, I'll only worry about her more. Gabriel's eyes train up to me.

"Oh hey, Dakota. Didn't see you there." He unwraps a bandage and proceeds to wrap it over the bruise. Marley whimpers at the touch and grips onto his arm. A spot of blood draws from Gabriel's arm when her hold becomes even tighter. He either doesn't notice or decides not to make a big deal out of it.

"Clearly," I say, while forcing a grin onto my face. Marley looks at me. She's beaming from ear to ear. "All better then?"

"The snake didn't get the chance to bite her too badly so she should be okay. Might be a bit weaker than usual for a day or so." I nod. As he speaks, Marley watches him as if she cares about every word that falls from his mouth. I envy her undisputed trust in him. As much as I want to, a nagging feeling tells me not to trust anyone, but myself. I don't know for certain that Gabriel has our best interests at heart. Every ounce of me wants to trust and love Gabriel. But you can't ignore gut feelings. They exist for a reason. You never know if someone has malicious intent, no matter how well you get to know them. Children are commonly taught not to take candy from strangers because you don't know their intent. That's the problem. I don't doubt there's good in the world, but sorting it from the bad is almost impossible.

"You'd better head to sleep, Marley. You'll need all the

strength you can get for tomorrow," Gabriel continues, attempting to stand up and set Marley down. She clings onto him, shaking her head.

"No! I want Gabe to stay," she pouts. Gabriel and I share a glance.

"Alright. Gabriel can stay," I say, turning to leave. A biting feeling of jealousy tugs at my heart but I shove it down. Jealousy is for the weak and that is the one thing I refuse to be. Weak.

"But where are you gonna sleep?" His voice is laden with concern. I can't help but laugh.

"Don't worry about me. The sky is looking quite appealing to lay under tonight."

"You can't sleep out there, Dakota. It's dangerous. Share with Enzo."

"Okay, okay. If you insist, your highness."

"Don't call me that." His voice seems to drop several octaves in the space of a second. I can't help but notice how angry I've just made him. His jaw clenches and his eyebrows cross. I raise my hands in mock defence.

"Sorry." I leave the tent. "Your highness," I mutter once I'm out of earshot.

# 30

I slept under the stars last night. There wasn't a chance in hell that I was going to sleep within five metres of Enzo. God only knows what that guy is capable of doing. I wouldn't have slept a single wink, knowing a stone-cold narcissist was right beside me. I felt much more comfortable underneath the canopy of the stars. The night was so clear. Thousands of shining dots lined the darkness. One shone brighter than the rest and I wondered if it could've been a planet. The idea that there could be extra-terrestrial life has always interested me. If there is some way of reaching them, I hope it's discovered in my lifetime. At one point, when I was far from sleepy, I'd tried to spot some constellations. It didn't help that the only constellation name I know is Orion, and even then, I don't know what it looks like. There was a pattern of stars that looked particularly like a wonky smiley face. I named it Zayathai.

I found myself waking up a lot earlier than usual, just in time to watch the sun rise. One thing I will give credit to the desert is the sky. Seeming as there's absolutely no signs of life for miles and we're positioned at the top of a dune, nothing blocks the horizon. No skyscrapers or villages or even a mountain. Just sand, sand and more sand. This gives me the perfect view of the arrays of colour that stretch across the open plane. A blizzard of sharp beauty casts itself upon my eyes and reflects off the cup of water I'm holding. I'm blinded by the grace of nature and baffled by its complexity. We as humans aren't meant to understand Mother Nature, I just know it. If we were truly meant to comprehend the world we live in, we would've done it by now. But we haven't. Life is a mystery. A beautiful, beautiful mystery. And I would like it to remain exactly that.

"I noticed you slept outside last night," Gabriel says. We're packing up our things and getting ready to continue our journey. I pause, facing away from him.

"Yeah, I didn't feel like sharing with your narcissistic friend." All my stuff had fitted perfectly into my bag before but now they won't. It's filled right to the brim and yet I still have a whole jacket to put in. I push and shove but it just won't fit.

"Dakota, it's not safe out here at night. What if you got bitten by a rattlesnake?" Gabriel moves closer to me. "Or worse." I blow a hair from my face and push the jacket with all my might. He watches as I continue to struggle with my rucksack.

"I don't need you telling me what to do all the time, Gabriel." He takes the jacket and the bag from me. "I know what I'm doing." Within seconds the coat is comfortably in my bag. He can barely hide the smugness on his face as I snatch the bag from him.

"Do you?" He doesn't wait for a response but spins on his heel and heads over to Marley. She's sat on a log by herself, chatting to Bunny as always. She giggles and chats with the prince while all I can do is stand and watch.

To Enzo's dismay, we decided to set off at the crack of dawn. He probably has a hangover from the despicable amount of alcohol that he poured down his throat last night. He muttered that he needs his beauty sleep, but Marley pointed out that his sleep doesn't seem to be making him beautiful. I had to stand in front of my sister to protect her from his wrath. Marley has recovered since yesterday, but she is still a little weak. Gabriel offered to take her bag but she'd refused, on the basis that she's a 'big girl'.

"My leg hurts," Marley groans, trudging beside Gabriel. She's clutching his palm in one hand and Bunny in the other. The poor stuffed animal is looking as rugged as ever. I doubt those blood stains would wash out too easily. Not that Marley would ever let me wash him.

"If you'd just let me take your bag…" Gabriel begins.

"I said my leg hurts, not my back," she interrupts, grinning up at him.

"Alright then. How about a piggyback ride?" Marley jumps at the chance. Gabriel picks her up, swinging her onto his shoulders.

"Good lord. Just get her a throne and some grapes, why don't you?" Enzo mutters, typing on his phone.

"She was bitten by a goddamn snake. Give it a rest," I snap.

Enzo rolls his eyes without looking away from his phone. Gabriel sighs and looks away from us. We all know how much he hates it when we argue. In a way it's like his two worlds are colliding. His best friend and…well I'm not sure how he sees Marley and me.

"I've been shot before and you didn't see me fussing over it."

"Were you six? I don't think so," I retort, scoffing.

"No. I was four," he responds, looking up from his phone and meeting my eye. This victorious gleam swirls in his eyes and I hate it.

"Well, I've been shot too. In the arm," I say. "By my mother."

"It's not a competition!" Marley exclaims, surprising us all. Everyone falls silent.

"So, you're a prince?" Marley asks as she bobs up and down on Gabriel's shoulders.

"Yes."

"Like an actual prince?"

"Yes," Gabriel repeats.

"You don't look like a prince," my sister admits, craning her head to look down at him. He makes eye contact with her glistening blue iris.

"And what does a prince look like?" he asks.

"Blonde," she says simply. She rests her hands on his dark hair, staring out at the dry planes.

"Shall I dye my hair blonde then?"

"No. Blondeness is a state of mind." Gabriel and I can't help but burst out laughing.

The dynamics among us has really shifted in the past twelve hours. I think the reality that we're going to be with each other for a lot longer has brought us closer. We're sharing more jokes, opening up more. It's almost as if we're building the foundations for a new family. My sister and I come from a home that we'd love to forget and Gabriel's royal upbringing doesn't seem as flawless as I thought it was. I don't know about Enzo. He is yet to tell us any more than his name. Enzo reminds me of someone. I saw him on a tv show once. He was boring. So very, very boring. But this colourless character holds a multitude of sins and secrets. Every ounce of his intelligence has gone to ensuring his appearance reveals nothing of his true personality. Drab clothes, rough hair and an uninviting glare. I do not see a man of dullness and monotony. I see a man who does not want his true character to be unearthed. No soul is truly this lifeless. His crass attempt at storing away his lifestyle doesn't fool me. I know that every inch of his skin crawls with stories and experience. This is not a boring, angry man. This is a man of culture and life, growth and hardship. I can't quite tell what, but something has made him shut down. What we see is not personality, this is self-defence. Defence against the cruel mistress that is society. It will tear you to shreds and leave you for dust without a second thought. In a twisted way I envy Enzo. He has decided not to open up his embodiment to ridicule and judgement at the hands of his peers. He is a closed book. As far as he's concerned, a closed book is a safe book.

I'm not sure how Gabriel decides where a good camping spot is but he always seems sure about himself. We find ourselves stopping a lot later than normal. By now even the sun has gone to bed. After all that practice, we manage to make quick work of putting up the tents. A low haze of warmth simmers through the air, carrying with it a dusty scent. In the distance, a feral horse releases a desperate whinny that makes my heart ache and burn. Ahead, the sun glows a fiery red, the blinding light piercing my eyes like lasers. Fatigue simmers in my veins as we settle around the campfire. Marley drops her bag beside me and sits down on it, whilst the boys faff around with their belongings. It takes us a good few minutes before we're fully calm.

"I have a surprise." Gabriel shuffles closer to Marley with his left hand holding something out of view.

"Ooo lemme see!" Marley claps in excitement and attempts to grab the mystery item. With the reflexes of a ninja, Gabriel whips the object in the air. I look up to see a bag with a multicoloured logo printed across the top: milly's marshmallows. A gasp leaps from my little sister's mouth as she clambers to her feet and tries to reach the sweets. Gabriel stands up to hold the bag higher, smiling down at her.

"Ah ah ah! First you have to let me change the dressing on your bullet wound." The grin that occupied my sister's face is replaced by a disappointed scowl.

"But it hurts so bad, Gabe, you don't understand!"

Angry tears spring into her eyes but she wipes them off with the back of her palm. I reach over to put my arm around her but she shrugs me off. "I'm not a baby, Dakota." It's easy for me to mask the pain she caused by doing that. Concealing my emotions is my speciality. Well that's what I thought but the look that Gabriel is giving me suggests otherwise. He opens his mouth to say something but is cut off by Enzo, who is sitting across the campfire from us.

"It may hurt but do you know what's worse? A wound infected with maggots and dry blood." I'm not sure if it's the reflection of the sun glare or his eye colour but his iris seems to glow red. Marley recoils into my side and this time she lets me embrace her. Putting down the marshmallows, Gabriel moves to kneel in front of Marley and holds out his little finger.

"If you let me do this, I pinky promise that I will be as gentle as possible. We'll toast the marshmallows as soon as we're done." She hesitates for a few seconds before interlinking her little finger with his. He smiles and gathers the medical equipment before coming back to kneel before Marley.

"Hold Dakota's hand, my love," he coos. Marley plants her small palm in mine. Her grip on my hand tightens as Gabriel comes towards her with those tiny medical scissors. She leans back further into my chest and Gabriel pauses. "Hey, it's okay. We'll stop if you need to, alright?" Her body relaxes and he takes that as a signal to lift her sleeve a little and cut off the bandage, which has begun to brown with the stain of old blood. Upon seeing the wound, I notice Gabriel grimace a little. It must be bad, considering Gabriel has been unfazed by watching people be burnt at the stake. I bounce my leg in a slow rhythm to keep my sister calm as Gabriel applies a fresh dressing.

"You're doing so well, Mar," I reassure her.

"Almost done," Gabriel adds. He swipes gently curled hair from his face and continues to patch up my sister. Minus the odd wince or whimper, Marley takes the pain very well. Soon enough, we've all taken our places around the fire, suited with a browning marshmallow. Enzo didn't strike me as the type of person to indulge in fluffy sugary treats but he's enjoying it more than anyone else. Granted he doesn't do much talking but even sitting with us is a good start. Marley sits on Gabriel's lap, merrily munching away and chatting to Bunny while Gabriel and I make conversation of our own.

"Wow I toasted my last marshmallow perfectly. Here have it." Gabriel holds the stick out to me, a bronzed marshmallow clinging to the end of it.

"Thank you but I'm okay. You have it." I do really want it but I feel obliged to be polite.

"I would believe you if your eyes weren't staring so ravenously at the marshmallow. C'mon, take it."

"But Gabriel I couldn't possibly–" My sentence is cut off as Gabriel slides the marshmallow off the stick and puts it in my mouth.

"Bon appétit, mon chéri." I blush as Gabriel puts his arm around me and pulls me closer.

"God, get a room," Enzo mutters. I giggle and Gabriel's body trembles against mine as he lets out a puffy laugh.

"My sincerest apologies, Enzo, are we disturbing

you?" Gabriel asks, still entertaining the remnants of his laughter.

"Quite," he replies, putting a final marshmallow in his mouth and heading to his tent.

Within a matter of minutes, I'm kicking my shoes off and clambering into Marley and I's tent.

"Good night," I yell. The zip of the other tent flies up and the material doorway falls open. Gabriel's face pops through it and he beams a cheesy grin at me.

"Good night, darling," he says, soft as anything. I squint my eyes at him.

"Ok, that pet name's a bit too cliché, even for me." He shrugs his shoulders.

"It was worth a try. Sleep well. We're one long desert stroll away from the forest." I nod, smiling. I wave and he waves back.

"Just make out already."

I'd thought Marley was asleep so it startles me when she speaks. I spin around. She's propped up on one elbow, the soft glow of a torch offering a dim source of light. I fight the urge to tell her that we've already 'made out.' She doesn't need to know that. Not yet.

"Excuse you. What me and Gabriel do is none of your business," I say, trying to be sure about myself.

"It is my business if you make me an auntie overnight." My mouth drops open.

"Oh please. I've done university-level biology. I know more about making babies than you do." I want to argue but she's right. Marley flicks off her torch and turns over.

"If you have a kid, you must name it Marley Jr," she

mumbles. A little yawn rises out of her before she nestles into the sleeping bag and falls asleep.

~

I must have left the door open slightly because the first thing to assault my senses is a streak of blaring sunlight. It pierces my eyes and drains my energy. An aggravated groan escapes my lips as I roll to face away from the sun glare. Marley is lucky enough to still be fast asleep. The second thing to assault my senses is the startlingly low voice of prince Luther.

"Rise and shine, Dakota." When I don't stir, he opens the door enough to climb in and shake me.

"Ten more minutes," I mumble.

"We don't have ten minutes to spare. C'mon, you know what they say, 'the early bird catches the worm'."

"I don't want the goddamn worm." My morning voice is so grumbly that it is almost the same octave as Gabriel's regular voice.

"Five minutes then you need to shake a leg." He kisses my hair and leaves the tent. Thank God Marley is asleep. A few minutes later, I clamber out of the tent, fatigued and lifeless. My sister follows suit and we ready ourselves for the final desert walk.

Marley is engrossed in reading and Enzo in his texting, giving me the perfect opportunity to talk to Gabriel.

"You know how you called me darling yesterday and kissed me this morning?" I ask as I tread beside him. He nods, smiling with an admirable level of triumphancy. "Yeah, that needs to stop." His eyebrows knit.

"Are we not…?"

"Yes, yes, we are, Gabriel, but Marley and Enzo don't know that. I'm not sure if or when I want my sister to know so can we hold off on the cringe PDA until then?" To be quite honest, they would've been stupid not to have guessed after Gabriel fed me a marshmallow and called me 'mon chéri' (whatever that means) but I digress.

"Cringe PDA? That hurt." He puts his hand over his heart and sucks in a sharp breath.

"You're mad," I say as I attempt to fight off a wild grin.

"Madly in love," he fires back. I can tell he's proud of his wittiness and it makes me hate and love him even more.

"Never say that again." He ignores what I say and puts his arm across my shoulder.

"No promises."

**31**

If I see one more cactus, I am going to go clinically insane. Even in my twelve years of staring at the same four walls, I was never this bored. When I imagined the sand biome, I envisioned life. I envisioned nests of scorpions scuttling by our feet. I envisioned a lazy stream of water, shimmering under the glaring light of our star. I envisioned a flock of roadrunners ploughing through the dust in the distance, a solemn sand cloud forming around them. I envisioned quails perched on solitary branches and eagles sweeping overhead. I envisioned snakes and addax antelopes and camels; ocelots, lions, Mexican coyotes. I envisioned life. Spare a lone snake, who slithered in the opposite direction, and a hundred cacti, I haven't seen anything resembling life. This desert is as dry as the hopes and dreams of the hundreds of Malsums who wish to take the journey that we have.

And that's when I see it. For the first time in days. Green. Not the dull green of a cactus. No, this is vibrant, clear as day. It stretches right to the sky, squeezing between the clouds. Trees and bushes and earth. Finally, we've made it. The penultimate biome.

# 32

Zayathai never felt like home. There was no comfort in the villages we resided in, or the houses we were supposed to call home. Our house was nothing to be proud of. The walls were white-washed and old, the floorboards long overdue for replacement. The bathroom...well the bathroom was horrific. That mysterious black grime lined every nook and cranny of the room. Some genius decided to buy a tacky yellow shower curtain, which was pretty much transparent. Nothing in our house served its purpose. The freezer was way below freezing point, the sofa was hard as a rock and the taps...my god the taps. The water pressure was so low that they could only produce so much as a dribble. Only two rooms in that house were up to standard: Mother's room and the chamber. Her room was like something out of a fairy tale. A king-sized bed, covered in at least ten unnecessary cushions, a wardrobe to hold her drab fashion sense. Even a vanity unit to apply that cakey, high coverage foundation that she wears with such pride. The chamber had to be perfect. Not because Mother cared about me, but because Mother wanted something with which to taunt me. That room is immaculate. Each metal wall is polished to shine. The keypad that locked me in is intricate and modern. The blood-shedding machine looks as though it was made by one of the world's most renowned scientists. I'll give it to my brother, he does know his way around technology. However, that never stopped it from hurting like hell as it sucked blood from my veins. A few beautiful paintings of hilltops and animals line the walls. A jar of sweets is placed just out of reach of my chair. She has made this room perfect so that I cannot complain. I provide blood for our clients and in return I get a beautiful room. It's all a mind game. A sick, sick mind game.

Our house was not falling apart because we couldn't afford to take care of it. Like most of Northern Zayathai, our house was falling apart because Mother didn't care to look after it. Many people lived in destitute conditions because they were simply too depressed to do anything about it. Mother had the capacity to make some much needed changes to our residence but she only cared about two things: herself and money. As long as we had a roof over our head to prevent the authorities sniffing around, she wanted nothing to do with us. Cassius was so brainwashed that even he couldn't see what was staring him in the face. She gave him this awful room, cold and damp. I decided to pay to glitz my room a tiny bit, which is the only reason why mine looks any better than his. She has left him for dust and still he follows her every move. For some reason, when I look at Gabriel,

I feel that same pain. For years, he has been following his mother mindlessly. But he has broken free. And he's broken free with a sword of anger, vengeance and determination.

# 33

The sound of jungle life flows into my ears. The squawk of birds, the purr of wild cats and the gentle breeze swishing through the trees. Zayathai never felt like home but I feel so much comfort in this forest. The leaves are like a roof overhead, the tree trunks the four walls. I notice this same comfort in the rest of the group, even Enzo. His broad shoulders seem to have relaxed and I haven't seen him text in almost an hour. That's a record. Even well into the night, I can hear the familiar click clack of texting coming from their tent. I can't imagine who he's talking to. Every other one of us was forced to destroy our phones, so that we were untraceable. Enzo wasn't. I thought about asking Gabriel why that'd happened, but I decided against it. He knows what he's doing and I feel as though questioning him would only rile him up. He'd assume I don't trust him and that's the last thing I want him to think. I do trust him. At least I'm trying to.

"So, you're telling me," Gabriel chucks a sunflower seed in the air and catches it in his mouth. "That you'd rather eat a live spider than go anywhere near peanut butter?"

"Definitely! Have you ever smelt peanut butter? It's vile!" I respond.

"But a live spider," Marley says. "It would be all skittish and furry." She pretends to gag.

"I bet spiders have a better aftertaste, though. I've heard they taste like chicken," I explain.

"That's disgusting," Gabriel says, laughing to himself.

"Not as disgusting as peanut butter," I say, shrugging. Enzo shakes his head and bears the first sincere smile I've seen him muster since we met. A low murmur of crickets settles around us as we head deeper into the bushes. I've been startled by numerous different terrifying animals in the past hour: snakes, wild cats, goddamn spiders. My good old sister adds to the hysteria by explaining the danger of each species in meticulous detail. Sometimes I wish she wasn't so smart. We fall silent and all that can be heard are ripe, autumnal leaves rustling and crunching beneath our footsteps. Jungle life consumes my heart and warms my soul.

"Doesn't it sound beautiful?" I say to no one in particular. I breathe in nature and drink the beauty through my eyes.

"You mean the helicopters?" Marley asks. Before I can respond, she points to the sky. Gabriel, Enzo and I stare at each other before reluctantly tracing our eyes to the clouds. In between the palm trees and birds are the distinct outline of three government aircraft.

"Dammit." Without hesitating, Gabriel takes Marley's hand and darts forwards. Me and Enzo sprint behind, watching the helicopters as we go. They cast a spotlight over the ground, far from us but not far enough. Our bags jostle and jump as we peg it through the shrubbery. The bushes become thicker as we descend into the epicentre of jungle life. Birds squawk overhead and little animals scuttle in the bushes. It makes me sick to think of the number of tiny creatures I must've stepped on by now. The glare of the helicopter lights seems to get softer as the jungle becomes denser. Nature protects us from the guards as the nearing on opaque canopy makes spotting us an impossible job. The whirring of helicopters recedes as they glide higher into the sky. Perhaps, they did see us but couldn't land. There's absolutely no space for huge flying vehicles where we've ended up. Trees surround us and the closest we have to a clearing is a little patch of dead grass that's just big enough for two small tents to be set up. Perfect. Once Gabriel decides we're in a safe place, everyone falls to the floor, bags still clinging to our backs.

"Can we stop for the day?" Marley grumbles.

"We've only just started," Gabriel replies. Marley groans and tips her head backward. I move sticky, sweaty strands of dark hair from my face.

"It might seem like a breeze to you, Prince Luther, but my legs are barely a quarter the length of yours. All this running really hurts. Not to mention I had snake venom in my system not long ago. I'm exhausted." She stares him right in those stunning grey eyes. "Exhausted." Gabriel looks to Enzo then to me. Enzo shakes his head but I have to sympathise with Marley. She really isn't cut out for all of this. Hell, I barely feel fit enough to be sprinting through uneven terrain every single day.

"I agree with her," I state, which nearly sends Enzo into cardiac arrest. His mouth flings about as he tries to form words to describe his anger.

"You people are spineless! It's as if you thought we'd just dance onto a minibus that would take us straight to another country. Suck it up because this baby mentality that you've got on is not going to get us onto that boat," the words spout from his mouth like a fountain of urine. Marley barely acknowledges him and I can't help but wrinkle my nose. Gabriel stares at the ground while his mouth makes weird movements. It's almost like he's talking without actually opening his mouth or making sounds.

"Sorry Enz but I'm with the girls on this one." I cringe at Gabriel shortening his friend's two syllable name. "How about we set up camp now–"

"It's midday, Gabe," Enzo cuts in. Gabriel turns to give his friend an authoritative glare that I've never seen him use before. Enzo's body seems to wither and that ballsy air about him evaporates.

"If you'd allow me to finish, I could explain my plan. A medium, if you will." The regal tone to Gabriel's voice has returned.

Throughout the journey he's always made himself the obvious leader, but I haven't seen him quite like this. He doesn't want our opinions. He just wants us to listen. Marley shrugs her bag off her back and cups her face in her hands. I find myself copying her.

"Setting up camp now will allow plenty of time for us to replenish our resources. I will find a fresh spring with Dakota, Mar can harvest berries and Enzo…" Gabriel looks around. No other job presents itself so he conjures up, "You shall sharpen the knives." We've only had to use the knives to cut up edible plants so I doubt they will be all that blunt. Everyone realises this, but no one says anything. Not even Enzo, to my surprise.

"Perfect," Marley and I say in unison.

"Whatever," is the only reply Enzo wants to make.

"Splendid. Come along, Kota. I suspect there is a water source nearby." Gabriel says this while tracing a finger over his wretched map. I don't feel like pointing out that the gushing sound of water is a much easier indicator than his little piece of crumpled paper. I've heard that in other countries they have this thing called GPS. It allows you to plan and navigate journeys from your phone. Genius, right?

Gabriel and Enzo shrug off their bags and stand up. The prince reaches down and takes my hand, tugging me to my feet. Marley holds her hand out jokingly to Enzo. He scoffs and turns his back on her. We've been alternating between who holds the tents in their bags, excluding Marley. It's by far the heaviest piece of equipment we have, so it's always nice when it's not my turn. Lucky for me today is one of those days. Enzo and Gabriel tug the tents from their bags and drop them to the floor. This is always the most irritating part of the day. As much as we're getting better at this, that doesn't make the lugging and arguing any less pleasant. Once we've constructed the two makeshift bedrooms, we set about our tasks. Marley doesn't need to be told which berries are safe to eat. Of course, she's read some books about poisonous versus edible plants. What a kid. It doesn't take us long to find the water source due to the tremendous amount of noise it amasses as the clear liquid descends from a steep cliff. A waterfall. Rocks of various sizes outline the pool of crystal-clear water that collects at the base of a violent stream. The pool is quite large. I reckon it would take a good few minutes to swim to the other side. Despite the rampant thrashing of water smacking the belly of the pool, the waterfall is somehow very peaceful.

"I've never seen a waterfall before," I say, staring in sheer amazement while Gabriel crouches down and begins gathering the water. We only have one pan and a couple of one-litre bottles with which to collect our supplies, but they'll suffice. Gabriel's hair falls forward and curtains across his face as the water *glug glugs* into his water bottle. He screws on the cap and sets it to one side. I'm so caught up by the scenery that I barely hear Gabriel when he asks if I 'feel like helping anytime soon.' I mutter my apologies and come to kneel beside him but my eyes don't leave the situation of the waterfall. Being amazed doesn't even begin to describe how I'm feeling.

"Nature. It's just...so stunning," I say more to myself than to Gabriel.

"Just like you," he replies a little too fast. I fight the urge to mock him, but the need is too strong.

"Clearly they didn't teach you how to compliment people at your posh kids' school." Gabriel stops collecting water. His eyebrows rise and his mouth drops open as he cocks his head towards me.

"Excuse you?" That authoritative voice is back again.

I found it funny when he used it on Enzo, but now my heart feels all jumpy.

"What?!" I hold my hands up in mock defence. "I'm just saying my paedophilic neighbour had better flirting skills than you."

"Ok that's it." Gabriel stands up and brushes himself off. "You're going in." I can barely make sense of what he's just said before I'm hauled into the air by the pits of my arms.

"Gabriel, don't you dare. I swear on everything you love–!" I cut myself off when I realise that all he seems to love is my sister and I. I'd prefer not to be cursed and I don't think Marley wants that fate either. I stare down at Gabriel's smirking face. My legs thrash everywhere to no avail.

"Are you sorry?" he asks in this condescending voice that makes me want to stamp his brains out.

"Not in the slightest!" I scream at him. A giggle escapes my mouth before I can cram it back in.

"Well, if you're not sorry, you can't be upset when I do this." He pulls me out of the sky and I slam into his body.

My legs curl around his thin torso as he takes a few rushed paces forwards and hurls us into the water. A sharp cooling sensation encompasses my body as we crash through the surface. My hair flings upwards as we fully submerge below the water. I'd thought it would be clear, but the surroundings are surprisingly murky green. I push away from Gabriel and claw my way up to the surface. Less than a second later, Gabriel emerges too. He swipes drenched hair from his face and shakes his head wildly. I take cover as his dark locks fling water all over the place.

"There could've been sharks in here!" I shriek through gulping laughter.

"All the better." He bites his lip to hide the broad grin that pines to spread across his face.

"You're crazy," I say as we tread in the lake.

"Crazy for you." This time I don't make fun of him. He moves closer and I allow him to take me by the waist. Our bodies collide with considerable force. As do our lips. Every ounce of me feels like it's drowning in Gabriel's love. Our mouths move in gentle synchronisation that feels like harmony to my aching heart. The only thing that makes us break apart is our inability to stay above water level as our passion starts to sink us. Still holding me, Gabriel turns and swims back to dry land with ease. We've only filled up two containers so we spend the next ten minutes working in soft silence. In my mind I'm freaking out over what's just happened, and I know for a fact that Gabriel is doing the exact same thing.

Of course, Enzo and Marley had questions about why we returned soaked to the bone. Gabriel had thought quickly on his feet and conjured up the excuse that I tripped on a rock and fell in, which prompted him to jump in and save me. Always making himself the hero. Typical. Marley had harvested many plants, including nettles. When everyone had shared confused glances, she told us that we could make nettle soup. It sounded disgusting, but I suppose it's nutrition. The broth is easy to make, so after I changed out of my wet clothes, Marley and I manage to make a decent amount by the time the sun sets. We're now sitting around the fire that Gabriel and Enzo have built, Marley cuddled into my side.

"This isn't that bad," I state as the spoon pours the pungent liquid through my lips. Marley's left eyebrow kicks up at me.

"Are you kidding? It tastes the same as how I imagine face-planting into dirt must taste," Marley complains. She drops her spoon into the mess tin and soup splashes over the edge.

"Even if it tastes bad you should still be grateful and eat it." For once Enzo is actually making sense. Marley eyes him with a deadly glance.

"I didn't ask for your input, Enzo." She spits out his name like it's manure on her tongue. He scoffs at her and returns to gulping down his portion. Gabriel's jaw hardens, but he says nothing. "Besides you can talk about gratefulness all you like, but I made this soup so I'm not entitled to eat it." Technically she's correct but Enzo completely dismisses her statement, choosing instead to reply with, "You're going to eat the soup and not act like a brat for once in your measly life." Why Enzo is getting so riled up over some plant broth I can't tell you. I suppose it's just another excuse to snipe at my sister.

"You can't tell me what to do. Kota, tell him!" She looks up at me with those big blue eyes. Her tiny lips are pursed tight together like she's sucking on a lemon.

"Mar, you do need to eat or you're going to get ill." I find my response quite a clever way at dodging an argument with Enzo. Marley doesn't seem to appreciate it nearly as much as I do. In fact, she hurls herself to her feet and storms past Gabriel. He stares straight forward as she flings our tent door open and zips it closed.

"Leave her," I mutter. I take another sip of the broth. "She'll calm down soon."

Gabriel and Enzo fall into conversation while I sit there, whirling the remains of my soup around with my spoon. My appetite fell just as quickly as it came and no longer masks the taste of the nettles. My sister is right. It tastes like dirt. Enzo takes Gabriel's empty mess tin and puts it on top of his.

"I'm heading to bed. Night," he says.

I say my farewell and add my tin to the pile. Gabriel stands and, to my surprise, heads to the wrong tent. He opens the door and climbs inside. I decide not to follow after him; Gabriel and my sister are probably talking. About what? I don't know. After tidying up our area, I'm not quite sure what to do with myself. Fatigue hasn't settled into my bones yet, but I wish it would. Besides walking and arguing, there isn't a whole lot that we can do. Entertainment-wise there isn't anything in the forest or any of the biomes for that matter. Each other's company is the best we have, which probably explains why an argument breaks out every ten minutes.

I try to fend off my curiosity but it gets the best of me. I walk over to the tent and whip the cloth door open. Huddled into Gabriel, Marley sucks on her thumb like she's two again. I haven't seen her do that in a long time. Not since dad left.

"...and then the dragon spat fire at her, but do you know what Lucy did? Using her magical powers, she

254

formed a heat resistant shield and…" Gabriel's voice trails off when he notices my presence.

"Please don't stop the story for me."

I slide myself on the other side of Gabriel and he puts his spare arm across my shoulders. He continues telling some elaborate tale about a girl with supernatural powers who fights dragons and…to be honest I'm not completely invested in the plot. My attention is more drawn to the man telling said story. He speaks vividly and does these silly voices for each character. Marley laughs every time.

"The end." Marley claps and cheers.

"Tell it again! Tell it again!" she squeals.

I can't tell you how relieved I am to see her acting like a child again. As much as I'm proud of her intelligence, sometimes I fear that it chips away at her childhood innocence. Not many kids know the ins and outs of science like the back of their hand.

"It's a bit too late, Mar," I chime in. She looks over Gabriel to scowl at me before nestling back.

"You'll tell me the story again. Won't you, Gabe?" She phrased that well. Too well. Surely, he can't back out of it now.

"I think you'll enjoy the story much better tomorrow when you've had a decent amount of sleep. Don't you think?" Genius.

"Fine," Marley mumbles. Gabriel starts to sit up but Marley grabs his arm.

"Wait! I need to ask you something. Promise you won't lie to me?" Gabriel runs his fingers through his hair and nods.

"I promise."

"Are you dating my sister?" I'm not even eating something but I still manage to choke. I sit bolt upright and so does Gabriel. We confer silently through pointed glaring. Marley watches us with squinted eyes.

"So you are."

"Yes. Yes I am." I feel a tang of betrayal that he didn't ask me what I wanted to tell her, but I suppose it's a tad obvious. Just a tad. Come to think of it, we haven't actually stated that we're dating to one another yet. I suppose the labels just haven't seemed important.

"I knew it!" she almost screams.

"We can't have been that bad at hiding it," I say, cupping my face in my hands.

"You both look at one another in this weird way and never leave each other's side. Plus, I heard you squealing and laughing when you were collecting water. Sounded awfully romantic for a platonic relationship." O k a y maybe she has a point. Gabriel takes this opportunity to slip his hand into mine. My heart feels all tingly.

"Are you ok with it...with us?" Gabriel asks. Marley shrugs and slips into her sleeping bag.

"I'm not bothered. Just don't smooch in front of me." She rubs her eyes with small, balled-up fists and releases a yawn. Within seconds, it seems she's asleep.

"Well, uh...good night?" Gabriel smirks when I say this.

"Good night," he replies. We'd hoped to get away with a departing kiss but Marley mumbles, "Ew I heard that." So not asleep then.

**34**

One thing my smart little sister forgot to mention was how quickly the weather changes in rainforests. Beforehand, the temperature was amazing. It was that perfect middle ground where the weather wasn't noticeable. Not too hot, not too cold. Just about right. The clouds are now closing over the forest, forming a humid blanket. As if being on the run wasn't enough, we now have hail and rain pelting down on us. Most of our stuff is okay but the most important piece of equipment has been compromised: the tents. As a result of hurtling debris, each one now obtains a few holes that we really could've done without. To add insult to injury the precipitation has made Marley's book go all crinkly. She certainly isn't happy about that.

"We need to get to high ground," Gabriel had said upon looking at the sky. That seems like a fabulous plan until you realise that there's absolutely no high ground in sight. Just trees and clouds and more trees.

"We're not gonna make it," Marley yells over the

clapping of rain against wax-sealed leaves and our thudding footsteps.

My sister definitely outdoes us in the brain sector but physically she's about as helpful as an umbrella with a hole in it. The poor thing tries desperately to speed-walk at the same pace as us, but her snake-bitten, four-foot self could never keep up. We charge through the vegetation, stamping on flowers and sticks and leaves. The once crunchy leaves are now soggy and soft. They squelch and squish as four sets of desperate shoes trample over them. A few leaves, brown with age, cling to the soles of my ironclad boots. Pools of water collect around our feet as we make a bid for safety. Enzo beelines ahead of us with his enormous footsteps. He completely dismisses our feeble attempts at yelling 'wait!' over the loud rainfall. For a while, he is easily in eyesight. We charge behind him confidently even though no one really knows where safety may be. Then he descends. Lower and lower and lower until all that's visible is the peak of his harshly gelled hair. We stumble down the slope after him. In an instance, the ground beneath my feet goes from soft to hard. Stone? Looking up and around me I notice what is now surrounding us: a cave. A huge opening to a cave.

"It should be safe here," Gabriel explains as he takes his camouflage hood down.

His voice bounces off the walls and slithers through my ears. He sits beside me, arm discreetly placed around my waist, holding me close. Marley and Enzo sit on the floor opposite us, careful to keep a good one metre distance.

"How did you know where to go?" I ask Enzo. He shrugs.

"Saw a decline in the ground. Ran towards it. Just common sense."

"What would you know about common sense?" Marley mutters. She's looking over Bunny, trying to push his left eye back into the socket.

"Coming from the girl trying to salvage a stuffed animal," Enzo fires back. I sigh and rest my head on Gabriel's shoulder. We've come to realise that any time Enzo and Marley start arguing, we're about to be in for a long ride. Gabriel looks down at me and rolls his eyes. I smile and nestle my head further into his shoulder.

A solid five minutes later, they are still going at each other.

"Can't you just accept that your precious Bunny is as good as gone?" Marley knits her brows at him.

"Bunny is more important than you'll ever be. He stays by my side no matter what." Enzo scoffs and leans his head against the wall.

"Scoff at me one more time, I dare you."

"Mar, don't rise to it," I say. I'm way too tired to break up their argument properly. It's become a daily occurrence and I'm not going to entertain it.

"Mar, come over here," Gabriel says, beckoning her with his left hand. With a dramatic grunt, she heaves herself up and trudges over to him. He takes both of her hands and looks into her soft, blue eyes.

"Not that I agree with him, but you can't hold Bunny when we're out walking anymore," he says. He eases the toy from her hand and puts it beside him. Her face drops and a frown settles on her lips.

"Why not? If you wanted a turn holding him, you could've just asked!" she exclaims.

"No, it's not that," Gabriel says with a hint of amusement in his tone. He drops her hands and reaches into his bag. A moment passes where only the odd drip of water from the ceiling or shuffling of his bag can be heard. Whatever he's about to give her wasn't broached with me first so it better be something child-friendly. He takes out a small handgun and sets the backpack on the floor. My eyes widen as he sets the weapon in her tiny hands.

"Not a chance." I attempt to snatch it, but she turns away from me.

"Nope! Gabe says I should have it so I'm having it," she tells me defiantly. He beams at her like a proud dad.

"Gabriel, I told you how I feel about weapons." He puts his arm back around me and leans close to my ear.

"They're closing in on us. She won't be safe without one," he whispers to me. We both look up to see her pointing the gun at Enzo. He snatches it out of her hand and checks the safety lock before handing it back. I don't even trust myself with a gun. Mine is tucked safely between some clothes, deep in my bag.

"But what if it goes wrong?" Gabriel gives me one of his careful looks. Something about people challenging his intelligence really rattles him.

"Dakota, do you really think I'd give her the gun if I didn't think she was sensible enough to have it?"

"She's six! "I almost yell.

"And three quarters," Marley interrupts.

"And three quarters," Gabriel echoes, smirking.

"This isn't funny, Gabriel."

"I know, I know. Just trust me when I tell you that she'll be better for it."

"Fine," I breathe out. Gabriel grins.

"Mar, let me get you a waistband to put your gun in. I'll hold onto Bunny for safekeeping, ok?" My sister nods. I'm surprised that my sister is willing to let someone else look after Bunny. Then again, Gabriel isn't just 'someone' anymore. She probably trusts him more than she trusts me.

I sit, knees huddled up to my chest, watching Gabriel wrap a tool belt around Marley. I sip some nettle tea that we managed to make earlier. My sister watches Gabriel carefully as he assists her. She really does think the world of him now. I suppose he's the dad she never had.

Speaking of dads, you're probably wondering what happened to ours. Silas was his name. Silas Calaway. He was a good man, strong as anything. Not to mention, he could make a mean tiramisu. If you asked me to list every flaw to that man's name, it really wouldn't take me long. Aside from his horrific singing skills and inability to draw, the only flaw I can think of is his Malsum blood. He was my safety net. Mother made me bloodshed and he held me, while I cried afterwards. The day he was snatched away from me was easily the worst day of my life. I remember that day like it was yesterday. He had, in fact, been making tiramisu with me when there was a knock at the door. Mother got there first, cradling Marley. When she saw who it was, she backed away into the living room.

The three armed-men didn't ask permission to come in. It's like they knew exactly where he was. Like they could smell him from a million miles away. They practically knocked the kitchen door down.

"Silas Calaway," the shortest one had said. "You're under arrest on suspicion of treason."

Treason. I was only seven but that word had played on the tv many times. Dad didn't have a criminal bone in his body, so I knew this had to be a mistake. I did try and tell the guards that but one of them had told me to 'pipe down'. Dad had silently agreed, offering me this look that told me this wasn't a situation that I wanted to get involved in. I cried as soon as the front door closed. So did Mother. Cassius did what he normally did and went to his room. Probably to cry without putting a damper on his toxically masculine reputation. We all wept because we knew that getting arrested meant you weren't coming back, no matter how small the crime was. The state never misses any excuse to cart people away or to kill them and use them as a deterrent. Petty crimes are rarely committed when people know they could end up with their neck on the chopping block for it.

But Dad did something that people hadn't done for years. He came back. Not for long, and he did so silently, but he came back. It was like watching a ghost as he trailed through the house, skin grey and ageing, as he collected a few of his belongings. We never heard him speak again but we received a letter from the royal family.

*Dear Mrs Calaway,*

*I write to you on behalf of the monarchy. As I'm sure you will be aware, your husband was taken into custody on the suspicion of treason. He has been prosecuted and found guilty for what he is. However, after an extensive conversation with Mr. Calaway, we have come to a consensus that suits us all. Silas has given us a tip that leads us to a Malsum, Carter Mitacron. In return he will not face a sentence, but will join the royal forces instead and serve the monarchy. We are pleased to welcome Silas onto our forces and I'm sure he's delighted to be here.*

*Yours truly,*
*Kathleen Mayflower, private secretary of Queen Dianne Escobar*

When Mother had slammed the letter on the table and stormed upstairs, I'd taken the opportunity to read it myself. At first, I was relieved for Dad but that was before I realised whose freedom he'd traded for his own: Carter Mitacron. His childhood best friend. I'd met Carter a number of times. He was one of the most hilarious people I'd ever had the pleasure of talking to. Dad and Carter were like brothers. Like family. The fact that Dad had turned on him so quickly made my stomach churn. I guess you can't, and should never, trust someone completely. That would be stupid.

I'd read about people like Dad before. The exceptions, they call them. People who managed to bend the unbendable system that Dianne runs. Only people with the most extraordinary negotiation skills could escape the death penalty or avoid being sent to prison. Not just anyone could snitch on someone and get away with it. You have to be convincing. You have to make them want to spare you. It never occurred to me that Dad might be one of those people. I do miss him sometimes, but most of the first time I just feel anger. Carter was a friend. If that was what it took for Dad to betray him, was their friendship ever real?

We sit quietly in the cave for a few more hours, Marley reading and Enzo texting, while Gabriel and I huddle together for warmth. Despite the relaxing ambiance of aggressive rain hurtling against the outer shell of the cave, I can't seem to relax. A sudden chill comes over me as the shoddy state of my clothes becomes apparent.

"You're still shaking, Dakota." Gabriel removes his arm from across my shoulder to offer a concerned look.

"Letting go of me sure isn't going to help that," I respond, nestling back into his side. A slight twist of irritation whirls through my stomach as Gabriel slides away from me to open his bag. I sit back and cold, hard stone meets my sodden jacket. So much for wind and waterproof. "Seriously? What could possibly be more important than cuddling me right now?" He doesn't respond but gives a disapproving shake of his head and continues to look through his belongings. After a minute or so, he retrieves a pair of black thermal socks and gets down on one knee in front of me.

"I don't have any spare clothes for you but these should at least keep your feet warm." After giving him a thankful smile, I reach out to take the socks but Gabriel clearly has other ideas.

"No, it's okay. Stay where you are, Kota, I'll put them on for you." A shy laugh curls around my tongue as he eases off my left shoe.

"You don't have to do that, Gabe. You're not my servant." He looks up at me with those beautiful, dark eyes and a playful smile glitters across his lips.

"I know that, but you're cold and tired so let me do this for you." I lean back against the wall and I can't help but laugh at the ridiculousness of it all. How such a silly, cringeworthy gesture could make me feel so cared for. The warmth of the fresh, dry socks against my blistered skin feels like what I imagine heaven to be. Gabriel comes to sit back beside me and plants a gentle kiss on my forehead. Marley conveniently looks up from her book at the same moment and grimaces, putting the encyclopaedia higher up so she can't see us. I nestle back into Gabriel and we relish in a few calming moments before we collectively decide to set sail. The rain seems to have passed a lot quicker than I anticipated. The air is rather fresh now. What's that smell called? Petrichor, I think. That earthy scent combined with the sharp, unmistakable musk of rain. I'm not particularly fond of petrichor but I sure can appreciate the beauty of the elements. My area of Zayathai was surrounded by so much concrete that experiencing sights of a palm tree or the gentle musk of dirt was very rare. However, it really does take the fun out of it when Marley gives you the Latin name for absolutely every plant that we pass.

"…and of course, there's the legendary combretum rotundifolium.

But what really catches my eye is the theobroma…"

"Nobody cares," a voice says. Not mine. Not Gabriel's. Not even Enzo's. Someone else's. He's standing before us, dressed head to toe in clothes embroidered in the Escobar symbol.

A smug, round face looks on at us. He has puffed, rosy cheeks and beady eyes. He can't be much taller than me, five-foot-ten at best. He's quite rotund, as one might say. I remember once reading this contraband English classic that I found in the attic. What was it called? I can be so forgetful sometimes…Lord of the Flies! That's it. Clearly the story wasn't all that good because I don't remember a great deal of it, but there was one character that stuck in my mind. A chubby, red-faced little boy. Piggy. What I am witnessing right now is an adult version of Piggy. A thin patch of blonde hair is planted on his head, far back from where his hairline used to be. This man is an absolute mess and it begs the question, why did the army send him out as their first line of attack? Pretty stupid, if you ask me. I can diss him all I like, but he is ready to fight. His left hand is pressed in a tight fist and the other is clasping an AK-47.

"You guys really thought you could escape. It's quite cute, if you think about it." He takes a step towards us and we collectively take a step back, except Gabriel. He moves to the front, towering over the man. My instincts tell me to grab him and get out of here, but I don't. All I can do is hold onto Marley's hand as tightly as possible.

"Where are the rest of your buddies, huh?" Gabriel looks down at him with venom leaking from his pupils.

"Oh, they're on their way, don't you worry. I've just been sent to watch you until they can close in. In the meantime, let's get to know each other. I'm Arthur Manning. I'm the man who's going to get a big cash reward for returning you, dead or alive." He looks past Gabriel and offers a condescending wave to us all. No one returns the gesture.

"Tough crowd," he mutters.

"You think you're so funny." Enzo's voice is harsh as ever. I don't think I've seen him this bothered by another human's presence. And that's saying something considering the multiple times he's yelled at Marley.

"As a matter of fact, I do. Soon, not only will I be a funny guy, but I'll be a mega rich guy." He puts his gun between his knees, in order to pretend to fan money everywhere while we all watch on. His eyes scan over the group and land on me. He knocks past Gabriel and ambles towards me. Gabriel spins to face us, breathing in sharply. I shake my head at him, urging him to stay calm. I drop Marley's hand and push her towards Enzo. To my surprise, Enzo pulls her close to him.

"So, you're the pretty lady that Gabriel's fallen head over heels for."

"Who says—"

"Oh, purrrleaseee. It's all over the news. Prince Gabriel goes on the run with his next conquest," Arthur muses. I look over to Gabriel who doesn't dare to make eye contact. Arthur takes my hand and, for some god forsaken reason, I don't pull away. I just stand there, frozen in place.

"I normally question Mr. Escobar's taste in women but you...you're a real eye-catcher." He leans into my ear, bad breath smothering my face. "What do you say? One quick kiss and I won't hand you in to the authorities."

BANG.

Arthur keels over, falling into me. I jump back, letting his body sink to the ground. Standing behind him, gun unholstered, is Marley.

# 35

We all stand over the body, staring down at the lifeless creep. His patchy, red skin has become a blanket sheet of white. His eyes are wide open and glassy, while his mouth hangs open. He looks shocked though there's still a smug edge to the frown he's now wearing. The injection wears off as soon as you die, so it's quite satisfying to see him look not so perfect. It's ironic to think that he's spent his life arresting and hunting down Malsums, yet he dies wearing a frown. I really want to feel something for him but not even an ounce of empathy worms its way into my emotions. If anything, I'm glad he's dead.

"What did I just do...?" Marley asks, voice quivering like a phone line in the wind. She crumbles beside him and feels his face. "Cold," she mumbles, looking up at us. For the first time in a while, Enzo can hardly fight a smile.

"Nice job, kid." He goes for a high five, which she completely ignores. Enzo returns to texting within twenty seconds. Marley picks up Arthur's hand and squeezes it, as if he's actually going to return the action. Of course he doesn't. She drops the hand and it crashes to the floor with an empty thud. Gabriel moves closer and puts his hand on her shoulder.

"I killed someone," she whispers. "Oh my god, I killed someone." Gabriel tugs my sister to her feet and pulls her into a bear hug.

"He had it coming, Marley. You did the right thing," he says, taking an arm away from her to stroke the top of her hair.

"The right thing? Are you mad!" I almost screech. Gabriel draws his tongue along the top row of his teeth and sighs.

"So, you'd rather he killed us first. That's what I'm hearing," he responds, cocking his head to the side. I shake my head, eyes squinted.

"If you think I condone my sister becoming a murderer then–"

"She's not a murderer, Dakota." I scoff but there's not an ounce of humour in the sound that leaves my mouth. It's harsh and it's angry.

"If she's not a murderer then how do you explain *that*?" I point to Arthur but Gabriel doesn't look at the body. He just tightens his grip on Marley.

"Gabe," Mar says, her voice muffled against his body.
"Yes?"

You might wanna let go of me."

"What's wro–" He doesn't even get to finish his sentence before she coughs violently and projectile vomits right onto his shoes. Gabriel jumps away from her and looks down.

"Sorry," she mumbles, wiping her mouth with the back of her sleeve. Gabriel looks to the sky and inhales a gentle breath.

"It's ok. It's…just vomit." He elevates one leg from the floor and waggles it in the air. The sick clings to his footwear, spare a little bit that slithers off and splashes on the ground.

"Gabriel, I need to talk to you for a minute. In private," I hiss. His lips curl into a grin and his tongue presses against the underside of his upper teeth.

"Lead the way." I grab Gabriel's arm and storm a few yards away from Enzo and Marley.

"Ok this cannot happen!" I order.

"What?" he asks in an attempt to play innocent.

"This, this! All of this!" I wave my arms around in a sudden wave of hysteria. "Jeez, Gabe! I-I mean what are we doing out here? I'm covered in mud, m-my shoes are soaked and oh my god my sister just killed a man! Are we crazy? I can't travel across the world! I'm not Christopher flaming Columbus. We can't do this! Let's turn around. Yes! If we go back now maybe we can–" I cut myself off and hold my head as if I'm in physical pain, hundreds of thoughts scattering through my mind and poking at my brain. Gabriel watches me as I experience what can only be described as a meltdown.

"Hey hey hey listen. There's no need to panic." He lifts my chin and offers me a warming smile. "We're at the final hurdle now, ok? We've got this." He finds himself laughing at my anxious expression. Gabriel pulls me into a hug and rocks from foot to foot. I tremble

271

and hyperventilate under his grasp, but I find a certain comfort in the embrace.

"We haven't got time for this!" Marley exclaims, stepping over the body. I'm quite taken aback at her sudden chirpiness, considering the quivering wreck she just was.

"Yeah, let's go already," Enzo says. Well at least they agree on something.

As we continue walking, I can't help but feel nauseous at how desensitised my sister has become to violence. She ended a life not even half an hour ago and now she's skipping along beside me and telling me facts about anteaters. Had she been in the same situation last week, she would've passed out at the sight of Arthur's body on the floor. She would've gone insane if she had been the one that pulled the trigger. This isn't what I signed up for. I wanted my sister to come out of this the same person as when we set off. I don't even recognise the girl who toddles beside me.

"I know we only just stopped but I could really use some soup right about now," I say.

"No, you're right. We literally stopped like an hour ago," Enzo says. "We don't have time for soup, especially with the army closing in on us."

He kicks at sticks and stones as we descend deeper into the forest. It's starting to get rather creepy now. The trees overhead have thickened, blocking the sun's desperate attempt to offer us sunlight. The floor's become softer, as if to suggest there's a bog nearby. I'd thought myself quite intelligent for being able to work that out, but Marley beat me to it. Since we started walking again, Gabriel hasn't let go of my hand. It's almost as if he's scared that he'll lose me. I've been walking with Marley and Gabriel for most of the journey, whilst Enzo trails behind or ahead. Gabriel's been telling me all about Dianne; all her likes and dislikes, favourite food, most embarrassing moments. You name it, he's told me. It does satisfy me that he's so open to sharing every aspect of her existence. This really does show that he trusts me. As long as I have Gabriel and Marley, I have all I need.

"Please can we sit down? Just for a minute," I plead. Gabriel looks down at me, as he often does, given the height difference.

"Fine. If the queen wants to stop, we'll stop." I stop dead in my tracks. I'm sorry, what did he just call me? Gabriel twirls me in a circle and I squeal in delight.

"Your throne, m'lady." He bows, motioning towards a rather unstable-looking log. In a slightly dizzy state, I take a seat. Gabriel dances towards a smaller log and points to it.

"And yours, my princess." Marley giggles and sits down. Gabriel squeezes onto my log and Enzo huffs, lowering himself to the floor. I know I'd said I was hungry, but I seem to be losing my appetite by the second. Marley and I were right; there is a massive swamp beside us. It globs and squelches in mossy elegance. A low hiss of some unknown creature trails through the air. We sit in silence. Marley is munching away at a tub of wild berries and reading, while I watch her with discretion. The gun on her belt taunts me like a carrot on a stick. Oh, the temptation to grab it and chuck it in that green abyss is overwhelming. That killing machine deserves no place near my sister.

"Let's play a game," Enzo announces. He slaps his knees and stands up. All eyes dart over to him, bewilderment swimming in each pupil.

"I don't know about you, but I fancy a round of guess who. Right, I'll go first." He rubs his palms together. He's planning something. I can tell by the satisfaction brimming in his eyes.

"The person I'm thinking of is small, about the size of a pig on its hind legs, I'd say."

"Enzo…" The warning tone in Gabriel's voice would be enough to make anyone shut up. Anyone but Enzo.

"Hey! No cheating. It's my turn," Enzo snarls in faux condescendence. "The person I'm thinking of is smart. Too smart, one could say." He advances on a hapless Marley. She watches him with wide, hungry eyes. "The person I'm thinking of is so annoying that even her sister prefers the presence of a guy she only just met over her." He advances on my sister some more.

"Enzo, stop!" Tears of fury lace my sister's cheeks and slither down her neck. An excess of rage sends her trembling.

"The person I'm thinking of will only be hushed by the wings of death. Maybe, just maybe, we should grant her that privilege."

In one fell swoop, Enzo snatches the book from Marley. Every one of us anticipates his next move, but not one of us is quick enough to stop it. With a careless flick of the wrist, Enzo tosses the encyclopaedia into the nearby bog. All we can do is watch as it makes its slow descent into the bowels of nature. It's only now that I notice something horrifying. My sister doesn't look sad. Her face isn't anxious or emotional. Marley is governed by pure, intoxicating anger. With a trembling yet somewhat steady hand, she reaches into her waist belt and wields her pocket knife.

"Woah! Marley, relax!" I screech in a moment of panic. She holds the knife out, her face cemented in concrete vexation.

"My encyclopaedia…" she whispers, head facing down at the ground. Enzo watches wide-eyed as my sister edges towards him. "My one and only book…gone." Her eyes trail up to meet his. For the first time since I met him, pure fear washes across Enzo's face. Releasing a war-like shriek, Marley lunges at him and makes a sharp incision down his right arm. Yelping in pain, he crashes to the floor, gasping and grunting.

"Marley!" Gabriel and I yell in unison. Marley takes one look at our exasperated faces and Enzo the fallen soldier. She makes a u-turn and darts into the thick of the bushes.

"Marley? Marley, get back here!" Gabriel bellows. He turns to Enzo. "Don't move." The prince takes my hand and we charge after her.

Again, the forest is almost silent. Maybe it isn't. Perhaps my crushing worry for Marley has blocked my senses because everything seems to have faded. My vision is blurry, my head light. For a split second I entertain the prospect that this is all a dream. Just a silly, silly dream.

A quick pinch to the arm confirms this to be far from true. We fight through vines and tall grass as if we're competing in a hurdles event. That's when we come to a clearing, rather wide. There seems to be a parting in the canopy, casting a spotlight upon the broken ground. Standing there with a face as hard as nails is Marley. Gabriel must've noticed the anger on my face because he tells me to stay put. Slowly but surely, Gabriel makes careful steps towards my knife-wielding sibling. She points it right at his chest but still he moves forward.

"Mar, it's me. Just put the knife down and we can talk," he says, calm undertones glistening through each syllable.

"You promised!" she shrieks. Her face is now red and drenched in salty tears. I find myself crying too as I witness the death of my sister's innocence.

"Marley, please," I whisper through sobs. She takes a quick, distasteful look at me before focussing back on Gabriel.

"You promised I wouldn't get hurt! You promised we'd make it out! I hate you!" her voice goes hoarse and it sounds like she's struggling to get each word out without scraping her throat. She gasps for air between words. Gabriel stops walking and kneels down to her level, shy a few feet from her.

"Marley…"

"I hate you….I hate you! I hate you! I hate you!" Marley ploughs towards him like a savage creature. He dodges numerous times as she attempts to slash at him. She manages to catch the lobe of his right ear before he can prise the weapon from her. He chucks it across the floor and grabs Marley, holding her tight. She thrashes her limbs around as if she truly believes she is strong enough to break free. My sister snarls, bites and attacks to her heart's content but Gabriel anticipates every move. Soon enough she gives up and her body goes limp. She crumbles to the ground and Gabriel goes down with her, still holding her in a tight hug. Marley wails like a newborn taking its first breath.

"I got you, I got you. Everything will be ok. I'll get us to safety." While my sister releases the result of a week's worth of pent-up frustration, Gabriel looks up at me. All I can do is shake my head. We've lost her. We've truly, truly lost her.

**36**

It's been five hours since Marley has said anything. Same goes for Enzo. You could call it a blessing because those two haven't stopped harping at each other for the best part of the journey. Every day, every hour was filled with their arguments. Countless insults and snarls, scoffs and retorts. And now I'd give anything for either of them to talk. Just a single syllable would do. This tranquillity isn't right. Both of them were born to talk and violence has silenced them. I feel sick to my stomach and I'm sure Gabriel does too. Both of their personalities have died. Enzo stares straight forward as we trudge through the foliage. He doesn't even look at his phone that he's been so glued to for the past few days. Marley's been trailing slightly behind, drawing on a crumpled piece of paper with a blunt HB pencil. Marley was never one for drawing but like I said, both of their personalities have died. Mother always had a saying for this sort of situation. Oh, I always forget this. Something about the devil and pointy horns? I can't quite remember but the point is to be careful what you wish for. I wished day after day for their silence and now I have it. But it hurts. It really, really hurts.

Night dawns on us much quicker than expected. Clearly our little fiasco took up a lot of time. We barely made it a few miles in a day and already we have to set up camp. Everyone's mood is dampened. Marley won't even look in Enzo's direction, let alone speak to him. She's avoiding everyone, in fact. The worrying thing is, I don't think she's ignoring us out of guilt. By the glimmer in my six-year-old sister's eyes, I think she's just upset that she didn't finish Enzo and Gabriel off when she was given the chance. Bar a few fleeting moments where her eyes flicker up from the paper, Marley remains drawing. I did try to make light conversation and look at the art but she'd hugged it to her body and snarled at me like a wolf.

It takes us the best part of an hour to put up the tents. Seeming as Enzo and Marley are in bad moods, they've decided to exempt themselves from all means of responsibility. This leaves Gabriel and I to struggle with the sad excuse of a living quarters. After a lot of lugging, complaining and swearing we manage to make something adequate to sleep in. The two drama queens sauntered straight past us and went to their respective tents, simultaneously zipping up the doors. It is freezing in this bush clearing but I'm not ready to huddle up in my sleeping bag just yet and neither is Gabriel. We haven't been able to talk alone in a long time. With a single glance from Gabriel, I nod and follow him into a tiny space a few yards from the camp. I bring the first aid kit with me. We sit on a log and I turn to face him. A gentle silence settles around us as I get out cleaning solution and q-tips.

"That's really not necessary. She barely cut my ear."

"Oh, shut up and let me do this." I move the hair that covers his ear and take a q-tip. I dip it in the solution and look up. Gabriel watches me with a calming gaze as I sort the antibacterial out. "This might hurt a little bit." He makes no reply but puts his hand on my knee. I brush the cotton with a steady hand against the wound. The prince winces and his hand clamps onto my knee.

"You're such a baby," I say, laughing to myself. I continue to clean and dress the wound while he watches me. His eyes follow my every move, interest glossing over his pupils. "You know you're staring, right?"

"I can't help it." His hand moves from my knee to my chin. He moves the hair that hangs over my face and looks deep into my eyes. "A face like yours isn't one to be taken for granted," I look pointedly at his soft lips, prompting them to embrace mine like a warm hug. His left hand makes its way to the back of my head and holds it with a gentle grasp. My vision of the world that surrounds us disintegrates as we share this wondrous moment. In unison, we move apart slightly. I reach up and slide my hand beneath the beanie, gently tugging it off. Gabriel arches a brow at me.

"Marley was right. You look better without it," I whisper. Our faces remain close as he bites his lip and smirks at me.

"Is that so?" I nod and drop it on the floor.

"Never leave me, Gabriel," I whisper. He huffs out a breathless laugh and kisses me once more.

"I'd sooner perish in the perilous waves of the Pacific, my love."

Gabriel takes my hand and together we move to the floor. We don't part as our heads reach the soft grass. The forest clearing grants us a small window of the overhead atmosphere.

We lay on the floor and look up at the clear night above us. Thousands of dots line the sky and twinkle like glitter. For a few moments we don't talk. Our hearts talk telepathically while we reside on the ground.

"Isn't it weird to think," Gabriel takes a berry from the box between us and pops it in his mouth. "That soon we'll live in another country?" I nod. "No more pain. No more insecurity. Just freedom. Sweet, sweet freedom." Each iridescent spec of his pupil glimmers under the sullen light that's cascaded on us by the moon. Grass and sticks tickle at my achilles and my nape. Bushes rustle around us as undisclosed creatures tread their way through the soft darkness. I slip my palm onto Gabriel's and he closes his fingers over mine. A thought braces my mind. My instinct is to shove it away into the back of my brain. The broken part. The part where sad thoughts belong, so as not to quash my denial. Such an instinct is pushed aside as my lips part and the words tumble from my mouth.

"What if we don't make it, Gabe?" Like a snake from a rockery, his hand slithers away from mine and rests on the ground. I lift my head to look at him. Though it isn't immediately discernible, I notice Gabriel tip his gaze away from both me and the sky. His eyes focus upon fractured ground and sunbaked dirt. Determined, I replace my palm in his. He pulls his hand away and rests it upon his chest. Accepting defeat, I rest my head back on the floor and wait. After all, patience is a virtue appreciated by all. Especially of a man as irritated as the one beside me. Moments pass before his hand returns to mine. I hadn't previously noticed but I've come to realise I held my breath for the entirety that his palm didn't hold mine. What has come of me? A girl woefully dependent on a hapless prince and his transcendent charm. It's enough to make me cringe at myself.

"Have you ever heard of Icarus?" I ask, breaking the silence.

"I haven't."

"He and his father had wax wings. One day he decided to fly towards the sun but he got too close and the wings melted." His eyes slide over to me. "The wings melted, Gabe. He fell out of the sky and drowned in the sea." That feeling of drowning that I'd suffered with for so long hasn't gone away. I thought that as soon as we passed those gates, I'd feel that weight lift from my shoulders. It feels heavier. It feels like it's going to crush me, spirit and all. Gabriel's hand squeezes mine.

"Through the rain and clouds, the dust and despair, the magnificent ugliness of our escapade, one attribute among each of our very hearts pushed us through," Gabriel says. His voice somehow manages to be gritty and soft as he rolls to face me. "Belief. If you, Dakota, do not solely believe that we will defy the confines of the Zayathian borders, we'd be just as well turning back. Without belief in our journey, no passion will drive us home. So, for the love of God, my sweet angel, let only optimism plague your soul." He wipes away the tears that I didn't realise were trailing down my face and we kiss once more. Our breathing appears somewhat disturbing in the tranquillity of our surroundings. Our faces remain only centimetres apart. Gabriel looks to my lips, caressing them with his glance. My eyes search his and for a moment we are silent.

"I love you, Dakota Ann Calaway." My heart stops for a moment. Not because he said that he loved me. Not because I reciprocate such a feeling. But because I have never told him my middle nor my surname. I wait some painstaking seconds before replying.

"I love you too, Gabriel Reese Escobar."

# 37

Marley won't let go of her gun. I've tried everything: asking politely, grabbing it when she isn't looking, trying to prise it from her grasp. Nothing is working. Just a few days ago she wouldn't even go near a toy gun and now here she is, clutching a shotgun like her little life depends on it. I suppose this gun replaces her encyclopaedia that was so helpfully chucked in a swamp by Enzo. I still have no idea what his motive was. What sicko goes out of his way to seek vengeance on someone over a third of his age? Marley had asked to be allowed to carry Bunny again and Gabriel didn't refuse. I'm not going to say he's scared of her because he's clearly not. What I will say is that now all three of us are treading on eggshells around my little sister. It feels as if she's ready to explode at any moment. Although I say that, she hasn't said an awful lot to suggest that. In fact, she's barely said anything at all. Every question asked to her is responded with a grunt or a shrug. All she cares about is Bunny, the gun and whatever drawing she's been so engrossed in for the past day or so.

How the guards haven't caught us yet is nothing short of a miracle. We managed to even sleep through the night without them finding us. The truth of the matter is, everyone acts like Dianne's guards are the cream of the crop. The top honchos, if you will. It always occurred to me that they were more show ponies than anything. Every one of those uniformed men are perfectly qualified to jump through the Escobar's hoops but that's about it. Sure, they carry guns but that doesn't actually indicate any skill. Just for perspective, my mother can use a gun and she's about as useful as a car with no wheels. Honestly, I think her men are nothing but a fear mechanism. Not to hype myself up but I think I'd stand a decent chance in combat against one of them. Maybe I'm underestimating them. There's never really been a chance for them to display talent, if they even have any. As far as I can remember, Zayathai has never been under attack. We don't engage in conflict with the rest of the world. We're the peacemakers. The calm country. Ironic. Although, as much as we can gloat that they haven't captured us yet, that's not to say they can't. We've resorted to redirecting our trail a little bit. The new route is more covered so we're less likely to be spotted.

Nobody told me how hot a forest can actually get. I'd assume it'd be a little bit humid but chilly on the most part. Boy was I wrong. I hadn't thought it a big deal when I took my camouflage jacket off but Gabriel's now looking at me like I just punted a guinea pig off a bridge.

"The guards are closing in on us and you think *now* is a good time to destroy our cover? You do confuse me sometimes, Dakota," he says from behind me. My name sticks to his tongue and seems like it has to be torn off. I tie the jacket around my waist as we traipse through the forest, exposing the black tank top I've been wearing underneath. It's barely dried off from when we got caught in the rain and has acquired a rather musty aroma. Enzo leads the line and Marley walks ahead of me, still drawing. I try to get a peek at the artwork but it's hugged too close to her body. She pauses for a moment to move a twig that blocks her path. I'd thought she'd hold it for me but she doesn't so the thin wood pings into my face and hits my eye. A burning sensation shoots across my whole face and my left eye feels all fuzzy. I blink rapidly and suck in a curt breath. Normally I'd say something to Marley but, like I said, we're treading on eggshells.

"As if me exposing an ounce of my bare skin is going to lead them to us. They've had multiple chances to catch up to us and yet I see no guards," I look around me in a theatrical manner. "And besides, maybe if you'd thought this through you would've made camouflage t-shirts. But you didn't so deal with it." I feel guilty as soon as I say that. This isn't Gabriel's fault. I'm just…I don't know. I guess this whole Marley situation is riling me up. I'm never this angry.

"I just want to keep you and Marley safe. That's all."

The guilt grows even wilder inside my stomach. I wish it away but it remains there in a curdled heap. We walk on in silence. Small animals dart around us: rats, ferrets…bunnies. I'm about to point out the rabbits to my sister but the words get caught in my throat. I hold my hand to my neck, surprised. Hesitation. Normally,

I'd never think before I spoke to Marley. Except when it comes to explicit jokes, I didn't feel the need to be cautious around her. She's my little sister. My blood. But now here I am. Maybe I am scared of her, of the monster she's become. The girl that ambles in front of me is not my sister. She is a stranger. The Marley I knew, cared. She felt things, emotions. The Marley I knew fainted at the sight of a burning body. This stranger before me has killed a man and didn't think twice about it. Despite all this, I still feel the same motivation to get her out of Zayathai that I did before. I don't care what version of Marley I escape with, as long as she's safe. I reach down my top and clasp the pendant in my palm. For Marley. I'm doing this for Marley, whoever Marley is.

The opening expands into a wider berth so we can walk in twos. Marley and Enzo walk side by side in radio silence, while me and Gabriel tread behind them. My arm is interlocked with his and I dedicate each inhale to his intricate scent. As we tread along the beaten path, I wonder how many people must've attempted this journey. We aren't the first and we certainly won't be the last. I know of many people who have tried and failed. We learn about them in history class. We learn about how they were killed, slaughtered like wild beasts. I'm not sure about the ones that succeeded. I'm sure it's no surprise that their achievements aren't documented in any history textbooks across Zayathai. As far as Dianne is concerned, those people don't deserve the time of day. Come to think of it, maybe no one has made it out. That would make more sense, considering all of the security. Now I really feel stupid. What made us think we were any different to everyone else? Slaughtered like wild beasts. That'll be us soon.

Gabriel had described our final camping spot to me last night. It sounded amazing. A secluded space with a little lake and a smaller number of bugs than the rest of the forest. No more murky drinking water and bed bugs. So, you can imagine my devastation when we had to change our course of action. Now we're setting up camp in a subpar patch of land for what feels like the millionth time. It's a small clearing in all of the shrubs. Overhead is a gap in the trees that's a lot bigger than the ones in our other campsites in the forest have been. It's still not huge though but it's enough to admire the stars.

"Marley, you need to help. Just because you and Enzo had a little spat, that doesn't permanently dismiss you from your duties. Even Enzo has gotten over himself so you should too," Gabriel says, arms folded. Marley ignores him completely. She seems quite comfortable, sitting on the floor with her gun and Bunny placed in her lap. The pencil rests in her hand as she glides the lead across the A4 paper. "Marley." Gabriel's fingers make weird motions at his sides, as if he's trying to fight the urge to ball them into fists. I put down the tent pole that I'm holding, pick up two small boxes and step over the heap of belongings on the floor. I place my other hand on his forearm and he looks down at me.

"C'mon. Let's go find something to eat for dinner." I know Gabriel wants to force Marley to help out but something about my touch breaks down his anger a little.

He nods and follows me, taking one of the boxes from me. We tread a few metres into the bushes. I've gotten used to finding nettles and berries so it doesn't take me long to spot a good place to uproot some plants. I start to harvest white beam berries from a tree. Gabriel tears nettles from the earth with his bare hands. How that doesn't hurt him, I have no idea. We work in a comfortable silence.

"I told you the gun was a bad idea," I say with my back turned to him. Well, that was a stupid thing to say. He was just about to calm down. The rustling of leaves stops.

"Don't turn this on me. How was I supposed to know your sister was going to go psycho?" he snorts. Of course, he is right but that doesn't make his words sting any less than those nettles must be stinging his hands. I spin on my heel and storm towards him.

"My sister has not gone psycho, Gabriel. She's scared, is what she is. Scared because *you* didn't protect her like you promised to." My teeth are pressed together tight and my words are airy. With every few syllables, I jab at his chest, pure rage firing through me. On the final word, he grabs my wrist.

"I'm doing the best I can with the situation and you know that."

"Well do better," I hiss, wrenching my arm from his grasp. The vigour at which I do this causes his nails to break the surface of my skin but I don't care. These wounds are nothing compared to the ones I've suffered at the hands of him and the diamond dagger that sits in his waist belt. "For the love of god, I *need* you to do better because over there is a frightened little girl that I will do anything, and I mean anything, to protect." I stride past him, clutching onto the box of berries. His gentle yet heavy footsteps follow behind me. When we arrive back at the campsite, Enzo has set up their tent and finished mine. He offers something that really catches me off guard. A smile. An inviting, comforting smile.

Marley has already decided to go to bed. We'd thought about asking if she'd like some soup but there'd be no point. She doesn't want to speak so it's unlikely that she wants to sit around the campfire with a steaming bowl of a soup that she hates. I say 'steaming'. As the guards have made themselves very apparent, we've tried to keep the fire as small as possible, so we can't be spotted by the helicopters. This leaves us with lukewarm soup and borderline hypothermia.

"So, what's your story?" I ask Enzo. We're sat cross-legged in a triangle pattern, huddled around the feeble flame. His broad shoulders are hunched and his muscles look smaller than usual, almost as if they're cowering.

"I'm not sure how you want me to answer that," he says before slurping a large proportion of his soup into his mouth. I try to ignore the gurgling sound. I hate noisy eaters.

"We've been around each other for days now. I can name three facts about you." I hold three fingers up. "Number 1: your first name." I knock one finger down. "Number 2: you're always texting." I knock the second finger down. "And number 3: you hate my sister for no reason." I point the final finger at him. He smiles again when I say this. His image distorts as the gas rises from the fire and dances before my eyes. Enzo brings his knees up to chest height and rests his arms on them.

"She's got a point," Gabriel says. He drops his empty mess tin on the floor and it lands with a clatter that makes me cringe inside.

"Alright then. Here's three more facts about me. My surname is Varsowast, I hate carrots and I have a very good reason for hating your sister. She's gobby and irritating." I feel like throwing myself through the fire just to tear his eyeballs out. The only person that can throw even the tiniest of insults at Marley is me. No one else.

"You're lying. Never in my eighteen years of living have I seen someone despise the existence of a child. A literal child." Enzo's face hardens. He drops his knees and clasps his hands together. He nods his head slowly. I take a small sip of my soup. A taste similar to spinach that I've come to know all too well coats my tastebuds. I put the mess tin down, unwilling to put myself through the torture anymore. Instead, I reach for the berries and pop one in my mouth. The powdery-sweet sensation pushes out the nettle taste.

"Okay. You want the real story. I'll give it to you." He leans closer so the fire almost touches his eyebrows and locks eyes with me. Everything inside of me says to look away but I don't. I'm entranced. "I had a little sister of my own." Gabriel looks down at the floor. He's heard this story before. I can see it in his face.

"Had?" My voice comes out as barely a whisper. I know where he's going with this but I still find myself asking.

"Yes," Enzo says. "Had." I thought it was just the gas

291

distorting my vision but Enzo's hands are shaking with vehement aggression.

"I don't understand–"

"She died, Dakota. Your mother isn't the only one to have shot her kids." My mouth flutters like a struggling moth but no words form. Enzo's quivering hands pick up a stick and he starts snapping it into tiny shards. "Isabelle was her name. She was blonde and smart as anything."

"Just like Marley," I murmur. He nods.

"When I look at your sister, all I see is what I've lost. She was the one thing I really cared about. The one…" His words are choked by tears. Gabriel says nothing but reaches out and takes Enzo's left hand. "So, no I don't hate Marley for no reason." Gabriel is holding his friend's hand with a firm grip but Enzo still manages to pull away with ease. He clambers to his feet and I notice a few solitary tears trickle down his face.

"Enzo…" Gabriel breathes.

"I'm going to bed. Good night." And with that he's gone, slipping into the tent, zipping up the entry. Gabriel stands and begins tidying. He blows out the fire, which had almost put itself out already. I collect the tins with hands that have now developed a quiver of their own. I'm not sure how Gabriel is feeling right now. I don't know if he's angry at me or the situation but I can tell he's not happy.

"If I'd known about Isabelle I wouldn't–"

"I know," he cuts me off. "Just don't make those excuses to Enzo. You've just ripped open wounds that he spent so long trying to heal. Don't expect him to accept apologies anytime soon." Sensing my guilt, Gabriel places a kiss on my forehead. "If you really feel like begging for forgiveness, don't do it tomorrow. Not on the last day of our journey. It can wait." He walks past me and into their tent. I'm not sure if it's five minutes or five hours before I move from the spot that he left me at and shuffle into our tent.

I remember that chilling feeling that had run through my bones at the thought of sleeping anywhere near Enzo. That same fear enters my body as I slip into the sleeping bag beside Marley. She's fully unconscious so I have the perfect opportunity to take the gun. But I don't. My eyes trail over to Bunny. The hole where his left eye is meant to be is riddled with dry blood, as is a lot of his body. Stuffing leaks from various parts of the toy, some of it a bright white, some of it stained with blood and dirt. The one eye that has prevailed, hangs on for dear life. I flick Bunny to the side and pick up the thing that's really piqued my interest. The drawing. As soon as I turn it over, I wish with every ounce of my being that I hadn't. The picture shows Marley being embraced into a hug by both me and Gabriel. Each of us has one arm around Marley but the other is in-between us and her. Each of us has a hand on the grip of a long sword. We've shoved the weapon into Marley, so much so that it impales right through to the other side of her body. A speech bubble sits above my head and one above Gabriel's. Mine says, "I'll always protect you."

Gabriel's says, "As long as I walk this earth, you will never come in harm's way again."

# 38

Sirens. For years and years, we were called out of our houses by sirens of differing frequencies. A lot of the time, no one knew what was about to happen except that whatever it is would be bad. Really bad. I remember one time a siren called us outside because Dianne's grandfather had died. Every person for miles had to stand outside of their houses in silence, while they paraded his hearse down the street. They toured the whole of Zayathai within the week. I had only been about eight and I remember being so dreadfully tired. The first two hours were manageable but as the night dawned on us, my legs began to feel weak. No one was allowed to speak. We had to stand in the driveway and stare straight ahead. Guards paced up and down the street, guns unholstered. I'll never forget the jolt of fear that flew through me when someone was shot down the street for talking. For obvious reasons, me and sirens don't get along with each other. So, you can imagine the horror I felt five minutes ago when the loudest alarm I've ever heard sounded overhead. Marley hadn't noticed. She barely even stirred when the sound first blared in the sky. I had to shake her multiple times before she became even remotely conscious. I thought I'd reacted fast but Gabriel flew open our tent door within seconds.

"Move. Now." He didn't have to ask me twice. We're now flying all over the place, grabbing whatever we can. Marley picked up her tattered, probably bug-infested toy rabbit and her gun. That was all she needed. I finally take my gun out of my bag and put it in my waist belt. I feel like a traitor to myself when my finger brushes against the trigger. Me holding a weapon is no better than my little sister. Neither of us should be resorting to killing machines. That isn't who we are. Desperate times call for desperate measures, I suppose. The noise draws nearer and starts to ring in my ears. All of a sudden, my hair starts to fling about my head. In fact, everything is flying everywhere. I look to the sky and there they are: three huge helicopters. They're black and the Escobar cress on the side of each one taunts me. Lucky for us, the clearing is so small that they won't be able to land. They can hover but until we reach a larger area, they can't get us into the helicopters.

"Stop moving and surrender! We've found you!" a man yells. He's hanging out of one of the helicopters, megaphone to his mouth. That voice. I know that voice. It's the same one I recognised when we were hiding near the village. He repeats this message over and over again as they lower to the floor. Each time he speaks, his voice becomes more familiar in my brain. Oh my god. I stagger over to Gabriel, who's preparing his weapons, and take hold of his arm. My vision is dull and I feel dizzy. He freezes then spins around.

"What…what are you doing, Dakota? Grab your stuff so we can go!" he yells over the turmoil of wind that's being drawn in and thrown out by the helicopter turbines.

"My…my…" The words will barely form in my mouth. He squints his eyes at me and I can tell he knows something is wrong. Whatever's in his hands falls to the floor and lands with a loud thump. He takes both of my arms because it's clear that I'm about to drop too.

"Tell me what's wrong, sweetheart." Sweetheart. That's a new one. I'm not sure if I like it but it slows my nerves all the same. The man's voice continues to ring in my ears.

"My dad. The man up there he's…he's, my dad."

Tears begin to cloud my vision and spill onto my face. Gabriel looks up to the man in the sky then back down at me.

"We can talk about this later. Unless you want an unwholesome reunion with your father, we need to go right now," Gabriel says. His voice has dropped several octaves. He isn't angry but he's serious. My mouth flutters around and I manage to nod before stumbling back to my belongings. Don't think about him, I tell myself. We can talk about this later. I grab my knife and add that to my waist belt, along with a small bag of white beam berries. I don't know how long it's going to be before we eat again. I also don't know whether that meal will be on a boat or in a prison.

"Everyone ready?" Enzo yells over the commotion.

We all nod. "Three…two…one…go!" And just like that we're off, back into the dark depths of the forest. I get a feeling of déjà vu from when we escaped the helicopters in the snow biome. Something doesn't feel right about how they aren't catching us. I know I've said this before but if they were really trying, they would've caught us. What game are they playing?

Our feet stamp over the sticks and shrubs. A few times I'm sure I've stepped on a small animal but that doesn't slow me down. The memory isn't clear but at some point, I unholstered my gun. It's a lot heavier than I thought guns would be. In the contraband movies, they always seem to hold them with such ease, like they're made of papier-mâché. Holding the weapon makes running an even more tedious practice but it's worth it if I'm to feel safe. Because right now, despite having ten-foot-tall Enzo and the prince of Zayathai with me, I feel anything but safe. There's no way of telling if I'm going to wake up tomorrow in a cell, awaiting execution.

Marley has become a lot faster at running over the past few days. I guess it's because we're constantly on the move so she's had to get used to sprinting at the pace of three young adults. Now she's running ahead of me, hand pressed tightly into Gabriel's. It seems that even though she's angry beyond control, she'll still turn to Gabriel if she feels endangered. I can't help but feel jealous over that. I'm supposed to be her safety net. I'm her sister, not him. He wasn't there when she had to have blood extracted from her body. He wasn't there to cook for her when there was only a lemon and three popcorn kernels in the

297

fridge. I was. Perhaps I should just get used to it. If we do manage to escape in one piece then we may become a family in our new country. A family. Gosh I wonder how that feels. I've never felt like I had a family. Even though I love Marley to bits, she wasn't enough to piece the whole family back together.

Enzo is far ahead, leading the pack just as he had the day before. Gabriel and Marley are ahead of me and I'm starting to lag behind a bit. My legs feel all wobbly. I can't fall over. I refuse to be the weak link. The thrashing of soles against cracked, brown ground stars to soften.

"We've lost them. Let's take five minutes to catch our breath," Gabriel says. He's buckled over, panting like a dog. Marley falls to the floor. Blonde hair clings to her red, sweating face. Enzo doesn't look hard done by at all. If you looked at him you wouldn't assume he's just ran about two-thousand metres. I want to sink to the floor like Marley but I need to talk to Gabriel first. It's as if he's read my mind. I look up and he's looking directly at me. All it takes is a nod from me to know that we need to find some privacy.

"Dakota needs the toilet so I'm gonna take her," he says. Seriously? That's the best excuse he can come up with? I almost say something but he makes this face that tells me I need to just go along with it.

"Alright," Enzo replies. He flicks his knife around and inspects the blade. Marley doesn't even seem to be registering that we're talking. Gabriel grabs my hand and we walk a couple of metres away. We turn a corner and a huge bush offers us some privacy from them. As soon as we're out of sight, I crumble into him. I don't cry but my body seems to give way. He catches me and lowers both of us to the floor. He releases a hand from my body to play with my hair.

"I knew he worked for Dianne," I mumble. "But I'm his daughter, Gabriel. His own flesh and blood."

"I know, I know." He pulls me in closer and rocks me gently. My lips tremble, unsure of what to say next.

"He's a Malsum, Gabe. He escaped prosecution."

"An exception. I'm familiar," he responds, continuing to stroke my hair.

"Arrested by my own father. How will that look?" His hand moves away from my hair and to my chin. He lifts my face and looks into my eyes.

"Listen to me. All I hear you do is speculate over what could go wrong. I told you to be optimistic and to trust me but it's like you want to get caught." I drop my eyes to the floor. "Dakota, look at me." His hand grips my face a little tighter. "I said look at me. Thank you. Can you please just trust that we'll get out of here alive because your pessimism is going to be the death of you. Of all of us." I close my eyes and lean against his chest.

"I'm sorry, Gabe," I mutter. A few lone tears begin to run down my cheeks. "I'm so sorry." He rubs my back and shushes me.

"Don't get yourself worked up. In a few hours, we'll be on a boat and you'll never have to face this kind of fear ever again."

"Dammit, Enzo! Stop. Talking." We both fly from the floor. Marley may be in a permanent state of vexation right now but she isn't stupid. She knows that screaming and yelling like that will draw the attention of the guards. Something must've happened. Gabriel can't get to the scene half as fast as me. He may be a lot quicker than me in general but if my sister's involved then best believe I'll be there at the speed of lightning. When we arrive, I have to blink a few times to check I'm not dreaming. Lying on the floor, cowering with his head in his hands, is Enzo. And you'll never guess who's standing over him with a gun pointing directly at his head.

**39**

"Marley, what the hell do you think you're doing?" I hiss, cautious of the volume at which I speak. Her shrieking has probably given the guard's enough of a lead, without me adding to the noise. I'm about to take a step forward but Gabriel anticipates my move. He puts his hand on my right shoulder.

"Don't." That's all he has to say for me to listen. Enzo is trembling on the ground. You could say it's amusing that a grown man would be so scared of a child but Marley is more than a child. She's blinded by violence, intelligent beyond belief and so angry that she can't control it. Hair still clings to her face and she seems to be sweating even more than before. Her face is beetroot red. She shifts the gun in her hands.

"Mar, why are you holding him at gunpoint?" Gabriel asks. His voice is calm and collected but his face tells a different story. That's his best friend on the other end of that weapon.

"He wouldn't stop saying things!" she exclaims. "He needs to shut up or I will shoot." And we all believe her.

Underestimating the wrath of my little sister would be the biggest mistake any of us could make.

"Well, he's stopped talking now so you can put the gun down. Haven't you, Enzo?" Gabriel presses. Radio silence. "Haven't you, Enzo?" he repeats. Nothing. Is this man trying to get himself killed? Marley's hands quiver under the grasp of the gun. I can almost feel how tired her arms are. But that's good. Maybe it'll encourage her to put the lethal firearm down.

"She doesn't scare me," Enzo says, even though his voice is broken and croaky. "I've survived a gun wound before. She doesn't scare me." When he repeats that phrase, it seems as if he's trying to convince himself more than us. Gabriel's jaw flexes, then softens.

"Is your pride really worth your life? Just apologise," I chime in. Enzo moves his hands from his face to glare at me.

"I'd sooner tear my own eyeballs out," he responds through gritted teeth.

"We don't have time for this. Enzo, say sorry so we can get the hell out of here." Right as Gabriel says that, the distinct noises of treading feet and deep hollering sound in the distance. I reckon they're ten minutes away from finding us. That isn't long enough.

"He can apologise all he wants," Marley says. Every eye darts to her. "I'm still going to blow his brains out."

# 40

Marley fiddles with the trigger. Her eyes don't leave the situation of Enzo's head.

"I've waited so long to do this," she growls. "To make you hurt. I can't wait to see that stream of blood oozing from your body." My stomach does somersaults. It takes all of my willpower not to press my hands over my ears. I don't want to listen to this. Only a week ago, the most venomous thing to come out of Marley's mouth would be the odd expletive when she stubs her toe.

"Someone's spent too much time in front of the tv. Where did you get that monologue from? Probably a lame spy movie," Enzo teases, his voice muffled as he continues to cower.

"You see what I mean?" Marley asks, turning to Gabriel and I. Neither of us speak. She turns back to him. "Any last words?" Marley can't be serious. I won't believe it. I can't believe it. But like I said, underestimating Marley is a big mistake.

"Sure. I hope you burn in the depths of hell, you psycho..." The last word is flushed out by the bang of a gunshot. The sound rings through my ears and makes my brain ache. I feel dizzy but I manage to hold myself up. For a moment everything in my mind quietens. My vision blurs and I feel unconscious. But only for a second. Soon enough my senses strengthen and the noise hammers at my brain all over again. Enzo's body jerks a little before coming to a complete standstill. The wound in his stomach is nothing like I've ever seen before. It's so big, so gruesome. Even when I close my eyes the sight of that fatal gash doesn't soften in my mind. At least she chose not to go for the head. I don't think even my desensitised sister could bear looking at an exploded brain. Marley drops the gun, grinning like a Cheshire cat. She moves closer and kneels beside him. Blonde hair drapes either side of her shoulders as she leans closer to Enzo's already pale face.

"Looks like you aren't invincible to gunshots after all," she says. Her eyes glaze over his still body and she laughs to herself.

Gabriel sprints over to Enzo's side, though there's clearly nothing we can do to bring him back. My feet stay rooted to the floor. Just like Marley had described, a stream of crimson blood snakes along the dirt, smothering sticks and leaves. Gabriel presses his hand over the wound. He's hyperventilating and he looks five seconds from collapsing right beside his friend.

"No no no no no Enzo come back. Don't do this. You're ok." The blood coats Gabriel's palms and continues to flow from the man's stomach. Enzo has a smirk that still plays on his face, even after he's past the point of death. "Please wake up. Please." Gabriel cups Enzo's hand in his and does something I haven't seen him do before. He weeps. Long, gasping weeps that seem to hurl themselves from his mouth with every ragged breath. I come to his side and put my arms around him. He falls into me, just as I had to him mere minutes ago.

"He's gone, Gabriel. Let him go," I whisper. I cradle him, while his tears smother my shirt. Some of Enzo's blood gets on my hands. I feel as though wiping it off would do nothing. His death will always feel like it's my fault and getting rid of the blood won't shake that. I let Marley have that gun. I let her hatred for Enzo grow wilder than it ever should have. I am to blame. I fall back as Gabriel flies to his feet and storms over to Marley.

"You weren't supposed to do that," he growls. Gabriel's mouth fumbles as he tries to find the words. When nothing comes to mind all he can think to do is repeat, "You weren't supposed to do that!" He shrieks the last word and shoves her to the ground. Marley falls flat on her back. A single tear escapes her left eye and snakes down her face before climbing onto her collar.

"Gabe, stop!" I scream. I jump over Enzo and pull his arms behind his back. His breaths are inconsistent and shaky as he stares down at my sister. Before this she had seemed unshaken but Marley values Gabriel's opinion more than anyone else's. More than my own. Her eyes soften and it's as if she shapeshifts back into Marley. The proper Marley. The stamping of feet isn't so distant now. Five minutes and they'll be here.

Marley clambers back to her feet and tries to wrap her arms around Gabriel's legs.

"I'm sorry. I didn't mean to upset you," she murmurs.

"No! Get off me!" he exclaims, wriggling his arms from my grasp to push her again. "You knew exactly what you were doing and now Enzo is dead. Dead!" Gabriel bellows at her. Tears pool in the bloodshot sockets of my sister's eyes. Before I can comprehend the situation, she snatches up her gun and puts it in her waist belt. She takes Bunny from the belt and whispers something in his ear before darting into the bushes.

"Marley? Marley!" I scream.

"She has the right idea," Gabriel says, wiping his eyes. Before I can ask what he means, the stamping of feet becomes only five-hundred metres away. Two minutes. Then they'll be here to arrest us.

The fact that we've left Enzo's body in the middle of the forest barely braces my mind. I suppose it's a dead giveaway of our location but what were we supposed to do? Carry the lifeless, fifty-foot being with us? I don't think so. Hand in hand, Gabriel and I are sprinting in the same direction that I think Marley went. Not being able to see her is really starting to make me panic. She must know where she's going. Marley has sat down with Gabriel and studied the map tens of times over the past few days. But we took a detour. Oh heavens, we took a detour. She has no idea where she is. Gabriel is a pace ahead of me and the combination of blood and calluses on his hand makes it quite unpleasant to hold. I feel compensated by watching the satisfying motion of his hair bouncing in motion with his steps. If I'd known this trip would've encompassed so much running, maybe I would've invested in a treadmill to prepare. Not that we could afford one. I feel lightheaded beyond belief but I push that to the side. All we need to do is find Marley and get to the beach. A boat is waiting for us at shore. I can almost taste the salt of the sea on my tongue. The thickness of the bushes is getting a little softer now. My guess is that ten minutes worth of running will be enough to make it to the sand. Oh, I'd give anything for this to be over now.

Gabriel makes a turn that leads us off the path. I tug his hand.

"This is the wrong way, Gabe. She definitely stayed on the dirt path." I turn and try to walk the other way but his palm squeezes mine. I freeze. What is he doing? "Gabriel, we need to…there isn't enough time for games. I need to find Mar…" my voice trails off. I instantly forget whatever I was about to say because what I'm seeing right now is terrifying. Gabriel is still. And he's looking at me like I'm prey. Like he's the predator.

"I'm afraid I can't let you do that." His nails are digging into my skin and I'm sure he must be drawing blood.

"I…I don't understand. Gabe, if we don't move now, they're going to catch us." A rag appears in his hand that I hadn't noticed before.

"I'm so sorry for what I'm about to do to you. Just know it's the only way."

My brain doesn't get a chance to comprehend the situation before he drags me towards him. Gabriel slams my back into his chest and holds me with his left arm. His right hand presses the rag over my nose and mouth. My breathing becomes scarce and I become frantic, throwing my body around to no avail. As much as I try to fight it, my eyes begin to drag themselves closed. Sedatives.

# 41

The first thing I notice when my eyes flutter open is Gabriel. He's sitting on the floor opposite me, watching my every movement with an intense gaze and bloodshot eyes. His normally manicured hair is frizzy and unkept. Although he's normally quite pale, he's now akin to a piece of paper. The man I'm seeing before me doesn't look satisfied with himself. He looks destroyed. The second thing I notice is the aching pain in my wrists and back. My hands are tied behind me to the tree that I'm leaning against. The back of my t-shirt has drawn up a little, which allows bark to stick into my back and scrape at my skin. My head feels strange, airy almost. Then I remember the rag had something on it to sedate me. That same rag has been put in my mouth and tied around my head.

"If you promise not to scream, I'll take the gag out." I close my eyes momentarily then nod. If I'm to get out of this alive, I need to be careful. Gabriel edges closer and refuses to make eye contact with me as he takes the gag out and tosses it to the floor. He moves back to his spot about two metres from me, as if he doesn't want to remain too close.

"I should've known not to trust you." My voice comes out in a powerless squeak.

"You don't understand, Dakota. You really don't," he murmurs.

"Enlighten me, Gabriel." I find my normal voice back. It's boisterous and assured. "Please tell me what part I don't understand. To me it looks like you're a traitor." That trust Marley had in Gabriel. Now I know why I didn't feel the same way. I always knew in the back of my mind that it would come to this. The prince of Zayathai actually wanting to help us escape was all a stupid fantasy. Why did I listen to my heart before my brain? Stupid Dakota. Stupid stupid stupid.

"I didn't know I'd fall in love with you." Now that's the last thing I thought he'd say. "They told me there was a family who were making a huge earning off selling their daughter's blood. Many people work in the black market but do you know how much money your mother was profiting from you?" Come to think of it, I have no idea. The only customers I really came into contact with were Mr Warren and two ladies. They'd hand me a big wad of cash every time but I'd never counted it. Money had no value to me because all of it went to Mother and she only spent it on herself. Maybe one or two went to obtaining some food. The fact that hundreds of other buyers were purchasing my blood never really occurred to me.

"Thousands. Bordering on millions, in fact," Gabriel says. Holy... "They wanted to stop her somehow so one of the royal agents bought some of your blood. They did some tests that confirmed it was in fact your blood she was selling and not her own. They wanted to arrest your mother but my parents wanted a show. If arrested, your mother could claim that the undercover work was all your doing, seeming as it was your blood. It was much easier to just go for you. Bringing Marley into the equation was just for a bit of fun, to be honest. Kill two birds with one stone." he waves trembling hands around as he speaks.

"Why couldn't you just arrest me like the others?"

"Like I said, my mother wanted a show. More and more Malsums have begun to become more daring recently. The black market is booming and many people are less cautious about buying Malsum blood. Our rule was spiralling out of control. She wanted to make a spectacle of you, have you believed that you can escape with me. The Prince." I haven't heard him refer to himself as the prince in a long time. Not since we began our journey. "The main threat to our power has been hundreds of people trying to escape the country every month. Maybe not in the north but other parts of the country are out of Dianne's control. She wanted to prove that you cannot escape Zayathai. No matter how far through the biomes you get, we'll always be one step ahead. You and your sister were obviously the perfect people to use as a demonstration because Dianne hates your family so much for the boom in the blood industry." Gabriel only comes up for air for a few seconds before continuing. "They were going to arrest your mother right after this whole drama but we don't know where she is. Anyway, they're coming for you now. You'll be paraded around and used as a deterrent before being killed publicly." I can't believe what I'm hearing.

"So, all of this was a plan?"

"Everything. The random interactions that we were having weren't random at all. The secret services kept tabs on you so they knew exactly where you'd be at all times. All I had to do was be there." When I was gardening, at the dry cleaners, down Darkness Grove, at the party... none of that was pure luck. The universe wasn't bringing us together, Dianne was. How did it not occur to me that no one bumps into a member of the royal family as often as I did? Sure, Gabriel was always a major presence in our village and you might see him once a week, wandering down your street. Maybe once every ten years would someone like me actually have the pleasure of a conversation with the prince. We fall silent. Gabriel still avoids looking at me.

"Can I ask a question?" He nods. "Why did you bring Enzo? Who is...was he?" Gabriel flinches when I change the tense. I guess his passing hasn't truly sunk in yet. Gabriel brings his knees up to his chest.

"Enzo really was my best friend. I was made to bring one other person with me so they could text the guards with updates on where we are and when to close in. That's why the guards haven't caught us yet. The actual plan was to get you to this part, off the path and arrest you here. They didn't plan to catch us until we reached this exact spot. The helicopters are going to land somewhere in a huge clearing. The group of guards that has been following us will be here shortly to carry you back to the helicopter. The whole 'closing in' deal was all just to freak you out and to make good television. This has all been documented for the whole of Zayathai to see. Some of the footage was recorded by Enzo and some by the guards." Enzo's phone. The constant texting all made sense now. "I knew Enzo would make an impression on you both. Though I'd never anticipated he'd hate Marley so much. Or that she'd kill him."

"Had you not noticed her resemblance to Isabelle? You must've met his little sister before she died." A small, empty laugh escapes his lips when I say this. The fact that he still finds humour in all of this makes me sick beyond belief.

"Isabelle isn't real, Dakota. The only reason he disliked Marley was because she is so smart that he was immediately concerned that she'd work out our plan. I'm surprised she didn't, actually."

"Oh," is all I can say to that. Enzo was a good actor then. When he talked about Isabelle, the pain on his face was like nothing I'd seen before. Maybe I'm not as good at deciphering emotions as I had thought.

"But it all made sense," I say more to myself than Gabriel. "Four Malsums running away together. It all made so much sense." Gabriel shakes his head and stares at the ground.

"I'm not a Malsum, Dakota."

**42**

I replay his words in my head about five times before it makes sense.

"You never took the Mixi, did you?"

"Neither did my parents." Ok now I was not expecting that. "The sole purpose of creating the injection was to control the population. We don't need to be controlled. We are the controllers." I hate how he says 'we'. Like he's one of them. "Besides, if we took the Mixi then there's a chance we'd reject it, just like you. Imagine if Dianne was a Malsum. Her own worst nightmare." I suppose it makes sense but that doesn't quash the surprise factor. Gabriel still won't look me in the eyes. He finds anything else to focus on: the ground, the trees, the sky. Anything. We fall silent.

"Did they tell you to flirt with me?" It hurts like hell to ask this question. The pain worsens when he responds with a nod.

"But you said you loved me," I croak. My face is starting to streak with tears. I want to wipe them away but my hands are tied back.

"I do!" he cries out. "Don't you see how this is hurting me more than you?"

"I find that hard to believe," I scoff. I lean my head harder on the tree and I can feel my dark hair clinging to the bark.

"I truly do love you. When they showed me the picture in your file, I thought you were beautiful." My file. They have a whole set of documents on me. That makes my stomach hurt. "I tried to ignore those feelings but when I set about my first mission to meet you, at the party, you were even more stunning up close. This journey may have been set up but the compliments I've given you and how you make me feel are far from fake." I'm not sure if that makes the whole situation better or worse.

"So that's how you knew my middle and surnames. My file told you." My mouth curls around the word 'file' in a vile manner.

"I'd hoped you hadn't noticed when I used your other names by accident," he admits. A bird squawks above us which makes his final words considerably quieter than the others. Good. The last thing I want to hear right now is his voice. But I need to hear it. I need to know how I was so stupid that I'd fall into such an obvious trap. "Don't be flattered though," Gabriel adds. "We have a file on every person in the country." Now that's got to be one big cabinet.

A light seems to flicker on in Prince Gabriel's head. He reaches into his pocket and pulls out the antibacterial I'd used to clean his wound not long ago. His sparkling grey eyes watch me with a sudden wave of concern.

"You didn't sedate without a fight. There's a nasty gash on your head now." I hadn't noticed but somehow him mentioning it makes the wound ache. "I need to clean it for you. Promise you won't do anything stupid." I nod. He arches his eyebrows in a condescending manner.

"I promise." Gabriel climbs to his feet and advances on me. My hands are clammy with sweat and my heart is racing. Gabriel kneels to my level and looks me in the eye for the first time since I woke up. He opens the bottle and pours some antibacterial onto the gag. He must know how horribly unhygienic that is. Warm, smoky breath coats my face as he leans closer and moves black hair from my forehead to dab at the wound.

"Earlier you said you were sorry for what you were about to do," I say, which clearly surprises him. I guess he hadn't expected me to speak. The hand holding the cloth hovers over the wound in apprehension. "Well, I'm certainly not sorry for what I'm about to do." I draw my knees up and slam them into his chin. He stumbles back and crashes to the ground. I didn't think this through at all. Realising that I'm tied down, I begin thrashing myself in all directions in an effort to break from the tree. The gaffer tape wrapped around my wrists is too strong to be broken in a frenzy. In the time it takes me to freak out and roll around a bit, Gabriel recollects himself and kneels back beside me. Except this time, he doesn't pick up the rag. He puts his hand tight around my neck, cutting off my airways.

"Stop moving! Please I don't want to hurt you!" he screeches. Both of us are crying now. I didn't plan to calm

316

down but the lack of oxygen going to my brain is starting to mess with me. I feel weaker and I need to preserve my energy. Even though I stop wriggling, Gabriel's grip on my neck only seems to tighten. I don't think he's thinking properly anymore. He just wants me to stay still. Gabriel pushes my neck back harder and bark pierces my skin. My eyes roll back into my head a few times.

"Just promise me something," I whisper-slash-gurgle. Gabriel doesn't expect me to have enough breath to speak and it catches him off guard. His grip tightens. A strange, choking sound escapes my throat. "Promise me you'll never give up on yourself. Because beneath the smoke and the ashes, there's a young fire ready to ignite the world." His face softens and that's all I need. I've stunned him enough that when I buck my knees again, he stumbles back and crashes to the floor with considerable force. This gives me time to think. Keep a level head, Dakota. This is your chance. I remember sitting on the sofa with Dad once. We were watching a strange movie that involved a man that got kidnapped by a tribe. They'd tied his hands with gaffer tape. What had he done? Think, Dakota. Think. I remember! I squeeze my hands together then slam them against the tape. It uncurls from my hands and my arms drop to the floor. I clamber to my feet and stare down at Gabriel. He loves me, I know he does. I love him too but I can't let him catch up to me again. I've let my heart cloud my vision for too long now. Enough is enough. I reach down and grab the diamond dagger from his belt. This dagger has caused me and Marley more pain than anything else in the world. It's time to finally put it to good use.

I hold it above my head then drive it through his arm. Gabriel releases a mighty cry and lifts his head to look at the wound. Blood squirts from around the blade. I must've hit an artery or something. He tries to swipe at me but I duck. I tear the dagger from his arm and put it in my belt.

"I thought you loved me," he grumbles. That word. Love. It's the reason that I haven't used my brain for days. My love for Gabriel has made me stupid beyond control.

"I could've stabbed you in the heart, Gabriel. You could be dead by now. You *should* be dead by now. But you're not. Now don't you ever question my love for you again," I say through blubbering tears and snot. He rests his head back on the floor and stares at the sky. I take this opportunity to make a break for it.

The final stretch.

I just need to find Marley and get the hell out of this forest.

**43**

My legs are moving faster than I ever thought possible. It didn't take me long to find the beaten path. Now I'm on track. The trees are really starting to thin out now.

"Marley!" I shriek. "Marley, where are you?" My eyes scan the surroundings as I charge towards the exit but all I see is trees, animals and more trees. She must be here somewhere. Perhaps she's already on the beach. My best bet is to just get out onto the sand and hope that she's there waiting for me. My shoes are worn down and leaves irritate the soles of my feet. I can feel blood running down my back and I still haven't fully regained my breath. The spell of dizziness, caused by the lack of oxygen in my brain, hasn't subsided yet. It had better dull down soon because I feel like I'm not running in a straight line and it's becoming really difficult to stay focused. The path makes a sudden turn and when I go around it that's when I see it. The exit. A smile stretches across my bloody lips as I sprint for it. The sound of the helicopters has gone. They must have landed somewhere to wait for the guards that are on foot to retrieve me. Where they've landed, I have no idea. Gabriel said they were going to a clearing so…oh no. My feet take a final step before I stop dead in my tracks. I've reached the end of the forest. If I take one more footstep I'll be on soft, white sand. But I'm not going to do that. And why is that? I hear you ask. Because there's no boat.

Why didn't it occur to me that we were never supposed to make it this far? I stare at the open sea. I've never seen the ocean in real life before. It's beautiful. The soft blue glimmers under the gleaming sun and reflects into my eyes. The waves are different than I'd expected, bigger and louder. They crash against the sand then draw themselves back. I've never touched sand this soft before either. The sand in the desert biome was rough and orange but this sand is gentler. Curiosity gets the better of me and I reach down. My clammy, blood-smothered hands glide over the soft substance. Some of the tiny rocks cling to my fingers. I rub the tips of my thumb and index together and the sand sprinkles to the ground. I'm quite surprised by how close the neighbouring country is. It's not close but it's within eyesight. I take one step onto the sand then another. I know how to swim. I could…but Marley. I can't leave her in there. But maybe I could. I haven't been selfish in a long time and maybe I need to be. But then I remember. I reach down my shirt and caress the locket. The main reason I went on this stupid expedition was to get Marley to safety. If I don't leave with her, I have failed.

I know what I need to do.

# 44

I turn on my heel and sprint back into the forest. I fly down the path but a sudden bout of yelling ahead almost stops my heart. The guards are nearing. They're probably following the path to find us. I dive to the left and begin aimlessly legging it through the forest, not caring about the protruding sticks that tear at my legs and arms. Marley must've come off the path too. She wouldn't be stupid enough to follow it. I keep running and running and running and I'm going to keep running and running and running until I find her. That internal promise comes to a sharp end when I see it. Hanging from the tree by the nape of his torn, bloody fur is Bunny.

Rule number five of living in Zayathai: if you're going to try and escape, don't get caught. You'd be better off dead than in the hands of the Escobars.

To be continued…

# ACKNOWLEDGEMENTS

Writing this book was, to put it lightly, a journey that I will never forget. When writing this book, the main goal that I had in mind was to send a profound message about society. That being, the danger of our contemporary strive to be perfect. Of course the extent of this pressure in the fictional country of Zayathai is hyperbolic in comparison to what we experience but then again it isn't. And that's the problem. For too long we've underplayed the toxicity of the feigned perfection that we're accustomed to through the likes of social and mass media and I really tried to highlight this in Kalopsia. With this goal came immeasurable amounts of intrinsic pressure. So, without further ado, here are the people that I would like to thank for making my dreams become a reality.

First of all, Winston Forde, my grandpa and editor. This is the second book that you have helped me to produce and I couldn't be anymore grateful. Without you I simply wouldn't be writing this acknowledgement so thank you and thank you again.

To my parents, Steven and Beverley Forde and my nana, Phyllis Ebanks. Your eagerness to read this book was the cure to my chronic procrastination. All I ever want to do is make you proud and I hope this chaotic novel does that. Thank you for everything you do for me, I couldn't achieve the things I do without you all.

To my sisters, Tamsin and Alicia Forde. You've always been there to mess around, make up stupid dances or just have a talk and for that I love you both. Thank you for always supporting me and helping me to make light of some very tough situations.

To my best friends, Hannah Appleton and Jaimie Farquharson. You guys have stuck by me through thick and thin and never fail to make me laugh. I'll always not only appreciate you both but look up to you as amazing inspirations. Thank you for being there for me and enduring my horrific sense of humour.

Compiled by the WLTF Literary Agency
www.winstonfordebooks.com

Printed in Great Britain
by Amazon

10216392R00194